The Monastery

by

Seeth Miko Trimpert

This book is a work of fiction. Places, events, and situations in this story are purely fictional. Any resemblance to actual persons, living or dead, is coincidental.

© 2004 by Seeth Miko Trimpert All rights reserved.

No part of this book may be reproduced, stored in a retrieval system, or transmitted by any means, electronic, mechanical, photocopying, recording, or otherwise, without written permission from the author.

ISBN: 1-4140-6588-4 (e-book)
ISBN: 1-4140-6587-6 (Paperback)

Library of Congress Control Number: 2004090530

This book is printed on acid free paper.

Printed in the United States of America
Bloomington, IN

1st Books - rev. 03/10/04

No matter if these two truths appear to conflict, they cannot actually do so, for they dwell in different orders of reality and are incommensurable.

Morris Bishop

† *Prologue* †

It began like any other morning. She got out of bed, walked to the bathroom, peed, then moved to the sink to brush her teeth. Halfway through this ritual, her eyes finally open, she gazed at the bottom of the washbowl, contemplating as always that tiny bit of black mold that persisted in forming around the drain fixture. Without much enthusiasm she then raised her head to have a look in the mirror. Staring back was a complete and total stranger.

It was not, as one might think, early senility or amnesia. She was cognitively functional and perfectly rational. It was simply that for the first time in nearly twenty-five years the woman saw herself; not a reflection in someone else's eyes, not another's perception of her; just herself.

She could, and often did, see herself as her children did. There were three of them and to each she was someone different. She could easily see herself as her parents did, generous though their estimations were. And, of course, most often, she saw herself as her husband saw her… "the other half" of him, he always said. Interesting though that he never said that he was the other half of her. Nevertheless, this was going to be a banner day. This morning she could see only herself, sans embellishments and interpretations.

It was indeed odd to study this stranger and wonder who the hell she was. With a rising sense of panic, the woman realized that she not only did not know who she was but that she could, in fact, only vaguely remember who she had been those many years ago. When, she wondered, had her value, her importance, become contingent on the ever-changing space allotted her in Brian's life. It was a shape shifting thing which expanded, grew to fill his empty places, and then suddenly, without warning or apparent reason, was brutally compressed as other people, other things, more interesting, more important, entered his life and required space.

She was bitterly, agonizingly lonely, the emotion so great that at times it was an effort not to cry out with the pain of it. Her resentment had grown, at first unnoticed, but still relentlessly, like the kudzu which choked her swamp maple, until finally she was so angry that her chest hurt. The long hidden fury that raised her blood pressure and fed her ulcer had today burst through the barriers of civility and blossomed into an all-consuming rage. However, since she was alone there was no one to know it. Her hands shook as she watched the mirror crumple and twist into weeping. Unable to face the soulless stranger any longer, she crawled back into her bed and went to sleep.

†*Chapter One* †

October 4, 1319

The young lieutenant shuddered as he dropped the nearly dead girl at the monastery's heavy front gate. Turning, he reached for the age-blackened bell then mounted hurriedly, cantering toward the distant tree line, wanting to be away before its summons was answered. He would not rid himself of the memory of the night just past as easily.

The soldiers had come upon her an hour or more before dusk, wandering as though lost, in a darkening forest some miles to the west, the blood-lust of a battle won still pounding through their veins. Without thought or malice each man had used her in his own way, attempting to counter the horror of life's destruction with an equally vicious and violent parody of creating it.

All had not finished with her until nearly dawn and, but for the lieutenant, they'd have left her for the crows. When the order to "ride" echoed down the line, overcome with guilt, he approached his superior. Having sought and received permission to do so, he'd then thrown the girl over the pommel of his wooden saddle and turned his horse's head toward the distant monastery, determined that at least she would have a Christian burial.

His commander, a seasoned soldier, pitied the younger man, who had yet to learn that war was more than battle. "Make haste," he ordered quietly. "Rejoin the column before nightfall. It would not do to be about in these woods alone."

Seeth Miko Trimpert

As he rode away, several of the lieutenant's contemporaries laughed aloud and made sport of his softness. Older men, wiser and battle-weary, chided gently or kept their own counsel.

The bell pealed throughout the silent monastery, cracking its stillness like shattering glass. The Abbot, lost in morning prayers, started in surprise. He could not remember when last the bell had tolled. Other monks busily engaged in morning chores raised their heads at its sound, and the young oblate whose job it was to answer such rare calls scurried in the direction of the portal, his heart skipping in anticipation. His day already enlivened and its prospects improved, the boy opened the gate.

His mouth gaped as he beheld the nude, battered body of a girl who was, to all appearances, dead. Never before having seen a naked female, and truly believing her beyond help, the youngster took his time to examine her, even going so far as to actually touch a bloodied nipple. Enthralled by the scene for but a moment, he rose and straightened quickly at the sound of the Abbot's footsteps.

"What is it, lad?" the Abbot queried, but before the dumbstruck boy could mouth a reply the older man had seen for himself. "Fetch Brother Dominic," he ordered, "and Brother Bartholemew. Quickly, boy, quickly!"

As the boy fled in search of help, the Abbot knelt beside the broken body. He felt gently along the side of her neck, hoping that he might find a pulse. "Dear God, girl," he prayed, "what have they done to you?"

But what they had done was all too obvious. Her face was bruised, her lips swollen and split. There were teeth marks on her neck and shoulders and vicious bites around

The Monastery

both nipples. Under her nails was the flesh of her assailants. Her wrists and ankles were burned as though they had been tied with coarse rope and blood still leaked from between her thighs. The Abbot turned her gently to see back and buttocks; noting still more blood he dared look no further.

Brother Bartholemew arrived from the herbarium, Brother Dominic on his heels. The latter had run full-tilt from the infirmary where he'd been tending to Father Lucien's painful gout. Noting the now gathering monks, Brother Bart stripped off the rough woolen robe, which covered his breeches and work shirt, and threw it over the naked girl.

"Get her inside," the Abbot ordered, motioning to Bartholemew. But, as the younger monk stooped to lift the injured girl, Father Lucien limped into view, a single eyebrow raised, nostrils flared.

"Women," he stated clearly, "are not permitted within these walls."

The Abbot cast a withering look, which fell like a shadow at the younger priest's feet. His voice cold, he countered, "Shall we close the door then?"

Lucien looked away in retreat. "I suppose not," he conceded. "I only meant…"

Ignoring the exchange, Brother Bart picked up the girl, holding her against his chest. She weighed almost nothing. He took a single step in the direction of the infirmary before the Abbot stopped him, a hand on his shoulder.

"No," said the older man, "she cannot be among us. Put her in the Bishop's cell. He has not visited in so long I doubt he remembers we are still here."

Bartholemew changed direction and strode away. Dominic and the Abbot followed.

Old straw rustled and a small mouse scurried into the

room's corner as Batholomew lay the girl in the Bishop's bed. Dominic, who often acted as physician, was to make the girl as comfortable as possible; Bartholomew to assist.

"Clean her up and stay with her," the Abbot told them. "Surely she will not live until nightfall. I shall fetch the oils for Last Rites. There is little else we can do."

Dominic immediately busied himself gathering his herbs and salves. He lit a fire and placed a kettle on the small stove allotted for a visiting Bishop's comfort, preparing a basin of warm water laced with lavender before the kettle steamed.

Meanwhile, Bartholomew arranged the girl on clean linens and began the task of washing away her blood and the stench of the soldiers, first with trickling lavender water that ran pink and then with soft strokes, cleansing the wounds which Dominic would repair should she live.

It had been five years since Bartholemew had touched a woman but he had not forgotten. And this woman, he thought sadly, must have been lovely. When all was done but for her privates, he hesitated. Betrayed by his body, he was suddenly angry that what once had been pleasurable was now a source of shame.

Dominic saw his discomfort and took pity on his friend. "I can finish, Brother," he offered.

Bartholomew blushed. Turning away, he gazed out the window over the herbs to the vineyards beyond.

Dominic made quick work of completing the bath and then began careful application of his ointments and salves. Steam rose, mixed with the medicaments and permeated the moist air with the earthy scent of the garden. His task finally complete, Dominic pulled a sheet up to cover the girl's breasts and turned to Bartholemew.

The Monastery

"Watch her while I return to the surgery. That nipple should be stitched, and the bite on her back, as well. I shall need my smallest awl and some fine thread."

Bartholemew looked up in surprise. "You believe she will live?"

Dominic nodded, "She is young, though perhaps not so young as I had first thought. If they have not done great harm on the inside, she will mend quickly." Then he frowned. "Pray God she does not remember what has happened to her for that could truly make her die."

Dominic returned almost before he had left and settled to his surgery. With patience and great skill, he sutured the more serious injuries making tiny stitches which in time would leave no mark. When all were repaired but the tears caused by repeated rape and sodomy Dominic turned to his companion. "I shall need assistance," he said.

Bartholomew acknowledged with a wave of his hand. For the next two hours, desire pounding, he helped to position, reposition and hold the woman while his friend worked. Finally, shamed beyond silence, he muttered, "Aquinas is wrong. Concupiscence is not voluntary."

Dominic chuckled. "In your defense even Aquinas argued that *delight destroys the judgement of prudence.*" When Bartholomew looked doubtful, Dominic continued, "and Damascene maintains that *the involuntary act deserves mercy or indulgence, and is done with regret.*" He raised his eyebrows, a silent query, "But... do you regret?"

Angry now, Bartholomew growled, "Do you feel nothing then? Am I an animal?"

Dominic, stitching carefully, smiled in understanding. "Nay, I have felt it, too, that hunger... but rarely for a woman."

The morning passed.

The Abbot entered as the two monks were pulling an old, well-worn nightshirt over the girl's head. Laying her gently on the yet again clean linens, they covered her modestly in preparation for Extreme Unction, the last sacrament. But for her soft breathing she might already have been dead. Feather-light and rag-limp, she gave no other sign of life.

When the girl had been anointed and God's mercy invoked, the Abbot crossed himself, rose and clasped the shoulders of his two young friends.

"You have done well, my sons. Now we will see what God has in store."

Dominic's stomach growled

"Hungry?" the Abbot queried, trying hard to hide his amusement. Dominic was always hungry.

Dominic flushed, then nodded.

"Go then and eat. You have earned it, both of you. I shall sit with her. Ask Brother Francis to come to me in an hour. We shall watch her in turns. She must not die alone." Then thinking of a time long past when his own young wife had died without family or friends, he added quietly, "No one should die alone."

William Devon, Abbott of the Monastery of St.Fiacre, was a good man and a sensible one. He had come to religious life full grown, a mature man, fleeing a cruel world. Having lost his beloved wife in childbirth, he had spurned the well-intentioned counsel of family and friends to find another. He had wanted no other and so had chosen to disappear into the mysterious world of the monasteries, eventually finding some peace here where life was calm and moral uncertainties

The Monastery

few. Time, God's physician, had taken the knife-sharp edge off his pain.

His life was not, however, without its challenges. The Abbot had in his charge young men like Bartholemew, Dominic and their friend, Matthew, who had the spring sap of desire still rising within them. He had Brother Francis, young in body but old in spirit, whose pitiful confessions made clear that he lived in terror of both his body and his God. He had Father Lucien, the only other priest in their small community, who saw sin in every man but himself. He had Brother Luis and Brother Paul, both past middle life, hardworking and God fearing men; and he had Brother Toland who, like himself, had once been married. Ten men in all, if one counted young Peter, an orphan abandoned at the gate. Ten men who had come to God by a melange of paths. Some had sought Him; some He had called. Some had fled the world; some been sent from it to do a duty. All these men, who did not live as men, and now, now there was a woman among them.

At the sound of the bell for Sext, Brother Francis, soft, round and cross-eyed, stumbled uncertainly into the Bishop's cell, his flaming red hair awry and upright like the comb on a cock. The Abbot explained to him his task: he need only sit quietly with the child (a term he used deliberately) calling out should there be a change and, if not, waiting for his relief.

Brother Francis blanched and stammered, "Aaaa-alone? You ww-wish mmm-me to stttt-ay with her alone?"

"Yes, Francis" the Abbott replied, patting the little man sympathetically. "You can manage it. She cannot hurt you and the devil is not about just now."

Seeth Miko Trimpert

Then, chuckling to himself, he went to gather the other members of his flock to explain the vigil. Each man, excepting young Peter, would watch the girl for one hour before being relieved by another. Should she, God willing, survive the day, the cycle would begin again and continue until she had no further need of them or died.

Listening carefully to the plan, Dominic shot Bartholemew a teasing smile. "Like Perpetual Adoration," he whispered.

Father Lucien, seated behind them and ever the eavesdropper, hissed, "Blasphemy!"

The Abbott prayed silently. "Help me, Lord."

And so it began…

Brother Francis suffered the agony of his first hour of temptation, fretting and pacing. A chubby, carrot-headed little man with pale skin and a tonsured pate, he gave the impression of a bumbler, someone not quite bright. Perhaps, it was the lazy eye, which gave his face a simple look and caused him often to misjudge a distance, walking always with an uneven gait. Ever agitated and ill at ease, he fidgeted endlessly when required to converse and fled the company of his brothers at every chance, retreating to the comfort of his animal pens.

Francis dutifully checked the girl's breathing several times during his watch, but otherwise kept his eyes averted. When once she stirred briefly, causing the sheet to expose a bruised shoulder, Francis struggled mightily with his decision, but then, feeling autumn's chill even through his own thick robe, took pity on her and reached to cover her once again. Afraid to allow his mind to wander, he read from his Bible, skipping quickly over Genesis 3:6-13 lest the

The Monastery

woman tempt him, too.

When Brother Paul arrived for his turn, Francis breathed a sigh of relief and stammered heartfelt thanks. The Abbott, passing from his own rooms to the refectory, watched as the little monk stumbled away toward the chapel muttering his Act of Contrition under his breath.

Paul assumed his duties with an air of slight distraction. He checked the girl's pulse and felt her cheek to judge temperature. Finding her cool, he tucked an extra blanket around her and sat himself in an adjacent chair. Unusual as the circumstances were, he still had much else upon his mind. The monastery's cook, he was responsible for turning all produce and livestock raised by the others into palatable and life sustaining food. He'd left poor Peter to clear away the remains of the midday meal, but there was yet another to prepare before day's end.

Paul did not hold with the practice, common in many monasteries, of one meal at midmorning. The brothers of St. Fiacre's were farmers, hardworking men who toiled from well before dawn until the light failed. Such men needed food. In years past when monks appeared wasted and pallid and had often grown ill, Paul had made his case to the previous Abbot, a cold, hard man who would not relent. Then, they had kept to the ritual privations, spending their nights in prayer and their days in toil and hunger. Even young men had died. However, when that Abbot passed, Father William, his replacement, had readily agreed to Paul's proposed changes and the custom of three daily meals was instituted. As well, nightlong prayer vigils were largely suspended. Now they prayed, to be sure, but they also ate well and slept. The men were healthy and Paul was well pleased.

Seeth Miko Trimpert

In another life Brother Paul might have been a fine French chef, for his work was his passion and his natural ability substantial. He had escaped the crushing poverty of his small village years past, when as a boy, the ninth of twelve children, he had run away to join a group of Franciscans traveling through his land. He'd willingly become a virtual slave in exchange for food and a bit of kindness. Eventually, growing too fond of him, the leader had sent the boy to a Thomist friend to be educated in the ways of the Church. Paul might have lived yet in that first priory had not he and another of his age been found together exploring the gift that God had given them. His punishment was banishment to St. Fiacre's, the Elba of his world. However, young and infinitely adaptable, he had taken to his new surroundings and attached himself to the cook, a kindly old man of dubious culinary ability, who had died within the year, leaving Brother Paul the entirety of his comestible domain.

At the end of his hour, Paul rose, stretched his long thin frame, which appeared to benefit not at all from his efforts in the kitchen, and reported all well to Brother Luis, who replaced him.

Brother Luis dusted himself off and slowly surveyed the room, noting not only the now sleeping girl, but also the relative opulence of the cell allotted visiting Church dignitaries. It seemed to him quite ludicrous that he and his brothers should suffer the pain of chilblains in winter when a perfectly good firebox lay unused. Still, he did not complain. His life was as he wished it. He worked contentedly alongside Matthew, Toland and, sometimes, Bartholomew through the long growing seasons, producing what was needed to feed themselves and their livestock. When a small surplus could

The Monastery

be managed Father Lucien sold it, along with wine from the vineyard, in a distant town, allowing them the occasional small luxury they could not produce themselves.

Long ago, before a succession of brutal winters had lain waste to the vineyards and left them near starvation, the monks of St. Fiacre's had been expected to provide several bishoprics and, sometimes, even Rome with fine wine and delicacies. But in those lean years when there was nothing to send, the old Church royalty had died off. Papal power waned. Even now, the Pope was only three years pontiff and under political and philosophical siege. Few, if any, remembered what once had been available from far-distant St. Fiacre's. The monks had neither seen nor heard from their Bishop in years.

And Luis was more than satisfied with this state of affairs. Having passed three decades in his present life, he felt little need of outside intervention. Their group was an agreeable one, their Abbot sensitive and reasonable, and the cloistered nature of their life, shelter from the strife – he glanced at the girl – outside their walls.

His hour passed quickly. The girl moved once or twice and moaned softly at the pain of it, but did not wake. Brother Luis, of course, did not speak to her.

Brother Toland arrived tired and sunburned from his work in the fields. He reported to Luis that most of the corn was stored safely in the cribs, fodder for the few cattle and winter-feed for the chickens. The shocks were bound in one field; the other was as yet untouched. Clearing stubble was backbreaking labor.

"We shall ask the others for help tomorrow," Brother Luis said. "If we are to plant early next spring we must have the fields clear before the freeze."

Toland nodded his agreement and then turned to the woman. Having been early at his forge this was the first he had seen of her, although the monastery buzzed constantly of little else. "How is she?" he asked.

"Well enough," replied the other farmer. "She is, perhaps, a little feverish, but not burning. She moves a bit and cries out when she does, but has given no sign of waking. Dominic says she must have water but I do not see how you will manage it." He shrugged, his resignation evident. "We shall see." Then grasping his friend's arm in farewell he moved purposefully toward the door. It was growing late. "I can get another hour in the field before dark, if I hurry."

Toland looked carefully at his charge. Battered as she was, her beauty was there for all to see. Already the purple on her cheeks bled toward yellow. She will heal quickly, he thought, then amended, if she lives. Seeing nothing that required his attention, he sat wearily in the nearby chair, still warm from its previous occupant. Within minutes the toll of fieldwork and the soporific effect of the warm stove had overcome him. He nodded off and was snoring softly when Dominic entered the room. Noting the even rhythm of her breathing and the relaxed demeanor of her countenance, Dominic left his friend to nap beside the mending girl and tiptoed from the room.

Toland woke and checked the girl. He held the wet cloth to her lips as Luis had shown him and noted with satisfaction that she seemed to take some water.

He had, long ago, put aside the anguish of losing a young wife to another. Bitterly, he'd cast aside the world and its women. Watching the girl it crept back, that well-remembered pain. During the early years he had sometimes,

The Monastery

late in the night, felt the need of her. When it became more than he could bear, more than prayer might match, more than long hours kneeling on the cold stone floor could conquer, he had relented and dealt with himself brutally, more pain that pleasure, bringing scant relief. But those times were now rare. Her face had faded. Now when he woke with the need of a woman, it was any woman, not her. Toland shook himself. He must not think of these things. His peace was hard won, too fragile.

Bartholomew knocked softly and entered.

"I was expecting Matthew," Toland said, his voice rising in surprise.

"He is still in the fields," Bartholomew replied. "I shall take his place. Dominic and I finished today preparing the vineyard for winter. The vines are pruned and well protected with your fine straw. Even Lucien did some work."

"How ever did you manage that?" Toland laughed quietly, his sarcasm barely masked.

Bartholomew shook his head and swallowed the temptation of an unkind reply. "Supper will be soon. Ask Paul to save me something. I am starved."

"I will have something brought here or bring it myself," Toland promised. Then, pointing his chin toward the bed, he added, "I think she took some water from the cloth."

"Good," Bartholomew replied.

Brother Bartholomew began his vigil by coaxing the girl to take more fluid. She responded only by turning her face away and mewling like a baby. When he laid a hand upon her shoulder her agitation increased until he withdrew.

Left to herself, she soon quieted and the steady rhythm of her breathing resumed.

Bartholomew could not take his eye from the girl. Until the morning just passed, he'd thought himself finally free of this awful longing. Although he had not chosen this life, he had thought himself hardened to it. True, he was not without his sleepless nights but he *was* a man and those could be managed and confessed. But, now the loneliness and wanting had begun all over again.

As the last son of a wealthy lord whose lands lay in the north of England, near the Scottish border, religious life had been his lot. The first son inherited the land, English law. The second went to the King's Army. The third son, tradition decreed, went to the Church and, as fate would have it, Bartholomew was that third son. Of course, he had rebelled. He had loved the land. He had loved the tenant families. Their sheep, their sons and their dogs had all known him. And their daughters had known him, too, for he was tall and handsome, with broad shoulders, fine manners and an appetite for life and its shared pleasures which had curled their toes in delight. He had fought hard against this barren life until his father, in despair, threatened to disown him. For a young man of wealth and privilege, poverty and disgrace loomed large. Their Bishop, recognizing that Bartholemew would never make a monk near home, sent him immediately to the Continent where he had remained in a monastery of exiles, seemingly all but forgotten.

Bartholomew pulled himself from his reverie to greet a bone weary Matthew, who crept quietly into the sick room lest he wake the girl. He seemed barely able to move, exhausted from long days of swinging the heavy scythe. "Go

The Monastery

to bed, Matt," his friend advised. "I can do another hour."

A weary Matthew shook his head. "No," he answered, "I will take my turn. What shall I do?"

"Very little," Bartholomew replied. "Watch her and try to get her to take some water like this." He demonstrated, dribbling water drops onto the girl's lips with the damp cloth. "Call Dominic if she wakes. Lucien will relieve you at eight."

Matthew watched the girl as Bartholomew had bade him do. He was one of the few amongst them with a true calling. While still a boy he had heard the voice of God, telling him clearly and in no uncertain terms what he must do with his life. And he was only too happy to do it. With little exposure to the world and its pleasures – he had only known his homely, widowed mother and a baby sister – he was not haunted by what he had missed. True, he'd had a brief entanglement with another boy while still a novice, but a wise and kindly prior, seeing it for what it was, had moved him beyond the reach of the older boy and such was not repeated. No, it was not, as one might guess, sinful predilections which had brought Matthew into exile but honesty.

Several years after taking his vows, Matthew had been enlisted, due to his remarkable facility with numbers, to assist with the bookkeeping requirements of a large and profitable English monastery. It was child's play to discover the gross irregularities which routinely filled the purses of the Prior and his clerk. Ignorant in the ways of the Church, he had gone directly to the Prior with his findings. St. Fiacre's was his new home.

Seeth Miko Trimpert

Father Lucien arrived at eight exactly, righteous indignation painted across his sharp features. He nodded curtly to Brother Matthew as though he had caught him in some unspeakable sin and cut him off abruptly when the younger man attempted to show him how to give the girl water. Matthew made no further overtures but stopped in the infirmary en route to Chapel to suggest that Dominic might wish to look in on his patient during the coming hour. Dominic nodded, having already anticipated the need.

Fastidious to a fault, Lucien picked up his robes, as if contact with the floor of a room in which a woman breathed might somehow compromise his soul. He walked carefully around the cot looking down his long nose at the girl. He had no doubt but what her presence was the work of the Devil. Only a fool would think her God's work. One had merely to look to see that she was a whore. If God were about he would take her quickly; of that he was certain. The priest had no intention of participating in the prolongation of this Magdalene's life, a circumstance he had made all too clear, protesting vehemently his assignment of this hour and swearing that should she live he would not repeat it.

The Abbot, exhausted from a trying day, had given him a long, weary look.

"Have you no soul, man?" he had asked. "Is there not a drop of Christian charity within that heart of yours?"

But Lucien had been unrelenting. Jaw set, eyes blazing with presumed religious fervor, he strode from the Abbot's rooms. Now he sat stiffly, staring anywhere but at the girl who, after hours of healing sleep, was beginning to swim toward consciousness. She moaned softly. Twisting and turning, she pushed the coverings from her. The priest's eyes, once narrowed in condemnation, widened.

The Monastery

Lucien was not a man who denied himself, as his gout readily proclaimed. He ate and drank too well and invested hours, both his own and Peter's, in the maintenance of his person and clothing, sheer vanity. He did as little work as the Abbot would allow, claiming privilege due a priest. The pleasures of the flesh were his one abstinence. Women were evil, the source of all sin and he avoided them at all costs. Still he could not deny himself. He could not turn away.

For all the thin, sweat soaked nightshirt covered, the girl might have been naked. Lucien watched her move her head from side to side, her tangled hair curling at the edges of her face. Her tongue moved tentatively across cracked, bruised lips. And her breasts, dear Jesus, rose and fell with each breath. Lucien left his chair and walked to the cot. Drawing a finger across the girl's cheek he caught an unshed tear, then laid a hand on her chest, a nipple pressing against his palm with each inhalation. Thus he stayed for some minutes feeling, as any man might, a need to protect her, to hold her, to have her for himself.

Suddenly, Lucien jumped back as if stung. Upsetting the chair in his haste, he flew from the room, sprinting past several monks returning from evensong. He burst in upon the Abbot without so much as a knock.

"I will not be with her again," he roared. "I will not! She must go, William! The Devil is in this house! Do you hear me? The Devil! Cast him out, quickly, before he ensnares us all!" With that he was gone.

Noting Father Lucien's precipitous and premature departure from the sick room, Dominic straightened away the remnants of his work in the infirmary and, taking his guttering candle, went early to his watch. Young Peter, much to his dismay, had been forbidden to be alone with the girl and so she had now survived one full circuit of the monastery's inhabitants. Dominic was to begin the second.

In the throes of autumn's final chores, the monastery was very busy. Every able-bodied man toiled from dawn to dusk, doing the work of two, in order to ensure that they had stores enough for the coming winter. Even Father Lucien had been pressed into service. The Abbot knew that men cannot work long without sleep and so, aware of Dominic's relative disinterest in the fairer sex and confident in his abilities as a healer, had accepted the younger monk's offer to place his own pallet on the sick room floor allowing the others their night's rest.

Lucien, of course, was horrified.

Nonetheless, St. Fiacre's settled in for the night.

†††

April 10, 1997

The nursing assistants from the departing evening shift chatted idly while their charge nurse, Dylan Sinclair, reported off to the oncoming night staff. Nearly finished, he droned on, "321A is a Mrs. Brenda Ellis, a 77 year old white female. One day status post right hip replacement."

The night charge, MaryLee Simms, wrote hurriedly:
Ellis, Brenda – 77 yo WF
– 1d s/p R hip replacement.
As Sinclair continued, so did the night nurse:
drsg – DI, afebrile
Tylox q4h prn pain.
Finally, the last bed. The tired monotony of Sinclair's

tone altered, his voice rising to create a sense of expectation. MaryLee looked up from her notes, waiting.

"321B is Rebecca Kincaid, a 49 year-old, white female. Admitted yesterday. She's stable, afebrile. Has an IV of D5 and a half, running TKO."

Gathering his notes, he rose to leave.

MaryLee placed a restraining hand on his arm. "Hey, wait a minute. What's her diagnosis?"

Sinclair turned, eyebrows peaked. "She's sleeping," he replied.

"Come on, Dylan. Sleeping isn't a diagnosis. What's wrong with her?"

"She's sleeping," he repeated with a slight shrug. "Stable, afebrile, no apparent trauma. We are unable to wake her. She does not respond to voice commands, but withdraws from painful stimuli. And," he added with emphasis and a shade of sarcasm, "she is the patient of the great Dr. Miles Winston."

"The Chief of Staff?" MaryLee's surprise was evident.

Sinclair nodded. "One and the same."

"What are we doing for her?" MaryLee asked.

"Keeping her dry," Sinclair replied with asperity. "Her husband is Brian Kincaid."

"Senator Brian Kincaid?".

"Yup," Dylan answered. "Step lightly."

Despite her best efforts, it was 4:30 a.m. before MaryLee had the time to actually sit down and look at her charts. She had survived the piracy of one of her aides by another floor, an unsuccessful code and midnight and 2 a.m. medication rounds. She had also helped her now lone aide

Seeth Miko Trimpert

weigh six patients since the shared bed scale had arrived on their floor at 2:45 a.m. instead of at the scheduled 5:30.

Finally, she sat down with a sigh, her thrice-heated vanilla latte on the desk in front of her. She carefully charted all her medication administration, transferring the information from a crumpled worksheet in her pocket. Then she found the chart marked **Rebecca Kincaid***.*

She glanced quickly at the admission sheet. Sure enough – Next of Kin: Brian Kincaid. There were also three children listed: Brian Jr., Melissa and Evan. There was nothing else of interest. She flipped to the History and Physical. The H&P was where nurses often found the things they really wanted to know.

Rebecca Kincaid, nee Hanson, appeared to be the only child of a Professor and Mrs. Argill Hanson of Omaha, Nebraska. She was a graduate of Northwestern University, had a degree in history with an emphasis on the Middle Ages. There was a note indicating that she had specialized in Medieval Monastic Life. Her children were grown. There was no current or past work history noted. Being the wife of Brian Kincaid, MaryLee thought, was probably a full-time job.

As Dylan had indicated, the physical was unremarkable. Mrs. Kincaid showed no sign of illness or injury. Her vital signs were normal and stable. Her blood work was well within normal limits and there was no indication of trauma.

MaryLee headed for Room 321. Mrs. Kincaid was sleeping quietly, curled on her left side, knees to chest, her arms around them. When touched she pulled away and cried softly like an injured child. Left alone, she quieted quickly. MaryLee checked her IV and returned to the Nurses' Station.

† *Chapter Two* †

October 5, 1319

Morning came and the girl slept on. The monks began again their silent vigils and held fast through a second day. In the middle of the night that followed, Dominic, asleep on his pallet on the stone floor, sensed movement. Thinking that perhaps Bartholomew or the Abbot had come to check on the girl, as they had done the previous night, he opened his eyes. However, tonight it was the girl who moved about. Her attempt to right herself had drawn from her a sharp cry of pain. Not wishing to frighten her, Dominic sat up slowly. "Can I help you?" he asked softly.

The girl, still too disoriented to be startled, shook her head.

Dominic continued to rise, then padded toward her cot on bare feet. He watched as her eyes darted about seeking something familiar, some sense of where she was. Eventually, spying the unused chamber pot in a corner of the room she gestured shyly. Dominic fetched it and placed it within easy reach. The girl struggled but could not manage alone. "Let me help you," Dominic offered again.

Too exhausted to do otherwise, the girl surrendered what little dignity she had left and then crawled like a wounded animal back beneath the covers. Once again, she slept.

In the morning, when Dominic awoke, the girl sat painfully erect in the room's only chair. Eyes wide, her tears glistened.

"Are you all right?" he asked.

She did not answer.

"Have you a name?"

The girl hesitated as if uncertain. Dominic could see panic lurking behind her eyes. Then she nodded. "Cecilia."

Dominic asked no more. He prepared some tea, summoned Peter and sent him scurrying for porridge. He chatted disarmingly of inconsequential things while the girl ate what was offered, drank the tea and gingerly returned to her bed where she slept away the remainder of the day. Dominic cleaned and dressed her wounds, rightly thinking it less distressing for him to do so while she slept.

The Abbot, agreeing with Dominic that the girl was no longer in peril, suspended the vigils and cautioned everyone to treat her gently when she deigned to emerge from the Bishop's cell, which finally she did on the fourth day.

I sit now in the herbarium of what must be a monastery. The sunlight is warm and soothing. I keep very still as movement brings pain. Before me a tall, handsome man works the ground on his hands and knees. His hair is thick and black around a sun-browned tonsure and his eyes, so serious, are blue. He is patient, digging carefully and patting the earth gently as though it were his child. He wears the habit of a monk, kilted above his knees, though I know not what order. I am not of the faith. How I know this I do not know, since I have no sense of who I am, save that I am called Cecilia. I am sorely wounded, but have no memory of how I came to be so, although my injuries are those of a woman who has been ill-used by many. Despite the fact that there are many men here, nine and a boy, I do not believe they have caused me this harm for although they are nearly silent and mostly unsmiling, they are all, but one, kind and considerate. Still I am afraid.

She sat, looking frightened and forlorn, on a bench that had been brought for her. Bartholomew smiled at her and returned to his work.

Peter brought her tea.

The Abbot came to bid her good morning. Still she did not speak.

When the dinner bell tolled Bartholomew rose to take her back to her room. She did not eat with them. As he helped her to her feet she faced him, tilting her face upward toward his. Her brown eyes swam in a pool of tears, her lashes dripping. Grasping Bartholomew's hand in desperation, she whispered, "I do not know who I am."

Bartholomew hesitated for a hair's breadth in time, then, overtaken by his own humanity, folded her into a clumsy embrace and motioned to the gaping novice to find the Abbot and waste no time about it.

"You are Cecilia," he told her, gently stroking her back. "You have said so to Brother Dominic."

In the days that followed the Abbot talked with the girl for hours.

"Tell me about yourself," he encouraged, "about your people."

Cecilia had no response. She remembered nothing.

"Do you know how you came here?"

She shook her head.

"Have you family or friends nearby?"

She did not know.

Her history, her family seemed not to exist, a mystery,

lost along with the cause of her injuries in memory's cloud. Slowly, her body healed and her health returned but who she was and from whence she had come remained a puzzle.

When it was clear that she would recover, Father Lucien was tasked with making discreet inquiries during his trips abroad in the distant towns. Someone must know something, the monks had reasoned. But all had come to naught. Still, even Lucien agreed, a young woman with no family could not simply be cast out to fend for herself. With neither dowry nor virtue she would surely end a common whore and that the Abbot would not abide.

William considered Lucien's oft-made suggestion that they ship her off to a nunnery on the French coast, an idea which intellectually, pragmatically, had its appeal. But, a barren, loveless life for such a girl? The Abbot thought not. He would wait.

Life in the monastery took on the routine of early winter but with a new and subtle undercurrent. The monks went about their tasks, decanting the wines, managing the stock and preserving winter stores. They repaired harnesses, sharpened tools and mended items broken and discarded for lack of time during the busy summer months. They did their sewing and resoled their boots. But always, however dull the chore, there was a sense of expectation, for at any time she might wander into the room. Although unable to recall a past, the girl was intelligent and hardworking. She could darn a sock or make a soup. She would take on any job, never expecting to eat at the table without working first. And she sang while she worked, not amongst them of course, but when she thought herself alone.

When the men were otherwise engaged, Cecilia

The Monastery

explored the old monastery. It had clearly seen better days. Once the province of Carthusians, it had been built long ago on the same general, but much reduced, plan as Mount Grace Priory in Yorkshire.

Across the center of the priory lay a row of common rooms which, like a man's belt, divided it nearly evenly into two quadrangles: one for living, one for working. In the North quad, each monk had a small place of his own, which contained an upper workroom with sleeping room below. Each little house shared a wall with its neighbors, and all fronted on the covered cloister which in summer fringed a square of green.

For most of the Thomists the upper workroom lay unused since they, unlike their Carthusians predecessors, were not hermits. Thus they did not keep daylong to their cells, shunning the company of others as the monastery's previous tenants had done but worked, ate and prayed together, enjoying the company of their brethren, albeit in a restrained, sometimes even solemn, way.

In the South quad were the storage sheds, barns and the forge. Here, too, was a long building, once two dorters end to end, designed for the housing of the many novices and lay churchmen who had once done the work of a busy and prosperous Carthusian monastery, while their betters lived a reclusive life of prayer and contemplation. These now lay empty and dilapidated, the victims of long neglect. Only the barns, forge and workrooms, the province of Francis, Toland and the farmers, were well kept and busy.

Cecilia spent many of the foreshortened winter days in these explorations, out of the sight, but rarely the minds, of the monks. Only Francis would glimpse her from time to

Seeth Miko Trimpert

time, darting among the ruins.

One day, near Christmas, Father Lucien came upon the girl in the library. She was sitting beneath a north window in a pool of cold, thin light, humming, a book in her lap.

"Put it up, child," he scolded. "Books are rare and valuable things and not for the likes of you."

The girl flushed and reached high to return the book to its proper place, her breasts straining against the fabric of her shirt. "I am sorry, Father," she apologized. "I only wanted to read for a bit."

The cleric, already angered by his body's reaction to her, scowled. "Read?" he scoffed. "Surely, you cannot read?"

"Oh, yes, Father, I can," she replied. "Would you like me to show you?"

"Certainly not," the priest snapped. Then he turned on his heel and quickly withdrew.

As the winter months passed each man found reason to be near her. The Abbot taught her chess and, once she had mastered it, they played late into the night before the roaring fire, laughing delightedly when one finally bested the other.

Brother Paul taught her to cook, sharing with her jealously guarded recipes he would not have told to God.

Dominic gave her lessons in the healing arts. Together they made decoctions of hyssop for Brother Luis's weak chest. They made mustard plasters, and garlic poultices. They brewed willow bark tea for the Abbot's gnarled finger joints, which ached ceaselessly in the winter's cold. Herbs were dried, crushed, stored.

And always, always her voice could be heard chattering, laughing. She was undaunted by her companions'

The Monastery

reticence to speak, her enthusiasm slowly precipitating a thaw in the long winter of silence.

She followed Francis to the stables where she helped with feeding the chickens and the goats. The poor man stuttered and stammered, but finally managed to teach her to milk the cow, blushing furiously when he realized that his bumbled explanation of the function of a teat was most likely wasted on one who had them.

She helped Matthew and Bartholomew with the grapevine cuttings, which they planned to graft in spring and were now nursing through the cold months.

Peter she taught to read. Although the boy had already acquired the most rudimentary skills under the strict tutelage of the monks, he was a reluctant and less than apt pupil. However, for the pleasure of Cecilia's company he would willingly have translated Caesar's GallicWars, and so applied himself with great diligence. Now he could often be found book in hand, far-sighted eyes squinting painfully below a furrowed brow, his tongue caught between clenched teeth. Nevertheless, soon he could read and appreciate much of what was to be found between the leather bindings in the monastery's library.

Toland and Lucien, each for his own reasons, kept their distance. Toland was polite, though aloof. Lucien was angry and cold.

"Why don't they like me?" Cecilia asked. "Have I offended them?"

"You have not," the Abbot replied kindly, "but God has by creating you. Pay them no mind."

Lucien persisted in his arguments that Cecilia must go. One bitter evening when the Abbot put him off yet again, Lucien rounded on him, a nasty, knowing glint flashing in his green eyes. "You'll never put her out, William," he accused. "I know that. We all know it. You want her for yourself. Any fool can see it."

Accepting the truth of the accusation, the Abbot stayed his sharp reply. After a moment's consideration, he answered quietly, "I want her for us all, Lucien. She brings us alive."

And it was true. Since Cecilia had come Brother Paul's menus were more innovative, his sauces richer, his desserts more frequent. Fires burned in the common rooms at all hours, the chill of old stones banished lest it be too cold for her. Men, once solitary and silent, congregated in the locutorium where conversation and light banter slowly became the norm.

The other priest lowered his eyelids quickly in an attempt to hide his soul, but it was too late.

"Yes," the Abbot repeated quietly, "I want her for us all…and so, my friend, do you."

Lucien left without further comment.

As the other priest withdrew, the Abbot sighed. I really do not like him, he thought sadly. Forgive me, Lord, but I do not.

After Father Lucien's rebuke, Cecilia sought and received permission from the Abbot to use the library. Unlike many monasteries of its time, St. Fiacre's was not limited to an armarium, a small book closet with only forty or fifty precious volumes, but had a full library. Its shelves boasted both religious and secular works, bequeathed to the monastery by a highly educated and widely read nobleman who had died without heirs.

After several abortive attempts to find something she

could understand, Cecilia asked the Abbot to recommend a book.

"Your education does not do your intelligence justice," he told her, "I should like to see you exposed to the history and philosophies of the world beyond our walls." Then without apparent plan, the Abbot found and gave her *Mohammed: God's Prophet*. "Come anytime you wish, child," he encouraged. "Read whatever you like."

I find that I have grown content. I still know only that I am Cecilia but oddly I find that that knowledge is enough. I have a place here amongst these good men and have found ways to make myself useful. No family has yet come to look for me. Am I an orphan? Was I traveling through this land? Are my people now gone, thinking me dead? Shall I ever know? Am I free then to make my own way? The Abbot says that I am. He says also that my manner and education are beyond that of my station. Perhaps, I am a lady. The brothers call me "child" but I am not a child. Although I am not certain, I believe I am near eighteen, no babe, and though I should have had a husband I cannot remember one. Surely I would remember that.

The following week Cecilia returned the book to its proper place. Alone in the library, she scanned the adjacent shelves which contained other works concerning the Saracens and their faith. Her interest now piqued she chose another and still another, tucked behind several larger tomes and hidden from view.

That evening, back in her own cell, she lit a lamp and picked up the first of the new books. It was the story of a prince and his seven wives. The tale was so outlandish that Cecilia thought to put it aside. But then, reconsidering, she continued to read. The social and religious concepts were so foreign to her that the heavy volume seemed more like the fancy of a children's tale; still she read on into the night. Two days later she began the second. At first she was shocked, for this book, unlike the others, was explicit in its descriptions of the protagonist's activities with his wives and concubines. Alone in her cell, Cecilia blushed at the thought of such things.

I have begun a book which makes my blood pound. Last night I read until nearly dawn and was forced to make excuses for my poor appearance this morning. How could I admit to reading such things and then to my dreams afterward?

On a chilly Sunday afternoon in late winter, the Abbot dozed in front of the library fire. Lead gray clouds had descended at noon, making the sky a low dark thief, which stole the chapel spire. A savage March wind whipped at gravid branches and hurled raindrops like stones against the library's windows.

In winter, Sunday afternoon was a time for each man to do as he chose. Some read or wrote letters, some played chess or an odd game of sticks, which Cecilia had yet to master. Some, like the Abbot, simply napped.

Cecilia crept into the room, intending to return her books quietly and select others without waking the sleeping man. The Abbot, however, dozed lightly. Peeking from beneath half lids, he noted the titles tucked in the crook of Cecilia's arm. As she replaced her books upon the shelves, the Abbot settled himself comfortably and readjusted the rug across aching, arthritic knees. He poured himself a small

The Monastery

brandy, then as an afterthought poured one for the girl. When she turned to face him, he pointed to the cup and nodded encouragement.

"Take it," he said. "You are no longer a child and the warmth will do you good."

Cecilia sat and the two sipped quietly for some minutes before the Abbot spoke.

Finally, he asked, "How did you find the books?"

The girl thought for a few minutes before offering an enigmatic reply, "Interesting."

"Did you like them?"

Cecilia nodded.

"Why?"

"Well," she said, eyes alight with curiosity, "they are full of things I have never considered. The ideas seem new and yet they are old. I suppose they were always there. I just did not know it."

Impressed with her intuitiveness and ability to articulate her thoughts, the Abbot nodded.

"I like the religion, too" she continued cautiously. "It is not so different as it seems."

"True," the Abbot replied. "In many ways all religions are much the same."

Made brave by the Abbot's acceptance of potential blasphemy and, of course, the unaccustomed spirits, she went on less tentatively.

"I did not know one could be married to more than one person. I thought it was a sin." She looked at the Abbot, her gaze a bold challenge. "But, I suppose if their god says it is permitted to them, then it must be so?"

The Abbot answered carefully. "Cecilia, it is not possible for any of us to know what God says."

"But what of the Bible?" she argued. "Father Lucien says the Bible is the Word of God."

The Abbot frowned. How to put it? In the end, he answered as simply as he could. "The Bible, Cecilia, is only what men have said that God has said. *Men*," he emphasized, "men just like us."

Cecilia frowned. "I shall have to consider that," she replied. Without further comment, she rose and went back to the bookshelves where she spent nearly an hour selecting two more books. Then she left the Abbot with a slight smile and a kiss on the forehead.

†††

April 18, 1997

Brian Kincaid blew onto the unit like a whirlwind. He towered over a nervous little aide, demanding to know the whereabouts of Dr. Winston. Unable to find her voice in the presence of this imposing, impatient man, the tiny woman simply gestured in the direction of Room 321. Kincaid stalked down the hallway, leaving the staff and the black and white floor tiles trembling in his wake.

He entered his wife's room without knocking to find his daughter Melissa, Miles Winston, and some foreign fellow talking quietly. "This better be good," he snarled. "I cancelled an important speech to be here."

Ignoring the rudeness, Dr. Winston extended a hand. "I thought we ought to talk," he said.

Brian Kincaid waited. The others were silent. Finally, he asked, "Did you do the brain scan?"

Dr. Winston nodded.

"And?" Kincaid prodded impatiently.

Winston cleared his throat. "And... everything is normal. In fact, her brain activity is on par with what might be anticipated in a woman leading a very active life. She appears to be communicating, problem-solving, in short, living." He shrugged. "I don't know what else to tell you, Brian. She's not brain dead. She's sleeping."

"Bullshit!" Kincaid exploded. "She hasn't opened her eyes or uttered a fucking word in over a week. That is not sleeping."

"Daddy, please," Melissa whispered.

"Shut up, Melissa," her father growled.

Miles Winston frowned. "Brian, get hold of yourself. I have someone I want you to meet, someone who may be able to explain this." The physician gestured for the small East Indian to come forward. "This is Dr. Chopak," he introduced. "Dr. Chopak, Brian Kincaid, Rebecca's husband." Politely, he added, "He is understandably upset."

"Don't patronize me, Miles," Kincaid warned.

Gurinder Chopak's proffered hand hung in the air, then returned, unshaken, to his side.

No one spoke. There were only the sounds of the hospital's public address system and the new patient in the next bed, wheezing audibly. Kincaid shot her a disgusted look.

"All right," he said, finally. "I'm listening."

"Mr. Kincaid," Dr. Chopak began, his voice liquid and lilting. "Are you familiar with the notion of reincarnation?"

Kincaid snorted, then turned his back on the speaking man. "Miles, what the hell is this? I didn't come here to listen to voodoo."

Seeth Miko Trimpert

Dr. Winston, patience exhausted, snapped, "Damn it, Brian, for once in your life, will you listen!? I have no explanation for Rebecca's condition. This man may. You can listen to what he has to say or not. It's up to you but please, stop being such as ass. It wears on all of us."

Kincaid frowned, considered for a moment and then nodded. "All right, Doctor. Speak."

Calmly, Dr. Chopak began again, his English arranged in the odd and formal way of his countrymen. "Mr. Kincaid, yesterday morning your wife was heard to be speaking."

When Kincaid opened his mouth, the Indian raised a hand to silence him.

"She was speaking slowly, almost chanting, in Latin and, although the nurses are not certain, one, a Catholic, thinks she spoke the responses of the Mass."

"That's impossible," Kincaid countered. "She isn't Catholic."

Chopak shook his head. "That is of no consequence. I ask you now again, do you know of reincarnation?"

Kincaid glared, his reply a short, contemptuous, "No."

Chopak appeared to take a mental step backward, as though deciding that Kincaid's response compelled a prologue to his previously planned statement.

"Very well. Sir, there are some, I among them, who believe we are born and reborn, our souls living a series of lives. We believe also that our souls move through eternity seeking betterment, always striving, moving forward toward the light. With each of our incarnations we learn, accomplish. What is left unlearned in one life can be known in the next. The sins of one life may be atoned in the next. But, of most

importance is that each life have purpose."

Kincaid's face was threatening thunder; Chopak was unperturbed.

"It is usual for a soul to enter a child at conception or birth... there is debate upon this point," he conceded. "... and remain with that body until it dies. But," Chopak raised a slender, brown finger, "sometimes an unhappy soul, wandering without purpose, searching if you will, may depart prematurely, abandoning an unfinished life. I think, Mr. Kincaid, that your wife's soul has left her."

Air exploded from Kincaid's lungs. "Jesus H. Christ, Miles, is this what medicine has come to?" he roared. "Is this your answer?" He was incredulous. "A thousand God-damned dollars a day and I get this!?"

The woman in the next bed wheezed again.

Kincaid snarled, making a dismissive gesture. "Get her a private room, Miles. That woman is disgusting."

Then he left, seeming to take the air in the room with him. When it returned, flowing softly back into the open space, Chopak murmured, "A most difficult man."

"I am sorry, Dr. Chopak," Winston apologized.

Dr. Chopak made a small gesture, almost like a blessing. "It is nothing, my friend. Do not concern yourself. Mr. Kincaid is a man unaccustomed to opposition. He is, I believe, most always having his own way and cannot yet accept the possibility that all that he knows is but a castle built upon the air. He will be coming back. He has no choice."

† *Chapter Three* †

<u>**March 1320**</u>

Spring burst quite suddenly through winter's back door. The monks put in the crops. Brother Francis oversaw the birth of two calves, four lambs and several goats. His rabbits, prolific as ever, were as thick as the fleas on the monastery dogs and often graced the table at dinner. Cecilia made herself useful in the kitchen and its garden. She seemed never too long in one place, never too long with one man. She was everywhere and nowhere. She mended Lucien's favorite shirt; held a bleating lamb while Francis removed a tick from its ear; learned new ways to season vegetables grown stale and dry in the root cellar. She helped Dominic prepare his springtime salve, useful and widely sought after for stiff, sore muscles tired from hours behind a plow. She moved among them, placing a hand on one's cheek, brushing shoulders with another and once, ruffling Brother Bart's hair, causing him to blush beet-red. Her movements were innocent and yet, somehow, seductive in their innocence. Most of her time was spent in the infirmary where Dominic, somewhat less susceptible to her charms, was comfortable in her company.

In April she nursed Toland through a dangerous infection, the result of his plowing over his own foot when he lost his balance and became entangled in a harness. As the monk tossed and turned, fever raging, he called again and again for "Ellie". Only Dominic, Cecilia and the Abbot heard. The others were kept away. One night, near midnight, as one owl hooted to another, Cecilia wiped her patient's

The Monastery

face and gave him water. He was burning. Just as she had decided she must call Dominic, Toland sat bolt upright and grabbed her hand. His eyes were open and pleading. "Ellie," he begged, "why did you leave me? Why?"

Cecilia opened her mouth to offer comfort but no words came. She heard his voice again, hoarse and barely audible, "I love you so much," Toland rasped, tears rolling down his cheeks. "I miss you so."

Sitting on the edge of his cot, Cecilia wrapped her arms around the weeping man and lay her head against the scorching heat of his chest.

"Lie back, love," she said softly, "I love you, too."

Toland collapsed against the pillow, pulling her over him like a blanket. Within a few moments he had relaxed his grip and fallen into a deep, healing sleep.

When finally she was able to disentangle herself, Cecilia rose and turned toward the door. There stood the Abbot, obviously witness to it all.

"I am sorry, Father, I…" she stammered, but the Abbot placed a twisted finger against his lips.

"Do not apologize, child. You have likely saved his life." Then he turned and left, returning to his own cold bed.

By early morning Toland's fever had broken, leaving him drenched several times over. Father Lucien, stopping in the infirmary at dawn to offer Communion, noted a pile of wet linens near the door. Cecilia, perched awkwardly on the sickbed's narrow edge, spooned porridge, thin as gruel, over her patient's parched lips.

"Have you been here all night," the priest demanded.

The girl nodded and continued her task.

"And you changed Brother Toland's linens?" he croaked.

Cecilia didn't answer.

"You are the devil's handmaiden," Lucien hissed. "Leave at once! Now! Heed me, girl, or suffer the consequences."

The girl did not respond.

"Go!" the priest's voice rose to a shout.

Cecilia turned briefly, meeting his fiery glare with her own, ice cold. "No," she replied quietly.

Father Lucien spun and fled, cassock flying.

Within minutes he was back, still raging, the Abbot in tow. Lucien stormed for some minutes, his angry words hailstones against the wall of the girl's resolve. Cecilia sat, silent and serene, absently stroking Toland's limp hand.

When the other priest was finally out of breath, the Abbot addressed Cecilia. "May I see you in library?"

"Certainly, Father," she replied. "I shall be finished here shortly."

Cecilia and the Abbot sat quietly gazing at the warm, grey ash of yesterday's fire. There was no sound but the occasional pop of a dying ember, lurking beneath the grate. Neither spoke: the Abbot lost in thought; Cecilia exhausted. Eventually, noting the girl's pale face and darkening smudges beneath her eyes, the Abbot poured a tot of brandy into a small cup. "Drink this, child. You look as if you could use it."

Cecilia did as she was bid. Then she waited.

"Lucien is very angry," the Abbot began.

Cecilia shrugged.

"Do not under estimate him, child. He can be

dangerous."

Cecilia made no response, but the lines on her tired face settled into a stubborn look, uniquely feminine.

The Abbot sighed. A day long past flashed before him like yesterday. He was before the fire in his own home, arguing hopelessly against the wishes of his young wife, that same look upon her face. I remember that look he thought wryly. I will not win.

"Does Toland remember last night?" he asked.

"I know not," the girl replied. "His words say nay, but his eyes say differently."

"He was married once," the Abbot offered.

"I know," she replied.

He shook his head. "Go now and rest. Dominic will tend to Toland."

The world began to change…

The earth blossomed, livestock went on mating and giving birth and nine men and one young woman tested nature's bonds.

Cecilia cared for Toland, tending his wound, feeding him and reading to him when the strain of illness and confinement became too much to bear. She spent more time with him while Dominic was in the vineyard. When no one saw she stroked his brow, rubbed his back. Though he tried to hide it, she saw his arousal and felt him catch his breath at her touch. He did not, however, pull away nor did he touch her. Toland was not the only man who suffered.

When not engaged in her nursing duties, Cecilia spent most afternoons in the kitchen garden. Bartholomew watched her there. He watched as she crawled between the lettuce rows, skirts rucked up, her full breasts reaching earthward and peeking from the neck of her bodice. He watched until he thought he would lose his mind. He watched and she knew it.

And Dominic watched him watching her.

And poor Brother Francis could no longer even be in her presence without it precipitating an obvious erection. At dinner each night, he could be seen, hands clasped protectively in his lap, his food untouched, waiting for permission to leave the table.

And Lucien was at war with God.

Toland improved a little each day, although progress was slow. The fever, banished by sunlight, lurked at the edges of his consciousness ready to take ground whenever he slept, and with fever came the dreams. Toland had already cried out several times this night, his haunted voice echoing along stone corridors. Cecilia could bear it no longer. Determined to pull him back from his nightmares, she whispered quietly through the halls of the monastery's heart until she reached the infirmary. Dominic was already there. Together, they changed the sweat soaked nightclothes and bed linens, talking softly to their patient and to one another. When all was right again, Brother Toland caught Cecilia's hand.

"Stay with me," he begged. "Please."

She glanced quickly to see if Dominic had heard.

Clearly he had. "Stay with him," he urged quietly. "He needs you."

Cecilia gave a faint nod of acknowledgement as Dominic left, closing the heavy door behind him.

Without a word, Cecilia helped Toland remove his fresh shirt. Then reaching for the hem of her gown she peeled it off over her head. She wore nothing beneath. Bending,

The Monastery

she blew out the lone candle and climbed under the blanket beside the naked man.

Toland turned to face her on the narrow cot. At once she felt his hands slide over her body. His lips were warm. She was surprised when his tongue entered her mouth, but he tasted sweet and she did not mind. Her hands wandered over muscles grown slack with illness and felt them tense beneath her touch.

"I am not sure what you want," she said.

Toland's arms enfolded her and pulled her to him. "I am," he replied.

Near dawn Toland whispered, "Again?"

Cecilia giggled, "Hmmmm… and again after that."

Toland chuckled softly, teasing, "It will take more than one man to satisfy you."

"It will," she replied, kissing him lightly. "It will take all of you."

For a bare moment her words did not register. When they did Toland's shock was evident. "All of us?" he choked.

Cecilia nodded, unwavering.

Disbelieving, Toland shook his head like a wet dog.

Cecilia took on an obstinate look. "Muslims have many wives. Why may I not have many husbands?"

"We are not Muslim," he replied curtly.

"*You* are not Muslim," she countered.

"Nor are you," he argued angrily.

Cecilia did not relent; "Well, I may wish to be!"

Toland hesitated, unable to think of a suitable reply.

Cecilia took the advantage at hand and stepped into the brief, silent breach.

"Do you wish to leave this place?" she demanded. "These men? This life that you love?"

"I had not thought of it," he replied haltingly. "But I would…for you."

"Well, you need not," she answered reasonably, "for you can have me here."

Toland was quiet while he considered the possibilities. Then he frowned. "Have you been with the others?" he asked.

"No," Cecilia replied, reaching for him. "You are the first." Then, seeing, for the first time, the angry face of jealousy, she reassured him, "Toland, you will always be the first."

She was gone when he woke again. Washed and dressed, she had built a small fire in the library before the sun rose. When the Abbot appeared for breakfast she insisted that he meet her there at the completion of the meal.

"I must attend Chapter," he demurred. "Perhaps, later."

"No," Cecilia was firm. "I know you are busy but there is something we must discuss…now."

The Abbot did not argue. Cecilia rarely asked for anything. But almost before he was through the doorway, he regretted his decision.

Cecilia faced him, speaking in a quiet voice. "I spent last night with Toland."

Unexpectedly angry, the Abbot scowled. "Do you wish to make a confession?"

"I do not," she replied, a look of scorn on her young face. "There is no sin in love."

The Abbot sighed. "Will you leave us then? With

The Monastery

him?"

Cecilia's eyes widened. "Leave you?" she gasped, her consternation evident. "Leave here? I cannot leave here!"

"And pray tell, why not?" the Abbot growled. This was no way to begin a day.

Taking a deep breath, as though preparing to make explanation to a slow child, Cecilia replied, "Because I also love Bartholomew and Dominic. I love you. I even love Francis."

The Abbot's jaw slackened in surprise, his chin coming to rest solidly on his chest.

"I am like the men in your books," she continued smoothly. "I love you all."

Cecilia waited for a response. Getting none, she chided. "You are dishonest in pretending surprise, William. You gave me those books to read."

When the Abbot blushed, ensnared in a trap of his own making, she continued, "I am not so foolish as you think." With that she rose and walked toward the door. She turned to look back once. "We will speak further on Sunday, just you and I, before we tell the others." Then she was gone.

The Abbot remained seated. He thought about the girl and what she had said. "The girl", that's how he'd always thought of her. Young, frightened, malleable. Now, somehow, she was no longer "the girl." In a single night she had changed, transformed. She was a woman. The power had shifted and now it was hers.

The remainder of the week slipped by. Cecilia spent another night with Toland, then it was Sunday. The Abbot arrived in the library to find Cecilia already seated. Two pewter goblets of mulled wine sat on the table between their two chairs. She nodded in his direction and smiled, almost as though giving him permission to sit.

Determined to regain the upper hand, the Abbot cleared his throat.

"It is apparent that you have seen through my perhaps ill-conceived plan to introduce you to the concept of polygamy," he began.

Cecilia frowned at the unfamiliar word.

"Polygamy…" the Abbot explained, "… the practice of having more than one wife."

"Oh, is that what it's called?" she asked brightening. "I wondered if it had a name."

The Abbot nodded.

Cecilia returned to the conversation. "I did not see it at first," she admitted. "It was not until I began the third, or perhaps, the fourth book that I realized that the theme was the same."

"Why did you not say something to me then?" the Abbot asked.

Cecilia considered for a moment. "I was not entirely certain how I felt about it," she conceded. "It is true that I am drawn to some of the men, and I can see that they want me as well, but it had not occurred to me that I did not necessarily have to choose."

"You are drawn to *some* of the men?" The Abbot repeated. "But not all. What are we to do about that?"

There was no reply.

"Cecilia, surely you realize that even if each enjoys exactly the same measure of your attention, there will be jealousy. If you will favor only some, there will be murder for certain."

"I understand," she replied. "It must be all or none."

The Monastery

The Abbot tried to remain calm but beneath his dignified exterior his heart pounded without mercy and his breath remained trapped in his lungs, making the drawing of another quite impossible.

"Are you saying," he asked, "that you will be wife to us all? That you are willing?"

Cecilia nodded. "All except Peter. He is but a child and I am not a plaything. But," she wagged a finger under the Abbot's nose, "Each man must be a husband to me. Each must promise to love and care for me. I am not a whore."

The ugly word brought the other priest to mind. "And Lucien?" the Abbot queried.

Cecilia gave the Abbot an uncertain smile. "I will manage Lucien."

The Abbot thought otherwise, but allowed her brave assertion to stand unchallenged for the moment. Instead he said, "We are not all young, Cecilia. Will you have Luis and Paul?"

Cecilia nodded again.

"And me?" he asked, gazing at his boots.

Cecilia smiled and took his hand. "I will," she answered. "Gladly."

Throughout the remainder of the afternoon the two discussed how their plan might be accomplished and how it would be presented to the others. It was agreed that each man would have one night each month with her. She must be free to beg indulgence if she were unwell or indisposed and her wishes must be respected without question. Nights would be spent in the privacy of her room which none might enter without permission.

"And," she insisted, "I will have a new bed, bigger, and a bar for my door. I will be your wife but I will not be overrun. I will have privacy and respect."

The Abbot concurred. For a girl with little experience with men, she had uncommonly good sense, he thought.

The sun had gone and the stars were bright before it was agreed that after dinner on Sunday next Cecilia would occupy herself in the herbarium while the Abbot called the monks together and laid the proposition before them.

"Consider well, Child," the Abbot warned. "This path once taken will not easily be reversed."

†††

April 26, 1997

Dr. Winston made rounds early. He had a full calendar at the office and a hospital board meeting at five. MaryLee was glad to see him. "Your patient gave us a bit of a scare last night," she reported.

"How so?" Winston asked.

"Twice during the night her heart rate increased to 140. Her respirations were rapid and shallow and she was diaphoretic. She was moaning but we couldn't wake her. Both episodes resolved spontaneously. She's quiet now."

Winston nodded. "Please, call Dr. Chopak and ask him to meet me here this evening at seven." He spun on his heel and headed for the bank of elevators.

MaryLee nodded at the doctor's departing back.

†††

The Monastery
May 1, 1320

The following Sunday at half after two, with Cecilia in the garden and Peter in the scullery, the monks gathered at the freshly scrubbed refectory table. They were all well sated and most would have preferred a nap to their present upright position. The Abbot, however, begged their indulgence and each smiled in acknowledgement, unwilling to deny the kind man who was their leader and friend.

"I have asked you here to discuss a small problem," he began. "Cecilia."

Nodding heads came up.

"Over the past months Cecilia has become more and more important in our lives. There is not a man among us who does not love her."

There was a murmur of agreement throughout the room.

"But, we love her in a way that is not permitted us by the Church."

The Abbot saw Brother Toland flush.

"Papal edict notwithstanding, it is unnatural for man and woman to live together in this way. We find ourselves… yes, *we* find ourselves unable to work, to sleep, even to pray for wanting her."

The truth of this statement echoed in the silent hall.

"Things cannot remain as they are. We could, as Father Lucien suggests, send her to a nunnery, although I doubt she would go, or we can keep her here and love her."

The monks all stared in rapt attention, barely breathing. William Devon looked out across their stunned faces, then shrugged and smiled.

"What say you, Brothers? Am I mad?"

Brother Bartholomew was the first to speak. "Are you suggesting that we can *have* her?"

"Yes," the Abbot replied simply.

"Does she know of your plans?"

The Abbot chuckled. "She does. It was, in fact, her idea."

"And she is willing?" Luis asked, his eyes wide in amazement.

"She is," replied the Abbot. "Under these conditions: If she remains among us, it will be as wife. Each man will be entitled to one night each month in her bed. If there are children, they will be ours. We will be a family. Can we do it, Brothers? Do we wish to?"

The others remained stock-still.

Sensing that many had a need to say something, the Abbot invited each man to express his views. "Let us go around the table. Speak your minds, my friends, for if we undertake this it will change our small world forever."

Brother Dominic, sitting to the Abbot's left, was first. He spoke without hesitation or preamble, "I say yes. I want her to stay."

The Abbot moved on. "Brother Bartholomew?"

"Yes. I want her. I will take my night in her bed and be glad of it."

"Francis?"

Poor Brother Francis stuttered and stammered until finally, his face nearly purple with frustration, he nodded once and dropped his eyes to the floor.

The Abbot's gaze moved on.

"Brother Paul, what say you?"

Brother Paul smiled. "I say that I am far too old and set in my ways to change now. Of course, Cecilia must

The Monastery

remain here where she is loved and safe, but she is like a daughter to me and I cannot share her bed."

Eyebrows were raised in silent question.

Paul added, "I have no objection, however, to others doing so, so long as she is willing."

The Abbot nodded. "Brother Luis?"

The old farmer, uncertain, rubbed his work-roughened hands together, then smoothed his bush-like eyebrows with a wet finger. "We are not all young, William. Are you sure she wants us all?"

"She has assured me that she does," the Abbot replied. "All except the boy."

"Then I say yes," Luis replied. "Old fool that I am, I am as smitten as the rest of you."

"Toland?"

Brother Toland's blush was furious. "I have wanted her from the first," he admitted. "I have confessed it to you many times these last months, so I may as well confess to the rest. I have been with her and I will not do without her now. I say yes."

Like wind in dry leaves, a murmur of surprise rustled around the table.

The Abbot nodded and moved on. "Matthew?"

Brother Matthew hesitated before drawing a long, resolute breath. ""I took a vow of celibacy," he replied, "and I have no wish to break it."

"Then you must not," replied the Abbot. "But what of the rest of us?"

"I make no objection," the young monk replied. "Each man must make his own bargain with God."

"Agreed," said the Abbot.

The circuit was now complete except for Lucien who

sat at the Abbot's right hand. The younger priest's silence loomed over the table and all now awaited a tirade of cosmic proportions. Lucien's ecclesiastical career, based as it was on righteousness and condemnation, had come to a fork in the road. That he had been quiet so long seemed a minor miracle to most.

The Abbot drew himself erect. "Father Lucien?" he prodded.

The priest was a picture of agony. Like those of a schoolboy caught cheating, his eyes darted from one face to another. Then, shamed beyond endurance, he choked out one word, "Yes," and fled from the room.

The Abbot sent for Cecilia. Bartholomew found her in the garden. She returned with him to face the men. No one knew quite what to say. Finally, she spoke.

"I have made a calendar and posted it in the kitchen," she said quietly. Then she returned to her gardening.

Unpleasantness came almost immediately. Furious at being excluded, young Peter took his complaint first to the Abbot. The boy ranted and raved about his manhood. When finally told that the decision had been Cecilia's, he fled the Abbot's rooms in search of her. He found her in the wash house, removing garden grit from her hands. Grabbing her arm he spun her roughly, pushing his pimpled face into hers and nearly spitting his words.

"You cannot deny me," he raged. "I am a man and I will have my turn."

Cecilia was calm and resolute. "You are a boy," she countered. "A child. Your behavior proves it. And *I* decide with whom I sleep."

For her, the matter ended there.

The Monastery

During the next several hours, each man made his way to the kitchen on one pretense or another, glancing, with studied casualness, at the calendar as he passed. The Abbot's name topped the list and was followed by all others in alphabetical order. Nine men had nights fairly evenly dispersed over the next three weeks. Paul's and Matthew's names had a line run through them but were not removed, leaving open the possibility that they might change their minds. Then there was a week with no names.

It was amazing how quickly the unthinkable became commonplace.

† *Chapter Four* †

May 2, 1320

Monday dawned, the Abbot's day. William Devon, though he trembled to his marrow with anticipation, gave no outward appearance of uneasiness. He proceeded through the day's services, chapter, and a meeting with Lucien on the business affairs of St. Fiacre's in his usual way. The other monks watched, secretly amazed at his apparent calm and completely ignorant of his thudding heart and loose bowels.

Cecilia spent the morning with Francis in the barns. As she passed by the forge en route back toward the refectory for the noon meal, Toland reached out an arm and dragged her into the inferno. He was bare to the waist, his broad chest already regaining its muscular definition although he still walked with a limp. Crushing her to him he found her mouth. Then he whispered, "Why must I be last?"

Cecilia returned his kiss with feeling to match. She nipped at his lip, teasing. "And the first shall be last," she quoted solemnly and then burst into a fit of giggles. Seeing a scowl darken his handsome face, she touched his cheek. "Patience," she counseled. "In this game of love, you have scored first. Now you must let the others play. Your turn will come again and it will be worth the wait. I promise."

Cecilia ate early in the kitchen and absented herself from supper. She did not appear in the locutorium in the early evening. The room felt empty without her and the men soon drifted to their own cells. When all had gone, the Abbot, his chess pieces in hand, walked slowly toward Cecilia's

The Monastery

quarters. He knocked and entered at her bidding, placing the ivory men on her small table. "I thought we might play awhile," he said awkwardly.

Cecilia smiled. "That would be pleasant," she replied.

When night had truly fallen and the sounds of the resting earth could be heard about them, the Abbot took the girl's hand. "Are you certain?" he asked.

"I am," Cecilia replied.

"Are you afraid?"

Cecilia laughed softly. "No, William, I am not afraid of you, nor any man here..." she hesitated, "save, perhaps, Lucien."

The Abbot frowned. "If Lucien is unkind to you, I must know. No other man here will see you ill used. He will love you well or be denied. It has already been decided."

Cecilia nodded gratefully. "Thank you," she replied. Then she unseated herself and moved toward her cot. "This must be larger," she chuckled, "or someone will be sorely injured."

They made small talk, clumsily at first, but with increasing ease as they prepared for bed. William knew a woman's ways. He helped her with her laces and loosened the ties in her long hair, running his hand through the tresses as they fell down her back. He pushed them aside as his lips found her neck and worked their way slowly along her shoulder. Cecilia turned to face him, finding his body, always before hidden by his robes, firm and muscular. Though not young, he was strong and oddly appealing, the only accommodations to age the pepper-grey hair on his chest and his gnarled fingers, victims of arthritis. As they crawled into the narrow cot and pulled the blanket over themselves, the

Seeth Miko Trimpert

Abbot whispered, "Oh, how I have wanted you."

"And I you, William" she replied softly.

At breakfast, Cecilia and the Abbot arrived together. The priest helped her with her chair, as a knight might his lady, then proceeded to his place at the head of the table.

"Thank you, William," she said to his retreating back.

The eyes of the others widened at her use of his Christian name. Never again did she call him Father, nor did he call her child.

Tuesday and Wednesday were busy. The mill, which was some distance from the monastery, was in dire need of fixing and now that the crops were in Bartholomew, Toland and the Abbot intended to see to it. They left early intent on putting in a hard day. Once a source of income from the surrounding farms, the mill had some years past fallen into disrepair. At last inspection two paddles had been broken and four wooden cogs in the gear mechanism rotted away. Armed with hammers and saws the three trudged off across the field.

Once the work had been assessed, Bartholomew and the Abbot began the carpentry, sawing and shaving until two replacement paddles and a spare had been shaped. Toland returned to the forge. The waterwheel, which creaked and staggered drunkenly, unbalanced as it was, was stilled and fixed with a leather strap to keep it from turning. Bartholomew climbed out onto one of the more sound paddles, stepping tenderly lest it snap under his weight. He balanced himself precariously and began fastening a new paddle to the wheel. The work was hard, standing, as he was, on tiptoe and hanging by one hand while trying to work with the other. The Abbot

The Monastery

in the open doorway held as much of the paddle's weight as he could. The task, awkward and dangerous, took more than two hours to complete. When finished, Bartholomew swung himself into the mill and lay exhausted on the dusty floor, waiting for his trembling arms to recover their strength.

Near sunset Toland returned from his forge, brandishing several pieces of metal, reinforcement for the paddle stems. "Now," he bragged, "they will not break again." Bartholomew and the Abbot examined Toland's innovation, their eyes gleaming with approval. "You are a clever man, Brother Toland," Bartholomew said. "Tomorrow we will try them."

After supper and Vespers the monks gathered in the locutorium. A fire had been laid and, though spring was well advanced and the out of doors warm, they felt the need of it to counteract the cold of the stone walls. Cecilia was among them and engaged in a lively conversation with Matthew, who was expounding on the blessings of celibacy. Some turned aside in embarrassment but the Abbot listened.

Like a sinner newly saved Brother Matthew discoursed with great fervor. Cecilia listened, too, her countenance open and pleasant. When Matthew paused for breath, she asked innocently, "And have you always been celibate?"

"Oh, not always," Matthew replied earnestly, "only since 1139."

Cecilia raised her gaze to his face. "Oh, goodness," she teased, "nearly two hundred years? I would have thought you much younger."

The Abbot hid a smile behind his hand. But the younger man, having missed the gentle jest, proceeded gravely with a long and rather tedious dissertation on the

Second Lateran Council, which Cecilia bore with good grace, only the twinkle in her eye hinting that she was amused.

On Thursday, Bartholomew worked steadily through the morning. The waterwheel repaired, he had returned to his vineyard. Barely able to keep his mind on his task, his thoughts wandered toward evening, causing him to cut his thumb. Though the gash was deep he did not notice until blood from the wound dripped onto his sandaled foot. Nor did he hear the noon bell for dinner and would, in fact, have missed his meal had not his work mates pulled him along behind them. He ate sparingly, nearly nauseous with anticipation, returning to the field alone to complete the last of the grafting.

Near mid-afternoon, he glimpsed a small figure climbing the hillside below him. He watched it make steady progress in his direction, knowing that it could only be Cecilia. Fearing the worst, he waited, shoulders straight, face impassive. When she reached him she smiled. Then, grasping his hand, she pulled him toward the copse on the next rise. She did not speak but walked lightly, picking her way among the fallen limbs, not yet gathered for firewood. When they had reached the midst of the small wood and were well protected, Cecilia laid her shawl amongst the soft ferns. Then she turned to Bartholomew and reached upward placing her arms around his neck and kissing him softly. "You are nervous," she said, "and do not need prying eyes and ears for your first time with me. We will be together here where none can see. This is for us alone."

When he continued to stand, uncertain, in the middle of the clearing, Cecilia moved around behind him. She wrapped her arms around him and lay her cheek against his back. "You can touch me," she teased. "I do not bite."

The Monastery

He pulled her around to face him again. This time, hands trembling, he opened the laces on her bodice one at a time, freeing her breasts and lifting her until he could get a nipple in his mouth. He sucked and bit until it hardened, sending a wave of new pleasure through Cecilia. When he set her back on the ground, she loosened the remainder of her clothing and let it fall around her feet. Bartholomew sucked in his breath, whistling sharply.

"I had forgotten how beautiful you are." When she looked puzzled, he explained. "I helped Dominic care for you when you were hurt."

"Oh," she replied, blushing. "I do not remember."

The monk pulled off his robe and shirt and the breeches beneath. "I have not done this in a very long time," he said. Then with a modest smile he added, "but I used to be quite good at it."

"I shall be the judge of that," Cecilia chuckled.

"Am I still to have the night?" he asked

"You are," she replied.

"Then I beg you to forgive me for what I am about to do, but I will make it up to you. I promise."

With that he fell on her. His hands eager to find remembered pleasure captured her breasts and squeezed until she cried out. Then he pushed her knees wide and buried himself in her body. He bucked and pounded until finally he shouted and collapsed. Cecilia, pummeled and bruised, nearly wept with frustration. She pushed him away and sat up.

"I am sorry, Cecilia" he said, over and over. "I could not wait. I will make it up to you." Then he rolled toward her and scooped her, unwilling, back into his arms pulling her tight against him. As she felt his racing heart slow and listened to his breathing resume its natural rhythm she waited for him to fall asleep. I have misjudged him, she thought with some bitterness.

But he did not sleep. Nuzzling her ear, he ran a slow hand down her back. "Your turn," he whispered.

Supper is done and the men are at Vespers. I await Bartholomew in my room. Thoughts of the afternoon just passed make my belly feel as if it were home to a thousand butterflies. I wish he would hurry.

Bartholomew knocked.

"Come in," she called.

He entered and stopped to look around. He had not been in the Bishop's cell since Cecilia had recovered and was surprised to see the changes she had made. The room was warm and felt of home. A mattress of fresh rush and lavender scented the air. A kettle atop the small iron stove simmered, whispering steaming secrets. Two tallow candles lit the room with a soft yellow glow, smoking slightly and leaving shadows like furtive children to play about the corners.

"We missed you at supper," he said.

Cecilia smiled. "I thought it might be awkward," she answered. "Paul brought me a plate." Anxious to feel his body against her once again Cecilia opened the bed. She put out the candle on her writing table and, returning, reached across to snuff the one beside her bed. Bartholomew stayed her hand. "Leave it," he whispered hoarsely. "I want to see you."

The next night Cecilia spent alone.

The days were as busy as ever but it was impossible

The Monastery

to behave as though nothing were different. There was now a chasm between the men who had been with her and those who had not. The tension in a room which held them all made her teeth ache. Although Cecilia had had no plan to spend consecutive nights with a man in her bed, she now recognized that it was imperative to make them all feel equal and quickly. To that end she determined that she would spend the darkness of the week ahead making each of the remaining men her husband.

Night fell as she waited for Dominic. It was well past ten when she heard his faint knock. Impatient now, she crossed the room hurriedly and opened the door. Her eyebrows arched in question, thinly veiled annoyance creasing her brow.

Dominic spoke, "Lucien is unwell."

"Is he seriously ill?" she asked.

Dominic smiled. "I think not. He is doing battle with himself. To want you is to be like other men. It is almost too much for him to bear and he is making himself ill."

"I am sorry for that," Cecilia replied. "He need not come to me."

"Oh, he will come," Dominic chuckled. "But first he must reconcile his notion of himself created in the image of God with what he will soon do."

"Perhaps," Cecilia offered, "it is not man who is created in the image of God but god who is created in the image of man."

Dominic frowned. "Cecilia," he warned, "you have a wicked intellect. Be careful with whom you share your thoughts."

The two friends talked into the night arguing religion

and its implication in the lives of men. No other man would have spoken to her as an equal, but Dominic, less dogmatic than many others, allowed the possibility of Cecilia's theories and encouraged her intellectual explorations. He, too, had come to the monastery more of necessity than calling and was willing to question.

Peter Abelard's concept of faith born of reason was familiar to him and he shared it with Cecilia. But Cecilia, still plagued by the improbability of a personal god, kept returning to her original question. Eventually, Dominic conceded the point, "It is a rare man, Cecilia, who has courage enough to live alone upon this earth."

As the hour grew late, Cecilia finally donned her nightdress, shedding her clothes before Dominic with the simple gestures of a wife long comfortable in her companion's presence. Dominic, for his part, watched with interest, a flicker of desire crossing his pleasant face. Slipping beneath her coverlet, Cecilia patted the mattress beside her, causing the new straw to rustle. "Will you join me?" she asked.

Dominic sat down beside her still fully clothed. "I am not like the others," he said quietly.

Cecilia smiled. "I know. Now come to bed."

The night passed as Cecilia came to know her fourth husband. Dominic, unlike Toland and Bartholomew, did not burn for her. He did, however, crave the closeness and comfort of human contact and, when finally assured of her acceptance, bravely taught her ways to please him. Initially shocked by his desires, Cecilia hid her feelings and complied with his wishes, quickly becoming comfortable and then aroused as it became clear that he would not hurt her and that her pleasure was as important to him as his own.

At midnight, Cecilia sat up from a sound sleep. She

The Monastery

shook the snoring Dominic until, drowsy but coherent, he responded. She shook him again to be certain of his attention, then said, "When you said that few men had the courage to live upon the earth alone, you meant that if God did not exist most men would invent him."

Pleased that his enigmatic concession had not missed its mark, Dominic smiled and kissed her cheek. "Yes, Cecilia, that is precisely what I meant. Now go to sleep."

Strangely, by morning they had forged an alliance far stronger than the others. Near dawn Dominic roused himself from her bed and began to dress. He bent to place a light kiss on her lips. "Thank you," he whispered.

"You are welcome," she replied.

Cecilia lay abed for another few minutes until the bell tolled for Prime. Hurriedly she rose and dressed. Tonight would be for Francis and she knew that she must spend the day with him in the barns. Somehow, he must become accustomed to her. Wondering how this might be managed, she knelt quietly in the back of the chapel, lost in thought if not prayer.

The day was a strange one. For the first time since they had begun their odyssey strangers entered their world. Even before Prime a band of gypsies presented themselves at the gate. They were clothed in colorful tatters, their children hollow-eyed and starving. While Paul and Peter went about the business of feeding them, Dominic saw to their scant medical needs. Cecilia kept to her room, chafing angrily under the Abbot's edict that she must not be seen.

When the wanderers had gone their way, she went hurriedly to the barns in search of Francis. She found him stroking the flank of a small mare that labored, snorting and whickering, delivering a late foal. Cecilia watched from the shadows as the shy monk coaxed and cajoled, his voice steady and firm, not a trace of a stammer. Once again, she was amazed by his kind and gentle nature. What a good father he would make, she thought.

After the foal had emerged, his mother let him rest, then nudged him delicately until he stood, his spindly legs trembling under the weight of his small body. Francis backed away and rose from the straw. When he saw Cecilia, the calm assurance he had shown the mare dissolved. His face reddened; his stutter returned.

"Can you not treat me as you would your creatures?" Cecilia asked.

Francis shook his head and looked at his feet.

Cecilia reached across the wide space between them and touched his cheek. "I will see you after Compline," she said quietly. "Come early."

Cecilia retired to her room directly after supper, eschewing the company of the many in order to prepare a welcome place for Francis. She took great care in her preparations. There were daffodils in a pot on her small table and fresh lavender, provided by Dominic, under her rough linen sheet. She bathed carefully and donned a modest nightdress she had made herself. Then she waited, rocking to and fro, in a chair made for her by Paul. Finally, her patience exhausted, she wrapped herself in a light woolen shawl and ventured forth into the cloister. The night was cool, the summer not yet come. A gibbous moon shone through a thin wisp of cloud, shrouding everything in an eerie light reminiscent of fog. Cecilia waited for her eyes to adjust.

In the far corner of the cloister garth sat Francis, still as

The Monastery

stone, on a wooden bench. Cecilia watched. When convinced that absent some action on her part he would remain as he was throughout the night, she brushed deliberately against a rosemary bush, making a rustling sound and casting its clean, pleasant scent into the night. Francis looked up. Certain that he saw, Cecilia beckoned him follow her. She waited at the door to her room until he had passed through it and, turning, slid the bolt into place.

"Shall we talk awhile?" she asked the trembling man.

Francis shook his head.

"Come then," she said, moving toward her bed.

Francis followed, silent but for his ragged breathing, his terror plain.

Cecilia sat upon the side of her mattress and began to untie the ribbon at her throat. Francis's hands shook at his sides, then darted suddenly to his crotch in a vain attempt to cover a growing erection. Cecilia's eyes followed his hands, which then flew to his face to hide his humiliation. Realizing that left his now fully erect penis pushing tent-like against his robe, again his hands went back to his privates. The picture presented by the desperate man, hands flapping down and up and down again, as though he might at any moment take flight, was pitiful and heartrending.

"Do not be afraid," Cecilia crooned. "Francis, we will manage."

She stood and pulled her nightdress up over her head. The shy monk's gaze followed the hem as it rose past her knees, then her thighs. When the cleft between her legs became visible, he moaned. As the shift cleared her breasts and was cast aside, he shuddered violently, the front of his robe immediately wet with semen, which spurted forth as his body convulsed. A cry of anguish escaped his lips as he spun awkwardly toward the door. Cecilia's hand shot forward to stay his flight but missed. The weeping man stumbled forward, fumbling blindly with the bolt. She called his name but he was gone.

Snatching her discarded shift, she slipped it over her head. Shawl in hand, she followed him quickly and silently through the monastery until she faced his door. She knocked lightly and begged him to open it to her. He did not answer. All she heard was weeping. Eventually, she returned to her room.

In the refectory next morning Lucien walked behind Cecilia, brushing against her as he passed. His message was clear. She turned to face him, speaking quietly. "You will have to wait until tomorrow."

Lucien reddened, his face angry. "It is my night," he hissed. His tone drew the attention of the others at the table.

"Indeed, it should be," Cecilia soothed. "And I am heartily sorry to disappoint, but…"

Across the table, Francis sat gaping in horror. Surely she would not tell them. He would die of shame.

Cecilia continued, looking innocently at Lucien, "Last evening I was ill and Francis has not had his night."

Lucien scowled and made odd noises in his throat.

"Forgive me, Lucien. I am sorry." Cecilia lowered her eyes, casting a sidelong look at Francis from beneath her lashes.

Once again Cecilia retired early to her room. Compline came and went. The men gathered in the locutorium and then dispersed to their own cells. The monastery grew silent.

The Monastery

Francis did not come. Cecilia went again to his room but he was not there. She went to the barns. He was not there. She spent the night alone, thinking.

At breakfast Cecilia left her usual place at table and sat next to Francis. When she had decided that she must make them all equal, she had also resolved to show none affection or favor in front of the others, until all who wanted her had had her. This morning that resolution went to the wind as she touched Francis's face and caught his hand beneath the table. Francis tried to withdraw but she would not release him. Finally, taking a deep breath he squeezed her hand. She leaned sideways to whisper to him, "Next time."

The others stared and then looked away. Only the Abbot understood her actions.

†††

April 27, 1997

Brian Kincaid and Miles Winston sat at the small round table in one of the hospital's many Family Conference Rooms awaiting the arrival of Dr. Chopak. Winston had already warned his old friend against a repeat of his earlier performance.

"Dr. Chopak," he scolded, "is the world's foremost expert in cases of atypical reincarnation. He works without charge and is under no obligation to help us."

Kincaid snorted, "And I suppose there is typical reincarnation? Just the garden variety type?"

Winston exhaled slowly through pursed lips, making no attempt to hide his displeasure. "Brian, if you would only listen," he paused for emphasis, "with an open mind..."

Seeth Miko Trimpert

Kincaid had almost conceded. His well-ordered life was spinning out of control.

"All right, Miles," he said finally, "I'll listen. I'll be respectful and charming." In an instant, he rearranged his face into something pleasant and open. "Will this do?"

He's a chameleon, Miles thought, nodding wearily.

"Listen, to him, Brian. This isn't a game. He may be our only chance."

Suddenly Kincaid's eyes narrowed. "Miles, don't tell me you really believe this."

Winston met his gaze but said nothing.

Kincaid's shoulders sagged nearly imperceptibly. "All right, Miles," he repeated. "I'll listen. I want my wife back."

Gurinder Chopak arrived at 7:00 p.m., exactly. He greeted the two men politely, waving at them to remain seated. At Dr. Winston's nod, Brian spoke first.

"Dr. Chopak, I'm afraid I owe you an apology."

The dark man nodded in apparent agreement.

"My children and I are very upset about my wife's..." He paused as if searching for a word, then selected, "...condition. Nevertheless, I was rude when we last met. I hope you will attribute my behavior to concern for my wife."

Miles Winston listened impressed by the adroit way Kincaid had made excuses for himself without actually apologizing. Nor was that fact lost on Dr. Chopak, who inclined his head in acknowledgement of Kincaid's statement and took a seat.

"Mr. Kincaid, your opinion of my person is of no consequence. However, it is most important that you accept that I do have knowledge which may be of help to you."

Kincaid's retort was sharp. "It is my wife who is the

patient, Doctor."

"I beg to differ, Sir," Chopak countered. "Your wife has found her solution. It is you who are abandoned."

Anger flashed across Kincaid's face, but disappeared almost before it registered on the consciousness of his companions.

There was a light knock as the conference room door opened. A heavy woman in pink scrubs and a hairnet came forward, placing a tray with coffee and cookies in the center of the table. "Thank you, Mrs. Grayson. This is very kind," Dr. Winston said. The woman smiled and quietly slipped out again.

While Dr. Winston poured coffee he spoke to Dr. Chopak. "Doctor, Mr. Kincaid is not familiar with your work. It would be helpful if you could tell him, briefly, what you do."

Dr. Chopak placed his beautiful brown hands on the table in front of him. "Very well," he replied. Then he directed his comments to Kincaid.

"I study the unknown," he began simply. "Mr. Kincaid, there is considerable evidence to suggest that we are all souls on a pilgrimage through eternity... living, dying and living again. As we travel, move on, we seek the Light. When we achieve enlightenment, our journey is complete."

Kincaid frowned. "Evidence?" he challenged. "What evidence? How do you know this?"

Chopak explained. "For millennia there have been people who seem to have lived before, people who once were thought bewitched, possessed, even insane. Over the centuries, these poor souls have been subjected to the most cruel treatment - burning, drowning, exorcisms of all types and, more recently, involuntary commitment to mental institutions. However, since the late nineteenth century some of us have begun to understand that there is more to this phenomenon than meets the eye."

Kincaid looked askance, though, to his credit, he remained silent.

"Regression therapy, initially an hypnotic technique allowing an individual to revisit a traumatic past event in order to address its present consequences, has, in the hands of skilled therapists, allowed some to remember the events of past lives."

Chopak quickly summarized several notable and well-documented cases, then slid a reading list, several pages covered with a bold script, across the table toward Brian. *"You may wish to read some of these titles,"* he suggested

Frowning, Kincaid scanned the sheets before him.

"OK. Let's assume, just for the sake of argument, that I accept this…this…whatever it is. Tell me what it has to do with Rebecca. My wife has not died. Her heart beats. She breathes. So she hasn't moved on, as you so delicately put it. Has she regressed to a previous life? And if so, how do we bring her back?"

"Begging your indulgence, Mr. Kincaid, I humbly suggest that the question of importance is not where she has gone, but why. Your wife's soul, for reasons which I cannot know, and which may be a mystery to you as well, has left Rebecca and lives elsewhere."

When Brian made no answer, Chopak continued. *"Dr. Winston may have told you that my field is not reincarnation as it normally occurs, but atypical cases, those which do not follow the normal path. I believe your wife is such a case."*

Kincaid couldn't help himself; he was intrigued. *"OK, Doc. Let's hear it."*

The Monastery

Chopak smiled ruefully at the casual familiarity. Americans had so few manners.

Maintaining his own formal speech, he began his explanation.

"Mr. Kincaid, as I have been saying to you, most souls enter a body at the beginning of a life and remain thus incarnated until the death of the physical being, when they are once again free, roaming in a kind of limbo until they are incarnated yet again. Normally, incarnations begin with conception or birth and end with death."

Kincaid waved an impatient hand. "So you've said," he granted, "I got that."

Dr. Chopak seemed not to notice him. "Sometimes, things do not proceed in the normal way. On rare occasions a soul which is hopeless will depart from its body prematurely. Hope, Mr. Kincaid, is the anchor. Without it, a soul drifts."

"Do you mean..."

"Please, Mr. Kincaid," Chopak chided. "Your questions will be answered."

Kincaid took the mild rebuke without comment.

"I believe that your wife's soul is one such. Was she very unhappy?"

Kincaid shrugged. "Why would she be? She has everything."

Chopak raised his eyebrows, creasing his smooth forehead, and peering owl-like through black-framed lenses. "She was loved? Attended to? Needed? Was there purpose in her life?"

"Of course, she is loved, Doctor!" Kincaid snapped. "I love her."

"I'm sure that you do, Mr. Kincaid," Chopak soothed, "but did she know it?"

Kincaid was having difficulty with his temper. This man was mocking him. "Look, Doctor, if her mind has left her body…"

"Not her mind, Mr. Kincaid, her soul."

"Whatever," *Kincaid continued.* "Call it what you will. It sounds to me like we need a good psychiatrist."

Chopak shook his head. "Mr. Kincaid, mental illness is the sign of an ailing soul; outright madness, evidence of the soul's death. Your wife's soul is neither ill nor dead. This is not something which has happened to her, but rather a thing which she has chosen. Rebecca is but a body. The soul is many people, many lives. Try to think of this soul as merely inhabiting Rebecca's body. Now that soul has simply abandoned this body, this life, for one with purpose and a chance at happiness."

"You talk about her body as though it were a rental unit."

Although Kincaid had not meant to amuse, Chopak smiled. "In a way, Mr. Kincaid, that is precisely correct."

Kincaid scoffed, "Bullshit…"

Chopak's face showed considerable forbearance. "Even Plato," *he argued,* "saw man as a soul using a body." *His statement had a cold ring of finality.*

For the first time in many, many years Brian Kincaid was afraid.

†††

May 9, 1320

Much to the chagrin of Lucien, who spent the lion's share of his day vomiting, Cecilia spent her's in the barns

The Monastery

with Francis. Her skirts rucked up around her thighs, she mucked stalls and pitched hay for the larger animals. Spring grasses, though greening, were still too sparse to provide all that was needed, especially for new mothers feeding growing offspring. She gathered the eggs, which she took to Paul. While there she requested that he make a picnic for Francis and herself. Paul looked at her as if she were speaking a foreign language

"What is it you want, child?" he asked.

"A picnic," she replied. "Something simple. Do not trouble yourself overmuch."

"Picnic?" Paul tried the word; it felt strange on his tongue. "What is picnic?"

"A small repast; something we may eat in the barn or out of doors," she answered.

"How do you know of this picnic?" Paul queried.

Cecilia stopped, a look of consternation dawning across her face. "I do not know," she replied. "I cannot remember."

She returned to the barns, passing through the kitchen garden to pick lavender, which she crushed between her hands to freshen them and then tucked discreetly into her bosom. She worked steadily, always within view of Francis but without speaking to him. She hummed as she cleaned the rabbit hutch and played with the new colt. When the bell tolled for Sext, Francis departed for the service. Cecilia dashed to the kitchen to get her picnic while he was away. Francis returned to find her sitting on a horse blanket, an odd midday meal spread before her. She patted the blanket across from her.

"Come," she said. "I have been waiting for you and I am hungry."

Seeth Miko Trimpert

Francis, at first, was silent. But he, too, was hungry, so he ate. Halfway through the meal, Cecilia cut an apple, slightly bruised and woody from its long winter storage, and offered half to her companion. When Francis took it from her, she allowed her hand to graze along the side of his. He did not pull away.

"Tell me about the new colt," she coaxed.

Francis tried, nearly choking on his words as he struggled to talk to her. Slowly, he managed to tell her about breeding the small mare with the horse of a villager some distance away. Although it had been arranged by Lucien, on the appointed day Francis had taken her himself, afraid lest Lucien allow her to be bred with a sire too large for her. When he was satisfied that the sire was of an appropriate size and that the colt should not be too large, he supervised while his little mare was mounted and impregnated. Then he brought her home, consoling her like a beloved daughter raped by a stranger.

They finished their picnic without further talk. But the silence was more comfortable. Cecilia gathered the remains of their food, scattering small scraps for the chickens and pigs. Before Francis knew what she was doing, she had approached and wrapped her arms around him. He stiffened, but she held fast, snuggling against his chest and matching her hipbones to his. He was a scant three inches taller than she. "Hold me," she ordered softly. After several seconds, she felt Francis's arms creep around her. His head dropped to her shoulder; his arms tightened.

†††

May 1, 1997

Brian Kincaid sat on the right side of table, flanked

The Monastery

by his younger son, Evan. Across from them were Miles and Brian's daughter, Melissa. Brian, Jr., a young executive in one of his father's many holdings, had pleaded a business appointment and refused to attend.

Dr. Chopak was, once again, punctual, arriving at nine sharp. Noting that his status was now sufficient to warrant placement at the head of the table, he sat and composed himself, laying notes before him. He shook hands with Evan before taking his seat, nodding to Melissa whom he had already met.

Kincaid's demeanor had changed. "I've told the kids what you said at our last meeting," he offered. "They have some questions but we'll hold them until the end if you wish."

Chopak nodded. "Perhaps, that would be best. Some may be answered as we go along."

He looked around the table, attempting to judge the readiness of this group for ideas so foreign that they would be nearly unbelievable, then sighed. There was no time to waste. If he was correct and realities collided infrequently, it might already be too late.

Clearing his throat, he began, "I have reviewed Mrs. Kincaid's medical records most carefully. There is absolutely no sign of physical illness. But for one, her tests, including scans and blood work, are entirely normal."

Kincaid's heavy brow furrowed, "But one?" he questioned.

Chopak's raised finger counseled patience. "If you would permit, Mr. Kincaid, even this result is normal, merely somewhat unexpected. It is a matter I would prefer to discuss later with you alone."

When Kincaid nodded, Chopak continued, "I spent

last night at your wife's bedside. We ran a continuous EEG. I am most pleased to tell you that her brain activity is that of a normal person, leading a normal life. There are periods of great activity and others of quiet, as though she were sleeping.

"The nurses have documented several brief periods of increased heart and respiratory rates. There are also times when she perspires heavily, as though engaged in something physically taxing. But all of this is quite normal.

"She speaks from time to time in Latin..."

"I've told you..." Kincaid interrupted.

Dr. Chopak ignored him.

"She speaks from time to time in English, but an old English, and in some other tongue with which I am not familiar.

"She knows a lot about the Middle Ages," Melissa offered shyly.

"Yes," replied Chopak. "I know. In fact, I wonder if that is where she is."

Evan spoke for the first time. A young man, his voice rose and cracked. "That's crazy! Tell him, Dad. That's nuts!"

Kincaid, who'd had more time to become accustomed to the impossible, placed a hand on his son's arm. "Take it easy, Ev." Then turning his attention back to Chopak, "Doctor, if this is true, how did it happen? How did she get there? And how do we get her back?"

"How did she get there?" Chopak repeated. "Mmmm... a good question. Let us begin in this way. The world, or reality, in which we live is one of many. These realities exist independently in space. Under usual circumstances, a soul may not move at will from one reality

to another since it is necessary for the body to die in order to release it. Once free it floats in the void until called to another life. However, there is one known exception to this pattern. Periodically, two realities, by chance or design (he shrugged here indicating that he knew not which), will intersect, collide. When this happens an unhappy soul, one which is seeking, may pass over what my colleagues and I call the Dreamline, leaving one life unfinished and beginning midway in another which has no past."

"The Dreamline?" Kincaid prompted.

"Yes," Chopak replied. "The Dreamline is the personal intersect."

Every face was blank.

Chopak sighed. "Do you ever dream of people and places which are familiar to you and yet not. You are you, but your surroundings are strange; your circumstances unknown?"

Everyone nodded

"You are glimpsing another life, once lived or yet to come; you have seen across the Dreamline. But when you awaken, it was only a dream, something lost to you before breakfast."

His listeners nodded again.

"For those without purpose or hope, it is different. For them there is perception of the Dreamline as a portal in the boundary between realities. It is a chance for them to quit a place of misery and begin anew"

Kincaid's face grew hard. Dr. Chopak directed his next comment to him.

"You must understand, Mr. Kincaid, that this state is a choice. Your wife, had she been happy and useful in this life, would have experienced the convergence of her realities

as we do…as a dream. However, because she was seeking when they came together she saw them for what they are and grabbed at the opportunity to move on. Although she is not yet gone, if her next existence is pleasing to her, it is unlikely that she will return for any substantial length of time. She has escaped."

Kincaid, uncharacteristically, paled at the implications of Chopak's assertion.

The doctor continued without apparent concern for the other man's feelings.

"Sometimes when two realities overlap a soul will move back and forth freely for a time, but only until the realities begin to move apart again. Then a decision must be made."

Chopak's eyes moved from face to face, stopping long enough to impress each with the importance of what he was about to say. "When this happens, as it must, the woman you call Rebecca will have to decide where she wishes to be. She will chose the reality which brings her closer to perfection."

Rebecca Kincaid's family sat, mouths open, staring at the East Indian as he continued speaking quietly, his graceful hands, like birds, emphasizing every word.

"During this time of indecision, the body in whom the soul has interest is active while the other, though not technically dead, does not function properly. Are you understanding me?"

No one moved.

"This transition from one reality to another is not without risk. The trauma of birth seems not to be foregone but only experienced differently. The spontaneous establishment of another life is often violent and painful."

The Monastery

"Spontaneous! You mean she just...like appeared somewhere else?" Evan gasped.

Chopak nodded.

"Like Athena?" Melissa wondered softly. "Full-grown from the head of Zeus?"

Chopak smiled his approval. "I see you are familiar with beliefs other than your own."

Dr. Winston joined the questioning. "How do you know she experienced pain?"

"She cried out in her sleep for several days and withdrew from any touch. She kept her body wrapped tightly as though guarding against pain. I have seen these signs in others."

"What happened to her?" It was Evan now, his voiced choked with emotion.

"I do not know and it is unlikely that we ever shall."

"Can't she come back and tell us?" the young man persisted.

"If she does come back, she will not remember," Chopak replied.

He checked his watch. The meeting had now entered its third hour. The family showed signs of great distress.

"I believe," he offered sympathetically, "that I have given you almost too much to think about. Let's meet here again tomorrow at the same time." He turned to Brian. "If you will, I would have a private word with you and Dr. Winston."

Both men nodded. Brian waved his children toward the door. "Find a pay phone, Ev. Call your brother. Tell him to be here tomorrow at nine...no excuses. Then meet me at the car. Melissa, stop crying. It won't help."

Seeth Miko Trimpert

The younger people left. Brian and Miles stretched in their chairs, stiff from the hours of tension and inactivity. Chopak appeared unaffected.

"All right," Brian said, squaring his shoulders. "Let's hear it."

Chopak began, "The only unusual result in all of the testing we have done is an elevated HCG."

Brian looked blank, but Miles frowned. Annoyed at being left if the dark, Brian countered, "Which means what, Gentlemen?"

With a wave of his hand Chopak deferred to Dr. Winston.

"HCG, "Winston explained, "is human chorionic gonadotropin, a hormone elevated in the blood levels of newly pregnant women."

Kincaid blanched.

"It goes up eight or ten days after fertilization and then decreases between days 50 and 70 as other hormones take over."

Kincaid ran his hands over his face, scrubbing at his heavy beard which rasped against his palms. "Is there no other explanation?"

Winston looked at Chopak. "It is possible for a tumor to make the body mimic pregnancy."

"So she has a tumor?" Kincaid's voice was strained.

"No," Chopak said. "There is no evidence of a tumor."

"So you're telling me that she's pregnant?" Kincaid was incredulous.

"Not exactly," Chopak replied.

Brian looked from one doctor to the other in

exasperation. "Then what the hell are you telling me?"

Chopak placed his hands on the table. "Mr. Kincaid, your wife may be pregnant in the other reality. Perhaps, because she has not yet completely relinquished this body, it reacts sympathetically. I am only guessing you understand"

"Guessing?" Kincaid sputtered. "You're fucking guessing?"

Clearly apologetic, Chopak replied, "I have not seen this before. I have called a colleague in England. I am hopeful that he may be more knowledgeable." He raised his hand in a gesture of helplessness.

Brian covered his face with his hands. "Jesus Christ," he groaned, "This simply cannot be. This is impossible!"

Dr. Chopak made a steeple of his fingers. "Mr. Kincaid, centuries ago St. Thomas Aquinas argued that what is is possible. Believe me, Sir, this is."

† *Chapter Five* †

May 9, 1320

It was Lucien's night. Cecilia had put him off as long as she could. With each of the men who had preceded him she had at least felt safe. Lucien was different. His lust for her burned in him, feeding a terrifying hatred. Her bold assertion that she would manage him echoed now, the hollow boast of a frightened child. In the afternoon sunlight she had been determined and brave but as the day drew to a close she began to be afraid. The whole monastery was on edge.

Toland found her in the kitchen gardens and whispered to her, "Call if you need me. I shall not be far away."

Francis brought an early summer flower and wordlessly placed it in her hand.

The Abbot went straight to Lucien himself. "Take care, Lucien," he warned. "Do not hurt her. The others will not permit it."

Cecilia spent the early hours of the evening in the locutorium, talking and laughing with the men. She was nervous and delayed returning to her room. Retiring reluctantly near nine, she found Lucien hidden in the shadows near her doorway. "I thought you were at chapel," she lied. "I did not know you awaited me."

Opening her door, she indicated that he should follow her. Lucien scanned the pleasant room and felt himself drawn toward its comfort and the affection she offered. There was a nearly palpable sense of welcome and home. It was a woman's place, warm, soft and faintly scented with lavender. For just a moment he let down his guard. As his feelings softened he

The Monastery

reached out to touch her, allowing a finger to trace the line of her shoulder as she turned to open the bed.

Then he pulled himself up sharply. She was temptation; this was sin. He would not fall prey to evil but face it head on. Without warning he grabbed her from behind. When Cecilia let out a small shriek of surprise, he clamped a hand tightly over her mouth, cutting her lip on her own teeth.

"Do not act the shy virgin with me," he snarled. "I know what you are and shall not be deceived."

Lucien had arrived fully clothed and, but for the need to raise the skirt of his cassock, removed no clothing. Sin was a dirty business and to be done quickly. He was vicious and brutal, using her like the whore he thought her to be and leaving her bruised and weeping before even ten minutes had passed. Humiliated, she sat among the rushes on the cold stone floor, her head upon her knees, sobbing. She still wore all her clothing but her drawers, which were rent beyond repair. Lucien had come for one thing and he had taken it.

Brother Paul, setting bread to rise for breakfast, saw Lucien as he crossed the cloister at a brisk pace, nearly running from his sin. Dropping the half-kneaded dough and wiping flour-white hands on his apron, Paul dashed in the direction of Cecilia's room. He listened carefully until he heard her weeping. Knocking once, he entered.

At first, finding her fully clothed, he thought Lucien had spurned her. But when she turned her face upward he saw her bruised mouth. Muttering an unaccustomed oath, he settled on the floor beside her.

When her weeping slowed she pulled herself up, squaring her small shoulders and drawing a deep breath. "I need a hot bath," she said. "A very hot bath."

Seeth Miko Trimpert

Paul nodded and went to begin heating the water.

†††

May 2, 1997

On 2 a.m. rounds, the night nurse noted that the patient in 321A had become agitated. A quick check of vital signs revealed an elevated temperature and blood pressure. Although she made no sound, the patient's breathing was ragged and uneven as though very frightened or sobbing. MaryLee left a message with Dr. Winston's service.

At 3 a.m. Mrs. Kincaid's agitation had increased. She clipped an aide who attempted to reposition her with a fair right hook and curled, once again, into the guarded position she had maintained during the first week after her admission. Now she was crying pitifully and calling for someone named "Dominic". The floor staff gossiped amongst themselves; her husband's name was Brian. Dr. Winston's service was notified again.

At 4 a.m. Dr. Chopak arrived on the unit. Though clearly in command, his manner was modest and unassuming. MaryLee said that she was very glad to see him. "Why has Dr. Winston not been called?" Chopak asked.

"He has, Doctor. Twice," the nurse insisted. "His service says that he's been notified." MaryLee shrugged as though a physician failing to respond to a midnight summons were not unusual.

Chopak acknowledged her implied censure with a vague motion of his chin. "Please call Mr. Kincaid," he said.

"Now?" MaryLee was dubious. "It's 4 a.m."

The Monastery

"Exactly now," replied Chopak evenly. "Tell him he should be coming as fast as is possible." Then he withdrew to Room 321. Mrs. Kincaid's asthmatic roommate, he noted, had been moved.

He stood at the bedside chafing the woman's cooling hand. "Rebecca," he called. "Rebecca, can you hear me?"

The woman moved, but did not answer. Pulling the blankets up to keep her warm, Dr. Chopak sat beside the bed and gently soothed the woman, from time to time repeating her name.

For a while she continued to weep almost silently, saying only once in a sad, bewildered voice, "He hurt me, Dominic. Why did he hurt me?"

Chopak watched as the tension slowly ebbed from her body. Whoever is with her, he thought, brings her comfort.

Brian Kincaid arrived at 4:45, frightened and disheveled. When he saw Rebecca, deathly pale, Chopak holding her hand, he panicked. "Is she..." he could not finish his sentence.

"No, Mr. Kincaid," Chopak hurried to assure him. "She only sleeps. But something has happened to her. She has been injured and cries out for someone named Dominic."

Kincaid's jaw tightened. "Who the hell is Dominic?"

Chopak looked disappointed. "I had hoped you might know."

Kincaid stared at his wife. "Well, I don't," he replied grimly.

At the sound of Kincaid's angry voice, the woman began to stir again. "Sit and be quiet," Chopak cautioned. "No matter what happens, Mr. Kincaid, do only what I tell you."

Then he turned back to the sleeping woman and began again to rub her hand and talk to her. His words flowed like a song.

After several minutes, she opened her eyes. They grew more and more round as she looked about and saw nothing familiar. "Rebecca," Chopak soothed, "I am Gurinder. I am a friend."

"Gurinder?" she smiled at the odd name. "What an uncommon name. I do not know it nor your face. Are you a Saracen?"

Dr. Chopak's face did not register his surprise at the question. "No," he replied. "I am from India, far to the East."

Interest sparked. "Are you Muslim, then?" she asked. "Have you many wives?"

"No, Mistress," Chopak replied with a smile. "I am Hindu and one wife is quite enough for me."

Rebecca obviously shared his amusement. "Indeed, Sir, you are correct. The many can be trying."

With a slow, fluid motion Chopak motioned Brian forward toward the bed. "Rebecca, do you know this man?" he asked.

The woman kept her eyes on Chopak's face, refusing to see the man behind him. "You mistake me, Sir, and miscall my name. I am Cecilia."

Brian lurched forward. "Rebecca, it's me, Brian. You know me!"

The woman cringed. "He will hurt me," she whispered to Chopak. "Please," she begged, "do not let him hurt me again." Then she paused as though she heard a distant summons. A smile lit her face. "I must go," she said.

She closed her eyes and was asleep.

†††

May 10, 1320

Lucien's mistreatment of Cecilia whirred through the monastery like doves on the wing. Toland and Bartholomew vied for the right to take revenge, eventually resorting to a children's game to determine the winner. Toland prevailed.

The blacksmith sought out the priest in his cell. In a mighty rage he burst through the door to find Lucien kneeling at prayer. Picking him up, Toland held him aloft with one hand while methodically beating him senseless with the other. When finished he cast the bloodied priest in a heap in the corner and left without ever uttering a word.

Cecilia slept through the night. By the time she awoke, wrapped safely in Dominic's arms, retribution had been extracted. As the birds greeted the day, Dominic looked carefully at the woman's face. It was bruised, the marks of Lucien's fingers clear on one cheek, an oval matching the heel of his palm on the other. Blood filled a crack in her lower lip. He pulled her to his chest, kissing the top of her head.

"You play a dangerous game," he whispered.

She stirred.

"Are you awake," he asked quietly.

She nestled against him, causing an unexpected response below his navel. "I am," she answered. "Are you?"

"Apparently," he replied, chuckling, "but I shall not trouble you."

Cecilia hid her face in his chest. "It is not trouble,"

she replied, her voice uncertain.

Dominic missed Prime and did not mind.

At breakfast the table was silent. When Cecilia entered all eyes found her. Seeing concern in every face she nodded to each in turn. "I am well," she assured them. "I am fine."

Lucien did not appear until the meal was all but ended, young Peter already clearing away the leavings for the waiting pigs. Dressed in his usual finery, the priest held himself erect at the expense of great effort. Limping, he crossed the refectory to his assigned place. He moved like a man tortured, gingerly lowering himself onto his chair. When his chin rose from his chest, his face came into view. Cecilia gasped. He had been beaten without mercy. His mouth was so misshapen that it would not close over his teeth; the skin on one cheek so taut it split and the eye above it so swollen that it was but a slit surrounded by matted lashes. The other eye was a small green circlet in a blood-red orb. Cecilia looked around the table. All but Toland met her gaze; his head remained bowed.

Cecilia spent her morning in the garden, alone. She had no wish to discuss the previous night nor could she bear the looks of worry on the faces of her companions.

As it grew later and all had become involved in the day's work, she slipped away toward the forge. Toland, fierce and angry, labored in the heat of his fires, his hammer ringing as he punished the molten iron. She watched as now restored muscles across his back and shoulders rippled with each stroke. When the horseshoe on which he worked was complete and sizzled in the water bucket, she cleared her throat.

The Monastery

Toland whirled from the forge, dropping his hammer, and lunged across the room to catch her in a crushing embrace. Cecilia freed herself and groped for his right hand. It was bruised and swollen, the knuckles like raw meat. She kissed each knuckle and then his mouth.

"Are you hurt?" he asked.

Cecilia shook her head.

Half naked, he dragged Cecilia toward the loft, his desperation on the verge of violence but Cecilia was not afraid. She knew that within Toland was a need to love and be loved almost beyond enduring. Like flash fire he burned, savagely sucking all the oxygen from the surrounding air and leaving all within reach of him gasping for breath. For a time, Cecilia burned with him.

"Say my name, Cecilia," he pleaded. "Say my name."

"Toland," she whispered. "Toland."

†††

May 2, 1997

MaryLee made her rounds for the last time at 7:00 a.m. Earlier when Mrs. Kincaid had failed to respond to further efforts by the mysterious Dr. Chopak, he and the patient's husband had departed promising to return later. Mrs. Kincaid had been quiet since then. Now she was whispering, her voice hoarse and rasping. The nurse bent to catch the words.

"Toland," Rebecca breathed. "Toland."

MaryLee frowned and went to make a note in the chart.

†††

May 17, 1320

A week passed before Cecilia took another man to her bed. Brother Luis, older and wiser by far than the younger men, brought no pressure to bear. When days before Cecilia had approached him to a beg a brief respite, he had smiled and clamped a work-worn hand on her shoulder.

"Whenever you are ready, girl," he said kindly. "There is no hurry…no hurry at all."

When finally she did invite him, he came quietly, loved her clumsily and returned to his own cell sometime after midnight, unable to sleep alongside her.

Summer slipped over them and life fell into a predictable routine. From the outside came word that their religion was in great turmoil. The Princes of the Church vied with the Kings of the secular world for power and riches. There were now those within the religious realm who would defy Rome, or Avignon, when it was expedient. The primacy of religious courts was repeatedly challenged by civilian authorities. Even the peasants had begun to grouse and grumble under the burden of heavy taxes and tithes. Beyond the walls of St. Fiacre's life became more and more dangerous and uncertain.

In contrast, their own small world was calm and good. The mill was repaired and ready for the ripening grain. Game, after an unseasonably short winter, was plentiful. Spring had brought mild weather and adequate, though not excessive, rains. The crops were in and growing well. The

The Monastery

kitchen and herb gardens, now mostly Cecilia's domain, were filled with plants, bursting skyward, their bounty previously unmatched.

Cecilia, too, bloomed. She posted her calendars for the second month and then a third; Lucien's days clearly marked on each. When the Abbot saw the first of them, he sought Cecilia in her gardens.

"Walk with me," he said firmly. Pacing, he waited impatiently while she rose and dusted the earth from her hands. Then he walked toward the hills, his step brisk and vigorous.

Cecilia was soon breathless attempting to match his long stride. "William," she wheezed, "please, slow down."

The Abbot stopped and turned to face her. Taking her hand in his, he resumed, this time walking more slowly. As he walked, he talked. "Was it wise, do you think, to place Lucien's name among the others?"

Without pause, Cecilia answered. "There is no choice. He must not be my enemy." When the Abbot made no answer, she continued, touching his weathered cheek. "William, I am not the first woman to be bedded by a cruel man."

The Abbot faced her. "He will hurt you again," he said, worry creasing his already furrowed brow.

"I will manage," her voice quivered.

Giving her a rueful smile, the Abbot mused, "Toland will kill him."

Cecilia chortled, the tension broken. "Only if Bartholomew does not reach him first," she replied.

But neither the Abbot nor Cecilia need have worried for Lucien did not come, either that month or the next. When his night came for the third time, Cecilia resolved to make

Seeth Miko Trimpert

a move. Finding him alone in the chapel, she took a seat beside him close enough to make her presence felt, but not touching. At first he stared straight ahead. When finally he relented and looked her way, she could feel his breath upon her face.

"Must it be this way?" she whispered. "Can you not like me, Lucien, even a little?"

The priest did not reply.

† *Chapter Six* †

May 2, 1997

Dr. Chopak sat comfortably in his own office, Kincaid opposite him in a large expensive wing chair. Brian was surprised at Chopak's office. He had expected the spare rooms of an ascetic. But Dr. Chopak had surrounded himself, and presumably his patients, with the deep, rich colors of Persian rugs, set upon by a combination of pieces of exquisitely upholstered red leather furniture. Each was a work of art. The leather of the furniture was soft as warm butter, the turns and tucks in each piece artfully outlined with row upon row of burnished upholstery tacks. Light was provided by a collection of table lamps reminiscent of Tiffany. Each cast a soft kaleidoscope of color on the wall behind it. Hundreds of gilt-edged leather volumes graced ceiling high shelves, which covered one wall, lamplight reflecting off the gold embossed on their bindings. Even the scent of the room was faintly exotic. Brian felt himself relax.

Chopak began quietly, his voice a near whisper. "Mr. Kincaid?"

Brian opened his eyes. He was tired and wore the bewildered look of a child and, although the current situation was largely one of his own making, Dr. Chopak doubted he would ever understand.

"Mr. Kincaid, may we speak openly?"

Kincaid tensed slightly, his relaxed demeanor replaced by wariness.

Chopak's hands moved outward in a graceful motion of appeal. "Please, Mr. Kincaid," he implored, "there is no chance for us unless we can be frank."

A look of resignation joined the parade marching over Kincaid's face. "All right," he replied. "Tell me what I need to do."

"Would that it were so simple," Chopak replied.

Brian shrugged, acknowledging a difficult situation, but kept his eyes fixed on his companion. He was not a man to avoid confrontation.

"Dr. Chopak," he persisted, "where is my wife?"

Chopak crossed his legs, carefully adjusting the knife-edge crease in his handsomely tailored slacks. Then, resting his elbows on the arms of his chair, he once again made a Gothic steeple of his fingers and began to speak.

"Mr. Kincaid, your wife's conversations suggest that she may now be living in the Middle Ages."

Kincaid looked dubious. "How so?" he asked.

"Do you remember this morning when she asked if I were Saracen?"

Kincaid nodded, thinking back. "Yeah, what's a Saracen?"

"A Saracen, Mr. Kincaid, is… or was… an infidel, a Muslim inhabitant of the Middle East, the enemy of the Crusaders in Medieval times. It is likely that the coloring of my skin or, perhaps, my accent made her think me foreign. Saracens are probably the only foreigners about whom she knows." Chopak paused, then continued. "More interesting though is the fact that she knows that Muslims may have more than one wife, a practice strictly forbidden by Christianity. Only a Muslim woman or an uncommonly well-educated Christian one would know this."

The small man wrinkled his brow, as though puzzling out a problem. "I thought at first that she might be Saracen, particularly when she seemed amused by the difficulties inherent in polygamous marriages. It was as though she had experience in such matters. I thought she might be one of a harem..."

Kincaid reddened and choked.

Chopak waved a hand in dismissal, "...but, I was mistaken. Think, Sir. Someone, a man, hurts her. She calls for Dominic. Hours later she whispers another name."

Kincaid came out of his chair like a rocket. Pacing to and fro, he demanded, "Who? Who did she call for?"

Dr. Chopak gestured for him to sit again and waited patiently for the energy fueled by anger to subside. When Brian was seated once more, Chopak reached for a photocopy of MaryLee's shift notes. Reading directly from the paper, he responded, "She whispered 'Toland'. Does that name mean anything to you."

Kincaid looked blank. "Toland? Are you sure that's a person? Couldn't it be a place?"

Chopak handed over the nurse's notes. There in a spidery hand MaryLee had written:

5 a.m. agitated, HR 160, R 40 - labored

Whispering "Toland (sp?) I love you, Toland." ML Simms RN

Defeated, Brian slumped in his chair.

Chopak changed course. "Mr. Kincaid, what did your wife do with her time? What interested her?"

That Kincaid sat mute, staring, told Chopak more than anything the man might have said.

"You do not know," he said evenly.

"Of course, I know," Kincaid sputtered. "She managed the house, had dinner parties, got her hair done...I think. She visited the kids, her parents, her sister. She was

busy!"

"Yes," Chopak replied. "I can see that. But what was she interested in?"

Kincaid controlled his temper with some difficulty. How the hell was he supposed to know what Rebecca did with her time? Didn't he have enough to worry about?

"Mr. Kincaid, did you love your wife?"

"Of course, I did...do! Stop speaking about her in the past tense!"

"Were you ever unfaithful to her?" Chopak asked.

If the question surprised him, Kincaid did not show it. He set his mouth into a grim line and answered in an icy voice, "I hardly think that is any of your business."

Chopak, like a setter on the scent, pointed his chin forward. "I will take that as a yes," he said quietly. "Was your wife aware of your activities?"

"I am a very discreet man," Kincaid replied acidly.

"I will take that as a yes, as well," Chopak answered.

Kincaid opened his mouth to protest.

The phone rang, halting the tense conversation. Chopak reached for the instrument, a look of mild annoyance on his pleasant face. He spoke into the mouthpiece.

"Mrs. Pashar, I requested no interruptions," he chided.

The voice responded.

"I see," Chopak replied. He offered the phone to Kincaid. "It is for you. A Miss Quinn. She says it is urgent."

A guilty look crossed Kincaid's face. He turned his back and growled into the phone, his words unintelligible. Then Chopak heard him say, "Yes. Yes. Seven is fine. I'll see

The Monastery

you then." Briskly he replaced the phone in its cradle and returned to his seat.

"It would seem," Chopak commented blandly, "that discretion is relative."

The session was over.

†††

June 1320

In those first months, Francis, too, fought his devils. When his night came in June he waited so late that Cecilia had given him up before he knocked, a sound so faint that at first she thought she'd imagined it. She found him at her door, eyes downcast, trembling. Taking his hand she pulled him into the room and closed the door behind him. Knowing her mistake during their first visit, Cecilia immediately pinched out the candle. Darkness would provide cover for the shy monk. She slipped past him, careful not to touch, and climbed back into her warm bed. "Come," she invited. "Leave your clothes on the chair."

In the dark, Francis fumbled his way out of his robe, shirt, and stockings. Although Cecilia could see the outline of his body in the moonlight, in the blackness of her bed's corner, she was invisible. As the monk neared nakedness panic set in; she heard his breath, labored and shallow. She could almost hear his heart.

"Do not think of me," she whispered. "Think of your creatures. Think of the garden. Pray if you must, but do not think of me."

Francis tried. When he stood nude and fully aroused at the side of her bed, Cecilia patted the mattress but said nothing. Francis lay down, tense and shaking, and stared at a ceiling he could not see.

"Turn to me," Cecilia whispered.

Francis did as she bid. Finally, she dared touch him. He held his breath as her hand moved from his face to his chest. Suddenly, he convulsed, letting out an agonized sob. Warm fluid splashed across Cecilia's abdomen and ran slowly toward her hip. Francis rolled away, trying to escape, but Cecilia anticipating his need to flee, wrapped her arms tightly around his body, her face against his back.

"No," she said. "Stay with me."

Francis choked back another bitter sob, his shame nearly unbearable. "Please," he begged, "Please, let me go."

But Cecilia held fast, stroking his chest with the motion she had seen him use on his laboring mare. He struggled briefly but eventually, convinced she would not release him, and unwilling to fight her, he lay quietly. Cecilia pulled him toward her and onto his back. She kissed his wet cheeks then lay her head against his chest.

"Go to sleep," she murmured. "Become accustomed to me. I will be here when you wake." Then she went to sleep.

Francis slept little, the nearness of the woman a source of cruel, unrelenting arousal. Near dawn he attempted to disengage himself from her arms and a leg which lay across him, but she only tightened her grip. Deliberately moving her leg over his hips she found what she sought.

"Do not move," she ordered in a husky whisper.

Carefully, with minimal contact, she levered herself over him. Francis moaned, "Oh, Lord…" Then, without warning, she lowered herself onto him, sheathing him

The Monastery

entirely before he realized what she was about. His eyes widened in surprise.

"Now," she whispered urgently, "Now, Francis."

The monk's hips flexed once involuntarily before he stiffened, breath held, and began shuddering. His teeth chattered.

Cecilia smiled in the lingering darkness and lay against his chest.

It had slowly become accepted that the man who slept with Cecilia did not attend Prime. It was an acknowledged dispensation, allowing those who wished it a little extra time with her. True, some preferred to return to their own cells before dawn and arrive at breakfast alone. But others shared the morning rituals of washing and dressing with Cecilia, enjoying the feeling of being married, and then accompanying her to breakfast, laying one last claim by holding her hand or pulling her chair as the Abbot had done. Each man had his own ways and Cecilia, accepting them all, made no complaint.

This morning Francis thought to scurry away. Cecilia stopped him. "Stay," she begged.

Too shy to object, Francis did as she asked. He dressed, his back turned, then performed his morning ablutions in her small basin. Cecilia, unwilling to hurry, donned her clothing slowly, one piece at a time, insuring that nothing was lost on Francis. The effect of watching her dress was predictable and, though he was embarrassed, he did not turn away. She was pleased. When ready she grabbed his hand and pulled him toward the refectory. "Be quick," she teased. "I am famished."

As they reached the refectory doorway Francis

retreated into himself. His shoulders rolled forward and he bowed his head.

Cecilia stopped abruptly, her annoyance obvious. "Are you ashamed to be with me?" she demanded.

"Nnnn-no!" the little monk protested.

"Then stand up," she ordered. "Raise your head." Then more softly she added, "You are as much a man as any here."

† *Chapter Seven* †

July 1320

On a brilliant summer morning in late July, Cecilia sought the Abbot in the Chapter House where he often stayed, long after the other monks had gone on to their daily work, managing the business of the monastery and planning a safe and secure future for them all. This morning he was tallying the projected income from last year's wine production and trying to estimate how much grain might result as income from the newly repaired mill. The lean years seemed to be over and with abundance came fiscal responsibility.

These business tasks of the monastery were often shared with his fellow priest, Lucien. Though a difficult companion, the younger man was still a shrewd and savvy businessman and cellarer of their enterprise. The monastery's envoy to the outside world, he too saw the possibility of prosperity in the little community's future.

Sometimes, when the Abbot worked with him, he could almost see the hungry little peasant boy Lucien once had been. Selecting a life in the Church had been his only chance at advancement. But for that, Lucien, like others of his class, would have seen his brilliant mind wasted, his back bent by a lifetime of cruel work in the fields of his master. Religious life was the only opportunity for education for a boy of his station and Lucien had grasped it certainly and held on for dear life. Little wonder the problem of Cecilia was so great in his mind. For if Lucien were not a priest, he was nothing.

Cecilia found the Abbot chewing on a frayed quill

and staring at a sheet of figures. She knew the business must be serious. Paper was a valuable commodity, used sparingly on only the most important tasks.

"William," she hesitated, "May I speak with you?"

The Abbot's name, he knew, was lettered boldly on Cecilia's calendar for the day. Afraid she might wish to beg indulgence, he frowned slightly, anticipating disappointment. At forty-seven he had thought himself old, but his nights with her, more important than he had foreseen, made him feel young and alive. Although stimulating company, in truth it was the softness inherent in a woman which drew him to her. Women were different. They thought differently, moved differently, worked differently. They saw the world through different eyes and only by the grace of their being willing to share their unique perspective might a man see these things as well.

Cecilia moved behind the Abbot and kneaded the knots from his shoulders and neck. He leaned into her, eyes closed.

"You work too hard," she admonished. "This day is too glorious to spend squinting over figures. May we not walk into the hills?"

"Are you not unwell?" His voice rose in question.

Cecilia frowned. "Whatever gave you that idea?" she asked. "I am perfectly well."

The Abbot started to explain but then waved away the thought. "Never mind," he answered. "I was mistaken. What shall we talk about?"

Cecilia sat down, smoothing her skirt, bowing her head and folding her hands primly in her lap. Then she ruined her Madonna-like pose with a mischievous grin. For a moment she looked like a happy child.

The Monastery

"William," she bubbled, unable to contain herself, "William, I think we are going to have a baby!"

Although it made no sense, the Abbot was surprised. After all, the girl had been sharing her bed with seven men for three months. Surely this was to be expected. Still, the fact of the coming child was startling. Pulling his thoughts together, he responded.

"You seem very pleased."

Cecilia made a tart face. "And you are not? Did we not say we would be a family?"

William Devon nodded. "Indeed, we did, my love. But the fact is rather different from the idea…"

Cecilia smiled indulgently. "How like a man," she chuckled, "to covet the idea, then eschew its fruition. Will the others be pleased do you think? I had thought to tell them one at a time but that gives advantage to those who know early. Perhaps, we might tell them today at the noon meal."

The Abbot considered for a moment. "Shall I tell them?" he asked.

"No!" Cecilia responded quickly. "I wish to tell them. It is my news…is it not?"

The Abbot nodded.

"Only you know now, although I do think Bartholomew suspects."

"And how would he know?" the Abbot challenged.

Cecilia blushed.

"Never mind," he countered. "I do not wish to know."

The mid-day meal was the most festive any could remember. When Cecilia left the Abbot she had gone straight to the kitchens to beg a special meal. Paul, who rarely denied her any wish, acquiesced with a smile. Cecilia rolled up her sleeves and began to help. By 1:00 there was a veritable feast. A mint sauce had been added to the lamb. Early summer vegetables spilled from the platter on which they and the lamb now steamed. The aroma of fresh bread wafted from the kitchen and mixed with the sugar-smell of a large, rich flan, cooling in a pool of liquid caramel. Several flagons of a wine, previously destined for the neighboring markets, sat open along the length of the heavily laden table. Cecilia and Paul surveyed their handiwork. "Excellent," Paul declared. "Now what do we celebrate?"

Cecilia gave him an enigmatic smile. "You will soon see," was all she would say.

The men filed into the refectory each taking on a puzzled expression as he saw the banquet. After the blessing, all took their places without comment and waited for an explanation. When everyone was seated, the Abbot tapped a knife against his goblet. "Brothers," he addressed them, "Cecilia has given us cause to celebrate, hence the table before you."

Without further ado he took Cecilia's elbow to help her rise from the chair beside his. She faced the men and smiled, her eyes passing slowly to the face of each man and lingering there until all but Lucien had met her gaze. "I have news," she said solemnly. "Good news. I am with child. We are going to have a baby."

In the deafening silence that followed, Cecilia grew uneasy. Finally, Paul rescued her.

"Cecilia, how wonderful!" he exclaimed. "This will make us a true family. I can almost hear the sounds of high voices and tiny feet." His mind already moving back to food, he continued, "We shall have to invent foods that do not require chewing. After all he will not have teeth right away."

Cecilia laughed, then looked around the table once again. William smiled and squeezed her hand. "We are pleased," he assured her, "just surprised."

Dominic got up from his place and came around the table to hug her. He was still the only one who showed her public affection without any sign of embarrassment. "We must take very good care of you," he said, kissing her lightly on the lips.

After a few moments reflection, Bartholomew smiled broadly, as did Luis.

Francis blushed when his eyes met Cecilia's but he did not look away. That could be my child, he thought, and his chest puffed out a little.

Toland and Lucien scowled.

Lucien's reaction was expected, but Toland's gave Cecilia pause. She had thought that he, above all, would be happy. His time with her was far greater than the others for she had known him first and had met him several times in the loft above the forge while others were working. It seemed most likely that the child would be his and so he should be most pleased. But jealousy knows no reason and so, he was not.

†††

May 7, 1997

Rebecca Kincaid slept peacefully through the afternoon. She was transferred at 4:00 from Kaiser Medical

Center to St. Vincent's, an expensive and highly respected long term care facility. Her physicians could no longer justify inpatient status in an acute care facility. After all, the woman was simply sleeping.

Brian Kincaid sat quietly watching his wife. He had arrived early for his meeting with Dr. Chopak. Rebecca lay motionless in the opulent stillness of St. Vincent's plush, private-pay unit. The room, discreetly decorated with chintz chairs and hunt scenes, was an odd and unsuccessful attempt by an American decorator to recreate the look of an English country estate. Still, it was immaculately clean and comfortable. And, of course, Brian thought bitterly, Rebecca had no idea where she was anyway.

He studied her face, the one that had been on the pillow beside him for twenty-five years. Today it was serene, unlined. There was no expression to be found there; no eyes crinkled with laughter, no forehead creased with worry. He tried to remember what they had talked about last, wondering vaguely if it had been the cause of this defection, but he couldn't remember. In fact, he couldn't remember any recent conversations with her. They must have talked, he thought irritably. Christ, they lived together! But he couldn't bring anything to mind, not a subject, not a word.

Gurinder Chopak arrived as scheduled and sat beside Brian in the room's other chair. Dispensing with formalities Brian asked immediately, "What are we going to do? This can't go on forever… can it?"

Chopak understood. "We need to bring her back, if we can, before the realities move apart again. I am surprised they have not done so already."

Kincaid's eyebrows rose as he waited for further

The Monastery

explanation.

"Mr. Kincaid, your wife's life proceeds in the new place. Blood work that was drawn yesterday indicates an HCG level returned to nearly normal."

"Then she isn't pregnant," Kincaid seemed relieved.

Chopak shook his head sadly. "She is, Mr. Kincaid. Other hormones have risen. Her pregnancy is simply farther along."

Kincaid's face fell then rose again as he mentally calculated. "But you said, or Miles did, that these levels don't drop until 50 to70 days into a pregnancy. You said that only a few days ago. Explain that!"

Chopak reached a hand to touch Kincaid. Under normal circumstances, he would never have done so; touching strangers was not acceptable in his culture. Still, the man almost cried out for comfort.

"Time, Mr. Kincaid, is an invention of man. It is arbitrary, contrived, and has relevance only where it is commonly understood. The concept or pace, if you will, does not transfer. One day to you may be one year elsewhere. There is no commonality."

"But if she has gone back in time, to a previous life..." Kincaid argued.

"She has not gone back in our time, Mr. Kincaid. She has moved forward."

Kincaid made the now familiar gesture of scrubbing at his beard with the palm of his hand. "I don't understand," he said. "I don't understand."

"Mr. Kincaid, Rebecca's soul has moved on to her next life. That it seems to us to be in the past is not relevant. It is in a separate place, not connected to us. She has not gone back to relive a life but rather gone forward... progress

toward the light. If she," he pointed a finger at the sleeping woman, *"is to live, then her soul must be lured back, and quickly. When the realities move away from one another she must choose. A soul cannot live in two disconnected realities simultaneously. She must choose one."*

Brian drew a sharp breath. "And what will happen to the other person, the other body, when she chooses?"

"The one not chosen will die," Chopak replied.

"You have seen this?" Kincaid demanded. "You know it to be true?"

Chopak nodded. "I have seen a man's soul leave his body for several days and then return. He remembered briefly where he had been but within hours, like dreams in the daylight, his other life had faded and by evening he could no longer remember anything. I have also seen a child scamper away to another life, leaving behind a small lifeless shell which struggled to breathe for several days and then simply stopped. The body cannot live without a soul, Mr. Kincaid. I have never seen a soul straddle the Dreamline for so long a period. We cannot have much time. We must hurry."

†††

August 1320

The dynamics of the monastery changed once again. Brother Paul, delighted with the prospect of children, plotted and planned with Cecilia. He clucked over her like a mother hen, but with such concern and kindness that she felt pampered. Matthew seemed in awe of the whole idea and kept his distance. Her husbands ran true to form.

William showed the courtesy and concern expected

The Monastery

from a man of his age and temperament. He was pleased with the thought of a child although he had no expectation that it would be his. He worried for Cecilia's health and wondered how they would manage the birth. They, nine men, without a midwife.

With the gallantry of an aging knight, Luis immediately absented himself from Cecilia's bed, promising to return when she felt up to it. No amount of coaxing would convince him that his action, however chivalrous, was unnecessary and so Cecilia graciously accepted his decision, trying to insure that she found other ways to show affection for him. On his assigned days, she took picnics to the field. She made him a new shirt. She put fresh flowers in his cell.

Francis's reaction was most surprising. On his first night after the announcement, he came to her room directly from Vespers. Never before had he arrived in even fleeting daylight. He closed the door and shot the bolt, turning immediately to face her.

"Cccc-could the child bbb-be m-mine?" he stammered, hope illuminating his face.

Although Cecilia was reasonably certain that she had been pregnant some weeks before Francis was finally able to join successfully with her she would never have said so. "Of course," she answered quickly. "The child is ours, everyone's."

Francis became insistent. "That is nnn-not what I mm-meant! And yy-you know it."

Surprised, and pleased, at his tenacity, Cecilia responded. "It could be, Francis, yes. But it does not matter."

"Per chance, it does not matter to you, Cecilia," he replied bluntly.

Seeth Miko Trimpert

Shocked at the clear, bold words, Cecilia's eyes widened and her face split into a grin. Cuffing him on the ear she laughed. "There *is* a man in there I see!" Then she pushed him back onto her new bed where they once again struggled to make love.

Dominic knew that there was little to no chance that the child was his, but was no less pleased by that knowledge. Cecilia brought such happiness to their world, that her child could not help but bring more. But he, too, worried about the birth. Much to Francis's chagrin, he began to frequent the barns, insisting that the little monk teach him about the birthing evolution of his various mammals. When an exasperated Francis pressed for an explanation, Dominic snorted. "We have to know what to do, do we not? I am physician to a gaggle of monks. What do I know of childbearing?"

Put that way, Francis understood and henceforth gave his full effort to insuring that when the time came Dominic would know all that he could. Both men only hoped it would be enough.

Several days after Cecilia had shared her news, when his night was still a week away, Bartholomew crept up on Cecilia at work in the garden. He knelt behind her and nuzzled the back of her neck. "Meet me later in the copse," he whispered.

Cecilia sat back on her haunches, wiping the sweat, which dripped from her nose. "Why?" she teased.

Bartholomew laughed. "You know why," he answered. "Do you not want to come?"

"Wicked man," she giggled. "I will come if I can."

The Monastery

Bartholomew smiled. She would be there.

It was not the first time he had lured her away from the others. There was a passion in her that was heaven. Completely uninhibited, she was willing to try anything. Their encounters were pure joy, for they truly liked one another and reveled in the breathless feelings they could create with their bodies. At first Bartholomew had spent his nights with her solely in the sweaty gymnastics of sex, but soon he found Cecilia interesting and so their time together had grown more pleasurable as they had come to know one another in more than physical ways. Although he was not exactly jealous, Bartholomew did sometimes envy another his time with her and Cecilia, though she would have denied it, did sometimes wish that it were he coming to her bed instead of another.

She did not, however, wish that when Toland came. Toland consumed her. He grabbed and groped, desperate to possess. In the beginning, the heat of his passion drew her often to the forge where they might steal a minute or an hour, but soon his intensity grew exhausting and sometimes a little frightening.

Today at dinner he brushed passed her chair. "Tonight," he growled, the urgency in his voice more command than request.

"Tonight is Lucien's," Cecilia replied evenly.

"You know he will not come," Toland hissed. "Let me come to you."

Cecilia gave him a level look, her voice firm and uncompromising. "No," she said. "The night is Lucien's whether he comes or not. Do not ever ask that again."

Fuming, Toland moved on to his place. He set his food down hard, cracking the earthen plate, and then sat himself, silent, scowling. Eventually he rose, leaving his food untouched and knocking clattering silver to the floor.

After dinner Cecilia put Toland from her mind and headed for the fields where she would meet Bartholomew. He was there, waiting and eager. They hurriedly stripped off their clothes and spent the afternoon like two children who have just discovered magic.

Long past midnight, Cecilia awakened to the rattling of her door. The iron bolt, a gift from Toland, was secure in its place. No one would enter without her consent. Cecilia covered her shift with a shawl as she passed across her room. The door rattled again. Knuckles rapped lightly.

Anticipating another unpleasant exchange with Toland, she asked, "Who's there?"

"Let me in," a voice whispered.

It was not Toland.

"Lucien?"

There was a long silence, then a sigh. "Yes," the quiet voice replied, "Lucien. Please, let me in."

She did not hesitate, but opened the door immediately.

Lucien looked dreadful. He wore no cassock, only simple breeches and a linen shirt. His thick brown hair was in disarray as though he had run his hands through it many times over. His green eyes were bright and feverish. Misery was written on his thin face. Cecilia's initial uneasiness disappeared amidst genuine concern for his well being.

"Lucien, you are ill," she said, leading him gently toward her bed. When he sat, she turned toward the door. "Wait here," she said hurriedly, "while I fetch Dominic."

Lucien grabbed her hand. "No, please." His words

The Monastery

were strained and harsh.

Cecilia squared her slim shoulders and turned back. As she faced him she drew a long breath and prepared to defend herself.

She needn't have worried. Without warning, Lucien fell to his knees. Wrapping his arms around her legs, he began to weep. "Forgive me," he begged. "Please do not send me away. Forgive me…" Shuddering sobs prevented further speech.

Cecilia stood, completely confounded. "Oh, my…" she said, stroking his damp hair. "Oh, my…"

Once started, Lucien seemed unable to cease. Finally, Cecilia nearly dragged him, still clutching her skirt, up onto her bed. "Lie down," she said firmly. "You are making yourself ill. If you do not stop, I *will* fetch Dominic."

Lucien shook his head. "No, please. Just let me stay here. I will not touch you. I give you my word."

Cecilia sighed. "You may touch me, Lucien. You may not hurt me. Why do we not talk? I believe you have much to say and I am a good listener."

And so he talked, though it was only a beginning. It would be many months before Cecilia understood that all that Lucien was hung on the peg with his surplice. He so relied upon his priesthood for his identity that anything which threatened it threatened his very being. It was not, after all, religious conviction that had kept him from her but a fear to death of returning to what he once was… nothing. Still, from that night forward he never missed his assigned time with her and no man was more gentle than he.

When morning came, Lucien rose early and fetched fresh water for Cecilia's pitcher. Her stomach, made queasy by the coming child, lurched. Lucien noted her distress and went directly to the kitchen.

"Cecilia needs tea," he told a gaping Paul. "Now, man. She needs it now!"

Returning, he helped her dress and then without further conversation retired to his own rooms to prepare for morning worship.

Cecilia sat in the back of the chapel among the lesser saints, watching as Lucien celebrated his mass. He intoned the ritual Latin, the Host held high. The monks chanted in response. There is only one man here who truly believes, she thought, and it is not Lucien.

☨☨☨

May 8, 1997

Brian Kincaid came alone to his wife's room and pulled a chair close to her bed. "Lure her back," Chopak had said. "Make her want to be your wife again." Was that even possible? He wondered.

He watched her turn her face from the light to the wall, then wriggle her bottom until she had made a place for her hipbone in the mattress. He had seen her do that a thousand times. Then she let out a long sigh and resumed an even, rhythmic pattern of breathing. Brian opened his briefcase. He would work.

Two hours had passed when Chopak entered the room. He took in the scene with an air of resignation. "Mr. Kincaid, what are you doing?"

Brian looked up, surprised, and then glanced at his watch. "Working. I've let far too many things go."

Chopak looked at Rebecca and then at Brian, his

The Monastery

meaning clear, "Yes, you have. The point of your being here, Mr. Kincaid, is to make her want to come back. Have you spoken to her?"

Kincaid shrugged. "Why? She's dead to the world."

"Not yet," replied Chopak, "but soon, perhaps."

The small, dark man sat on the side of the bed. He took Rebecca's hand and began rubbing it as he had done before. "Rebecca," he called over and over again. "Rebecca, come back to us. Rebecca, can you hear me? It is I, Gurinder, the Saracen."

It was nearly an hour before there was any response and then it was only agitation. Somewhere Rebecca heard him and though his voice upset her, she did not return to speak with him.

†††

Autumn 1320

Cecilia woke with a start. She had heard a man's voice, calling again and again. Unable to remember with whom she slept she turned to see, but the bed was empty. She was alone. By morning the dream was gone and though unreasonably tired, she had no memory of her sleep's disturbance.

When night came again, it was Bartholomew's time. He had pestered and teased Cecilia all day with promises of what he would do, but when evening came he found her exhausted. He felt an unexpected tenderness when he saw her stretched across her mattress, sleeping. They were more playmates than lovers and the emotion surprised him. Carefully, he undressed her and tucked her under a light cover, noting with interest the faint mound that was someone's son. Quite suddenly he wanted very much for it to be his, but the thought was fleeting. He undressed and climbed into the big bed beside her. When she responded to his overtures with a rippling snore he amused himself by tracing the contours of her face and body with a finger. He poked gently at the small mound, eyes becoming wide when it moved away from his hand. Eventually tiring, he went to sleep.

Near midnight he awoke to Cecilia thrashing about the bed. Catching her arms, he folded her into a tight embrace, whispering in her ear, "Shhh, Cecilia, shhh."

When she was finally calm and awake she spoke. "Why did you call me?"

Batholomew frowned. "I did not. You woke me with your movement. I said nothing."

Cecilia looked puzzled. "Someone called me, touched me."

"Not I," Bartholomew replied certainly.

Cecilia shrugged. "Perhaps, the child makes me dream," she offered. Then she nipped at his lower lip and rolled back onto her side, facing away toward the wall, smiling into the dark.

Bartholomew placed a hand on the nape of her neck. "Will you deny me?" he asked.

Cecilia, intending a game, was surprised at the seriousness of his tone. She turned back quickly. "Not you," she said softly. "Never you."

† *Chapter Eight* †

<u>May 12, *1997*</u>

Gurinder Chopak spent the early hours of his morning engaged in a transatlantic telephone call. Hunched over his desk, tapping insistently on a yellow pad before him, he concentrated on the questions at hand. Neither he nor his colleague, Nigel Haversham, had experience to lead them through the case of Rebecca Kincaid. The conversation was a serious one.

"She is clearly alive and well elsewhere," Chopak asserted. "This body is suspended but not wholly disengaged from the new life she leads. I believe that her weeping, guarding against pain and certainly the elevated HCG show that without doubt."

Haversham concurred. "Quite right. Gurinder, have you tried to get a fix on where she is? In time? In space? Is it a world known to us or not?"

Chopak replied. "I believe she is in our medieval period, perhaps in a parallel reality. Her speech is very formal, her choice of words odd. She asked if I were Saracen and then seemed to share a small joke with me about the difficulties inherent in polygamous marriages."

"Is she part of a harem? A concubine, perhaps?" Haversham asked.

"No," was the firm reply. "I thought so at first, but now I think she is the one with many husbands. She has named two men in her sleep talk and referred to yet another who has hurt her. They seem important... even the one who hurt her. She was so sad."

Haversham's reply was thoughtful. "Will she talk to you?"

"She has spoken directly to me only once. She was pleasant and seemed unafraid until her husband tried to intervene. Then she became upset and almost immediately returned to sleep." He thought back replaying the scene in his mind. "It was as though she had heard someone call her. Like a child late for supper, she picked up her head, listened and then said, 'I must go'. I've tried to reach her since then but can only manage to irritate her. I cannot make her talk to me."

"What about her husband?" Haversham asked. "Does she respond to his voice?"

"Not favorably," replied Chopak. "Initially, she refused to acknowledge his presence. When forced to, she seemed afraid. I am certain that there are difficulties between them, equally certain that they cannot be overcome quickly enough to help us."

Haversham, not one to waste words, was silent. The satellite link crackled.

Gurinder Chopak, just as sparing with words, waited. Finally, he asked, "Should I push? I have been fearful that to compel her to acknowledge where she is might precipitate a final decision to relinquish this life. I do not wish to force her hand. Still, there cannot be much time left to her."

"You're likely quite right," Haversham replied, his accent clipping the end of each word. "Then again, we've only seen what? Two dozen of these cases? Perhaps, there is time. Perhaps, she knows or intuits something that we do not."

"Advise me," Chopak said. "I must return to her soon. Give me your opinion."

"Do what you can to learn," Haversham said, without hesitation. *"These matters are beyond us. She will do whatever she must. I doubt we could change that even if we would. Remain neutral if you can. We cannot know what is best for her. A soul does not lift anchor without reason. Do not try to effect an outcome. You can only see one side of this coin. Try to see if she will show you the other."*

Chopak nodded as though his colleague could see him. "Thank you," he said.

"You are welcome, my friend. Good luck."

Nigel Haversham would have given ten years of his life to know the Kincaid woman. Chopak had the chance of a lifetime.

†††

January 1321

Cecilia slept poorly, night after night. The weight of her belly, now huge with an active child made her back ache, but it was the dreams that dragged her down. At Monday's breakfast she appeared so exhausted, teary eyes above black hollows, that Paul sent her immediately back to bed. He followed within minutes, her breakfast on a covered tray. When she had eaten to the old man's satisfaction and was tucked in snugly, Brother Paul trudged across the snow covered cloister garth to the Chapter House where the others were already discussing the results of the last growing season and making plans for the next. He interrupted without apology. "Cecilia is unwell. Something must be done."

All eyes turned to him. As they discussed the problem each man spoke. They had seen her toss and turn throughout the fall and into the winter. Several had kept away on their assigned nights thinking, wrongly, that it was they who disturbed her rest. Only William and Lucien now came to her regularly and then to offer comfort, not ask favors.

Paul was blunt. "I do not think she should be alone." The men nodded one by one. Vigils began again, but this time they were daylong.

Each man took his day and the night that followed. They kept her company when she was awake. They held her when she slept. They watched with increasing worry as the ghosts of her past haunted and pursued her, unaware of the cause, unable to help.

William took the first day. Between Cecilia's naps, the two played a desultory game of chess. After supper, when William made no move to leave her, Cecilia gave him a wan smile. "Are you not going to your bed?" she asked.

"I will stay," he answered. "But do not trouble yourself, Dominic will bring me a pallet on which to sleep."

Cecilia's tired smile widened. "You will stay?" she asked hopefully. "Truly?"

William sat on the bed beside her. She grasped his hand.

"Sleep with me," she begged. "I have been so lonely. No one comes now that I am like this." She gestured toward her bulging abdomen, poking gingerly at her navel, which pushed out like a large button. The Abbot knew suddenly that it had been a mistake for them to absent themselves from her bed.

"Silly woman," he chuckled, hugging her against him. "We did not stay away by choice but because we thought you would prefer it."

Relief made tears flow down her cheeks. "Really?"

The Monastery

she pleaded.

William nodded. Then he removed his clothing and climbed into Cecilia's bed. The girl immediately curled into his arms and went to sleep. But it did not last. By midnight she was thrashing about. The Abbot woke her. "What is it?" he whispered. "Cecilia, what troubles you so?"

It took some time to pull her back, but when finally she spoke her face took on the look of one haunted. "They will not let me rest," she complained. "They call and they call. They touch me when I sleep."

"The Abbot frowned. "Who?"

Cecilia looked bewildered and afraid. "I do not know," she replied. "They are strangers and yet… I feel I know them. Tonight there was a young woman. She cried as though her heart would break. She kept calling, 'Mother… Mother'. William, it was so pitiful. I wanted to hold her but my arms would not move."

Trying to comfort her, the Abbot folded Cecilia into a clumsy embrace and squeezed, suffering the kicks and pokes of the child, who tired of his long confinement.

After a few moments, Cecilia whispered. "William, I think I am losing my mind. Is this my punishment?'

William sat up and pulled Cecilia up with him. "No," he answered sharply. "You have done nothing to be punished for. You love us. We love you. You are a gift from God. Never say otherwise, Cecilia. Never."

Reassured by his words and the feel of strong arms around her, Cecilia went back to sleep. She did not stir again until morning.

Each day followed the one before it, as days are wont to do. Cecilia insisted on being up and about during the morning hours, but by afternoon she would consent to rest. Tuesday, Bartholomew was with her. Wednesday, Dominic. Thursday, Francis. Paul, too, took a turn and spent his night in her rocking chair. Only Matthew demurred although he gladly entertained her during the morning hours. In the middle of the following week Cecilia woke beside Dominic. She felt a sharp pain and then a rush of fluid between her thighs. Dominic woke as the wetness reached him. She lay very still until another pain gripped her belly. Dominic, his arm resting across her, felt the contraction sweep across her taut skin. He kissed her forehead. "Today we have a baby," he said softly.

Things went far better than the monks had anticipated. Cecilia had asked to have Dominic and Paul help her. In the end, they were assisted by Francis who was the only real expert on the matter. When Paul growled, "Something's wrong. Your animals do not scream in agony when they birth their young," Francis showed his innate understanding by answering simply, "My animals do not stand upright. Their muscles are looser and their pelvises larger."

Dominic and Paul looked at him in astonishment. This from the man they had thought simple.

The other monks congregated in the locutorium early in the day and remained, pacing and sweating, as the hours passed. As evening neared and Cecilia's screams grew hoarse, Toland made to leave. "I cannot stand it," he raged. "I am going to the forge." Bartholomew rose as if he, too, would go.

The Abbot's reply was quick and sharp. "You will stay," he said. "We will all stay lest someone forget the price of the pleasure Cecilia gives us." When the two men hesitated, the Abbot lowered his voice to a menacing tone. "Sit," he ordered, and the younger men did.

†††

May 25, 1997

Chopak had thought he was making progress. He spent three consecutive days and nights at Rebecca's bedside, one accompanied by her daughter, Melissa, who had wept pitifully. Although Cecilia had not spoken to him, he knew that she heard him for Rebecca was restless and agitated. When he touched her she pulled away. She mumbled almost constantly in her sleep, once asking, "Is this my punishment?" Punishment for what, Chopak wondered.

He ran a tape recorder. He made a list of everything she said and every name she mentioned. There were now seven: William, Bartholomew, Dominic, Francis, Lucien, Luis, and Toland. She had also mentioned Paul, but she spoke to him in a different tone. The others were lovers; he was sure of it. There is no misunderstanding the conversations of those who are intimate. Even without the words, the tone, the nuances are unmistakable.

Now she was gone. Over a period of several hours Cecilia had steadily withdrawn until Rebecca Kincaid relapsed into near coma. Now she did not even avoid painful stimuli. Something in her other life required her full energy and attention. There was nothing left for this one. Exhausted and disappointed, Chopak went home.

†††

Seeth Miko Trimpert

January 17, 1321

Two hours past sunset Cecilia delivered her first son into the waiting hands of Dominic who checked him over quickly for essential equipment, counting fingers and toes, and handed him off to Paul.

The old man handled the little creature as if he were a cloud, holding him high, fingers spread so that no part of him might escape. "Come, little one," he whispered. "Come to Grandfather."

"Grandfather?" Francis queried.

Paul gave his brother a pleased look and a nod. "This lad will have many fathers," he answered, "but only one grandfather… me."

At the sound of the babe's angry wail, the tension in the locutorium broke with a collective sigh of relief. Francis, knowing that his brothers were worried, hurried out to them. "It is a boy," he said proudly. "We have a son and his mother is well." Then he dashed back to help Paul. There was not a trace of his stammer but in the excitement no one noticed.

By midnight, all was finished. Cecilia rested clean and comfortable, her small son tucked in along her side. Her husbands visited one at a time and each left her, with obvious reluctance, to make room for the next man. Every man looked for himself in the child, but the baby, red face puckered and eyes shut, nestled beside his mother, more hidden from their view than not. Nothing could be told.

For seven days the baby ate, slept and grew but steadfastly refused to open his eyes. Cecilia, stubborn as her son, adamantly declined all inducements to name him, arguing that she would not give him a name until he looked her in the eye. On the eighth day, despairing that he might

The Monastery

be blind, she cried. When Bartholomew's efforts failed, the Abbot came to comfort her. As they sat, speaking quietly, the hungry child awoke. He fussed briefly and then at the sound of a deep voice opened his eyes for the first time. They were large and brown and so like the Abbot's that Cecilia sucked in her breath.

"Oh, William," she whispered. "He's yours."

The Abbott simply stared in amazement, watching as the solemn little face took in the room and those in it. Then his small chin began to quiver. It was all too strange. Cecilia put him deftly to her breast where he latched on with a tiny sigh, safe again in the familiar.

While the child suckled, his parents talked.

"Are you certain?" William asked.

Cecilia laughed. "How can you ask that? Look at him."

"Will the others know, do you think?"

Cecilia thought for a moment. "It is so obvious that, in truth, I cannot see how they could fail to know. But," she paused and chewed her lip, "some will not want to see."

The Abbot nodded.

"Still, over the years, he will undoubtedly grow more like you. Then even they will know, but by that time perhaps all will have sons and so it may not matter as it would now."

The Abbot frowned, his concern for the peace and happiness of their house plain.

Cecilia took his hand and kissed the gnarled knuckles. "William," she soothed, "every child will be someone's. With some it may not be obvious who fathered them. With others it will. It cannot be helped. God willing there will be many and so every man may have his chance at this happiness. Are

Seeth Miko Trimpert

you not pleased?"

The Abbot looked at his son and then at Cecilia. "You cannot know how pleased I am, my love."

With that William Devon rose and tipped Cecilia's face up to him. He kissed her softly, with just a hint of longing for the time when he might share her bed again, and turned to leave. As he reached the doorway, Cecilia called to him.

"His name is Will," she said.

The Abbot left before she could see the tear roll down his cheek.

† *Chapter Nine* †

Spring 1321

Life at St. Fiacre's changed once again. March was bitter and windy and kept them indoors when they were already tired of winter. The cold dragged on into April, delaying planting. Francis came in day after day, hands stiff and red, from hours spent in the freezing barns midwifing his creatures. Cecilia always had warm water waiting.

Still, they were all well and happy. Little Will was an endless source of amusement. He barely squeaked before strong hands lifted him from his basket. Cecilia moaned that he would grow up impossible but the monks merely laughed and continued to spoil him.

Cecilia regained her strength quickly and posted a calendar on the day that Will was two months old. Even before that Toland, Lucien and Batholomew had begun to hint in private moments that they had need of her. She had, in fact, let Bartholomew into her room two weeks past, late in the night when the others had slept.

As the first month of resumed relations proceeded Cecilia began to feel almost hunted. The men seemed oddly desperate. Their one night was not enough and each begged extra time. Finally, besieged and a little afraid, she spoke to William.

"No one was like this before Will," she complained. "What is wrong with them?"

The Abbot chuckled. "Each wants the next child to be his. It is the way of nature. It is the price of your kind of polygamy. When a man has many wives paternity is never in doubt."

Cecilia looked puzzled. "Is it so important?" she asked.

"Yes," William replied. "It is. Are you beginning to regret our arrangement?"

Now it was Cecilia's turn to laugh. "Never," she said firmly. "You forget, I am young and there is much and varied pleasure in loving and being loved by seven men."

The Abbot blushed.

Cecilia saw and realized immediately that although he was always her confidant, even the Abbot was a man. A man who loved her and, like the others, did not like to think of another in her bed. "I am sorry, William. I did not... I should not have said that to you."

William made no reply.

Cecilia returned to the topic at hand. "No, I am not sorry for my decision," she said. "I love you all." With that she kissed him, a reminder, if one were needed, that tonight would be his.

Much later, as she lay in the dark circle of the Abbot's arms she murmured drowsily, "When I am pregnant again, I hope you will all stop feeling this need to plow and begin again to make love." Then she went to sleep.

June 1, 1997

Dr. Chopak had been sitting at Rebecca Kincaid's beside for twelve consecutive hours. He had neither eaten nor slept, and for the first time since any had known him, the St Vincent's staff thought he looked out of sorts.

One more try, he promised himself. Just one more

The Monastery

and then I go home. Then, sipping the tea a kind nurse had brought, he picked up Rebecca's hand and for perhaps the thousandth time rubbed lightly, calling her name. Getting no response, he let his hand wander up her arm and squeeze her elbow. Still nothing. He touched her cheek and lifted her eyelid to check her pupils.

Without warning, the woman's hand flew to her face, slapping his away like a bothersome fly. Then she sat up and opened her eyes. Ignoring the room around her she glared at him.

"What?" she shouted. *"What do you want?"*

Chopak jumped back in astonishment.

"Well, do not just sit like an ass at the bottom of a steep hill. Tell me what I must do to be rid of you." The woman was clearly exasperated.

"Forgive me, Mistress..." Chopak began.

"I shall not," the woman snapped. *"I have a baby son, barely three months out of the womb, and seven husbands who wish to plant another in my belly. I am exhausted. And you! You will not let me sleep. What do you want?"*

Chopak's mouth fell open.

"Close your mouth," the young woman advised. *"You look like a fish on the bank."*

Chopak began to regain his composure. *"Mistress, I do apologize. I had no idea I caused you such distress. Do you, by chance, remember me?"*

The woman nodded. *"The Saracen with one wife, of course. But why do you pester me?"*

Chopak swept a hand around the room. *"Do you know this place, Cecilia?"* He tested the name.

Cecilia looked about. *"No,"* she replied, a faint note of fear in her voice.

"Do not be afraid," Chopak reassured. *"You are safe. Have you been here before?"*

Cecilia thought for a moment, then gave a tentative answer. "Some days before my son was born...there was a young woman, weeping?"

"Your daughter," Chopak answered.

Cecilia gave him a perplexed look. "I have only a son, and a babe at that."

"It was your daughter," Chopak insisted. *Then thinking to make her aware of her physical self and age he added, "Look at your hands."*

Cecilia looked at the hands at the end of Rebecca's arms. "These are not mine," she answered certainly. *"They are hers."*

Chopak thought it unwise to argue. "Very well," he conceded. *"The girl was her daughter, Melissa. She misses her mother."*

Cecilia's face was sympathy itself. "I know," she said. *"I tried to hold her but my arms would not move."*

Uncertain how to proceed, Chopak paused. Then, deciding, he continued.

"Cecilia, do you understand what has happened to you?" The young woman thought for some minutes.

"No," she finally replied. *"But this I do know: I am Cecilia. I am mother of Will and,"* she touched Rebecca's abdomen, *"soon another, though,"* she placed a finger to her lips to indicate a secret, *"no one yet knows. I am wife to good men who love me. I am someone of importance. I am needed. I am happy."*

Chopak countered, "Rebecca's family loves her, too."

Cecilia looked doubtful, thought for another moment

and shook her head disbelieving.

"Saracen," she said, "think on this. When I wake I will find Will in his basket beside my bed, his little mouth sucking in anticipation of my breast." Her face softened. *"And, I will find Lucien wrapped around my body, stiff with the need to love me. When she wakes... she will see only you."*

May 1321

Spring finally came and with it the long warm days which promise summer. Cecilia decided not to announce her second child as she had done Will, but to allow each man to learn of its existence through his own senses. It was a game she played with herself. Who was how perceptive?

Over a period of two months each man made his discovery. The Abbot, who perhaps loved her best, was the first. Late one night in early May when they lay in her bed talking, as was their habit, he absently stroked her smooth skin, allowing his hand to pause briefly on her stomach, "Again?" he asked softly.

Cecilia smiled.

"When?"

"After Christmas, I think, but not long after."

The Abbot frowned slightly. "You must be careful, Cecilia. A woman who bears a child every year lives a short life." When she did not answer, he pressed. "I do not want to lose you."

Cecilia hugged him. "I will be careful, William. I promise. But you must remember that those women have very hard lives. I do not. I am cosseted and pampered enough to be sinful."

"Nevertheless…" he persisted.

The others followed suit. Luis for a second time removed himself from her bed. Francis hoped again. Lucien smiled and was even more gentle, but said nothing. Dominic chuckled and patted her bottom. Toland was furious. Only Bartholomew asked. "Is it mine?"

As summer came to an end, farmers came from the surrounding countryside to do business with the mill. The Abbot, at first wary of having people see a woman in their midst, cautioned Cecilia to remain out of sight, but it was impossible. She was often in the fields or the vineyard. She was a part of the monastery's life and adamantly refused to remain "hidden like a thief". In truth, it mattered little since, the Church's official position notwithstanding, many a parish priest had wife or concubine and more than a few monasteries and convents had well-deserved reputations for debauchery. The farmers thought no less of the churchmen for having found solace in the bed of a pretty young thing. Few of them had been churched themselves though they lived faithfully with women they called *wife*.

As the months passed and the monastery became more successful, word of their prosperity spread. Once again St. Fiacre's found the hungry on the doorstep and, as always, the monks were generous. But even with all they gave away, when the snows came again, the storehouses and cellars were full.

The men spent the early winter months planning. Next year they would sell more wine, mill more grain, increase the livestock. Men with a family, they soon realized, had more interest in the things of this world, which understandably had more immediacy than the next.

The Monastery

†††

June 5, 1997

Gurinder Chopak and Brian Kincaid had fallen into the habit of meeting in Rebecca's room on Thursday evenings. This evening was no different. When Chopak arrived, Brian sat twiddling his thumbs and staring glumly at his wife.

"The nurses are all atwitter," he said, his voice dripping with sarcasm. "Is she calling out for even more men?" The expression on Chopak's face stopped him mid-thought.

"No! No! Not again."

Chopak made a helpless gesture. "It is so. She told me."

"She told you?" Kincaid shouted. "She told you what? When?"

Chopak did not try to soften the news. "She told me several days ago that she has a son and another child on the way."

"And why haven't I heard this happy news?" Kincaid demanded.

Chopak replied. "I left six messages."

Kincaid had no response. The yellow Post Notes were stacked neatly on the left side of his desk, next to the phone. He had been busy. Now he marshaled his thoughts. This situation was completely out of hand. Setting aside anger and arrogance, he addressed Chopak in a business-like tone.

"Look," he began. "I can't get a handle on this time thing. Make me understand."

Chopak acknowledged his confusion with a nod.

Kincaid continued, frustration creeping into his voice. "Rebecca has been like this for what? Six weeks? Her alter ego may have the morals of a mink but even they can't birth two bastards in six weeks!"

Chopak rose, closed the door to the room, then sat again and composed himself. He motioned for Kincaid to do likewise.

"Try this," he suggested. "Think of Cecilia's life..."

Kincaid interrupted immediately. "Cecilia? Who the hell cares about Cecilia? We're talking about Rebecca."

Chopak almost looked annoyed. "Think of Cecilia's life," he repeated firmly, "as a book. Let us say that our tale spans ten years time. Now think of the book's author. It may take one year of his life to write the ten years of his story's protagonist. And while he is writing, other things take place in his life which are, of course, completely independent of hers. Some days he may write all day. In one good day he may chronicle one year of her life. On another, he may not write at all. On yet another, he may write but one scene, a few hours of her life. There is no correlation between time in her life and time in his.

"Now, you, Mr. Kincaid, are a reader. If you are very interested in our story and have the time to do so, you may read it in its entirety at one sitting. In a few hours of your life, the ten years of Cecilia's may pass. But if the tale fails to catch your interest or you are very busy, it may take you several weeks to read it. And remember that while you are reading you are also engaged in other things, which are independent of the book. Your life and hers are not connected temporally, nor are hers and the author's. You all exist in separate dimensions. You are a sometime voyeur, nothing more. Still, her life is there, proceeding in an orderly fashion *which does not change in pace or course whether or not you read."*

Kincaid sat, thinking. "Is this possible?"

Chopak nodded.

"So this woman, the one who has Rebecca's soul, really does exist? Somewhere? She has a child, or maybe children?"

"Yes," Chopak replied. "She does."

"And you talk to her?"

"I have," Chopak said. Then he added ruefully, "but I annoy her."

"Can I meet her?" Kincaid asked.

Chopak thought for a moment. "We can try," he said.

†††

January 1322

Christmas came and went as winter winds howled around the monastery. Little Will caught cold and crouped pitifully through the long nights. When Cecilia, in the last days of her pregnancy, became too exhausted to care for him, Paul once again organized the men. They minded the tot round the clock for nearly a week until finally he awoke one morning, smiling, free of fever and breathing almost normally.

As her time grew nearer, Bartholomew, hopeful that this son was his, rarely left Cecilia's side. Only when Lucien or the Abbot came would he withdraw, for they would not relinquish their time with her and gave him no choice. And so it was Lucien who was with her when she went into labor and Lucien who stayed with her until Dominic was called. Unlike Will, this child came quickly and Dominic laughed aloud when he caught it. Paul standing ready to take the child frowned in disapproval.

Dominic paid him no mind. "Someone's son," he chuckled, "is a girl!"

Cecilia dozed lightly listening to her tiny daughter sniffle and snort in preparation for the cry, which would signal her readiness to eat. Little Will slept soundly across the room, having adapted quickly to sleeping through the sounds of his sister's night feedings. Bartholomew, too, slept soundly beside Cecilia. Much to her consternation, only days after her parturition he had asked to return to her bed. Frowning at his selfishness she had begun to chide him.

Bartholomew blushed, defending himself, "I am not asking to bed you," he replied quietly. "I only wish to be with you and the babe. Perhaps, I might help."

Cecilia could not hide her surprise. Bartholomew's reaction to the child had been a puzzle from the beginning. When his turn to visit had come, a scant few hours after the birth, he had approached with some trepidation. Having listened once again to hours of Cecilia's pitiful cries, he wondered if this time she would blame him for her suffering. But Cecilia had smiled tiredly, patting the mattress beside her, indicating that he should sit and placing the tiny bundle in his arms. Bartholomew's disappointment at Cecilia's failure to produce another son was gone at first glance.

The child was perfect; her skin warm and nearly translucent, her eyes a deep blue. She had a tiny mouth, which puckered like a rosebud and sucked constantly, making the sound of a hungry piglet. Her ears were little

The Monastery

flowers, which peeked from beneath a cap of black curls. Her hands, clenched into wee fists the size of a man's thumb nail, grasped tightly to Bartholomew's outstretched finger.

A feeling, unlike anything he had ever known, clutched at his heart. "Had you thought of a name?" he asked.

Cecilia giggled. "Anthony," she said.

Bartholomew shared her amusement. "Perhaps, you might reconsider?" he suggested. "She has the look of you, Cecilia. Would you call her for yourself?"

"No," she answered quickly. "She must have her own name. I would call her Maggie… if you do not object."

"If *I* do not object?" A look of understanding crossed his face. His question, asked months past, was answered.

Bartholomew spent nearly two weeks of nights in Cecilia's company. Although he often woke tempted by her closeness, he made no attempt to press for more than companionship. But as Cecilia resumed her normal routine, the others became jealous, thinking that he must be favored. Noting the strained silences and angry looks, Cecilia spent one last night with Batholomew giving him a breathtaking gift, taught to her by Dominic, in exchange for the nights of comfort he had given her. Then she sent him back to his own cell with a promise to post her calendars again within the month.

Bartholomew accepted Cecilia's decision without question. Then, lonely after weeks in close proximity to her, he worked long hours on any project he could find. At other times, restless beyond bearing, he struck out into the cold, walking for hours among the sleeping grapevines, across the hills, into the copse where they had first been together. His heart ached but he made no complaint.

Finally, taking pity on him the Abbot sought him out. "Can I help?" the priest asked.

Bartholomew looked up from the work at hand, his handsome face etched with unhappiness. He shook his head, his reply plaintive. "I had not expected to love her," he said sadly.

William Devon laid a sympathetic hand on the other man's shoulder. "I know just what you mean," he agreed solemnly.

Then he left the younger man with his pain.

When Cecilia posted a calendar commencing two weeks hence, the Abbot, concerned about the possibility of yet another pregnancy before she had fully recovered from two in quick succession, visited Dominic. Familiar with herbs and their possible uses in the prevention of unwanted pregnancy, the physician shared what he knew.

Then, agreeing that their understanding of the female body and its workings was insufficient to meet their needs, they went to consult with Francis. Taking in the heady, pleasant odors of Francis's domain, Dominic and the Abbot seated themselves on available hay bales. The three monks sitting thus, amidst the animal sounds and smells of the barn, quietly discussing the rudiments of some means of contraception were near comical.

Francis said what they all knew. "We nn-need to ask a w-woman," he stuttered.

Dominic and the Abbot concurred. The problem was that there were no other women and Cecilia, young as she was and still oblivious to her past, seemed to have no notion of what to do, nor any real concern for the consequences of doing nothing.

The Monastery

"We could simply stay away from her bed for a time," the Abbot suggested, his reluctance obvious.

Dominic frowned. "Some would," he conceded, "but others would not. And," he added, "Cecilia, as you know, sometimes acts the aggressor. She seeks us out…" The other men nodded. "A man would be hard pressed to say no."

Francis tried again. "Ff-females come intt-to season," he offered.

"Animals do, yes," agreed Dominic, "but women?"

Francis nodded. "They mmm-must."

The Abbot thought for a few moments. "Animals bleed when they are in season…" he reasoned.

His companions nodded again.

"Cecilia does not allow us in her bed when she bleeds and yet still she becomes pregnant. Women must be different."

Their discussion lasted until the bell tolled for Sext. In the end, it was Dominic who was elected to discuss the matter with Cecilia. He was, they reasoned, the one she trusted most in female matters. Was he not, after all, her midwife?

Before the day appointed for this awkward encounter, Dominic did further research in his herbals and in the library. Eventually, he had found some rather vague treatises on mechanical and herbal means of preventing undesired conception, which came with a dire warning of eternal damnation. Although the options seemed messy and their efficacy unproven, there was little choice. When the proposal was finally put to Cecilia, as delicately as Dominic could manage, she reacted as he expected.

"Ugggh!" she shuddered. "Why would I want to do that?"

Dominic explained, he coaxed, he begged, he cajoled. Eventually, the Abbot weighed in. "I will forbid the men to come to you unless you at least try to give your body a rest," he warned. "I will *forbid* it, Cecilia, and they *will* heed me."

Cecilia relented. It would, she conceded privately, be nice to be the sole occupant of her body for a while.

Their efforts met with unexpected success. Through the spring and early summer Cecilia grew lithe and strong once again. But for her milk-heavy breasts she looked like the girl who had come to them more than two years past. She could toil alongside the men and often did, enjoying the satisfying tiredness that came from hard work. Since the babies were not solely her responsibility, she had a freedom unknown to other women of the age. Young Will had been weaned to goat's milk when Maggie was born, leaving Maggie's feedings as the only task which fell exclusively to Cecilia. All others were happily shared for the children were the joy in every life, second only to the nights with Cecilia enjoyed by her husbands. Even Peter's stoney attitude toward Cecilia softened as he romped and played with her toddling son.

Summer routines fell into place. Long warm days were followed by their briefer nights. Remote as they were, St. Fiacre's still had visitors. The guesthouse was repaired and refurbished. The mill's patronage increased. Although Cecilia refused to hide herself and her children, she did accede to the Abbot's request that she and the children remain in the background and not flaunt their presence to those who might be traveling far abroad. With the Pope and his court at Avignon and the once heavily traveled Crusade routes now nearly abandoned, visitors from afar were infrequent and

The Monastery

Cecilia did not mind the rare inconvenience of remaining within the living compound and the cloister garth for a few days now and then. It was, in fact, Francis and Toland, not she, who complained bitterly when visitors overstayed their welcome. For the guesthouse was in the work quadrangle, alongside the old dorters, and Cecilia, otherwise a frequent visitor to the blacksmith and the barns, never came when there were strangers about.

Cecilia took the lovely summer to forge strong bonds with each of her husbands. Now that there were children it was more important than ever to love each man enough to satisfy him and make him love her in return. And she did love her husbands and her life, and wanted nothing more than to keep everything as it was.

The Abbot grew daily in stature. A strong, reliable man, he was her companion, her confidant. Together they discussed the future of the monastery and its family as any parents might. Although she did not always understand, he explained to her the business workings, what costs were incurred, what profits garnered by the work they did. He spoke to her about the Church and the turmoil, which had left St. Fiacre's on the fringes of its domain. When once a small contingent of armed knights had ridden past accompanying their war-like Bishop and leaving the monks like field hands in a cloud of dust, he explained how ungodly the men of God had become. Secretly, he was thankful that in his haste the Bishop and his entourage had passed them by without notice.

Bartholomew, too, became more and more important. Unlike the Abbot, whose religious life and love for Cecilia and his little son seemed to live comfortably, side by side in his soul, Bartholomew grew more worldly in his thinking and appearance. He was the first to shun the tonsure and let his black hair, once again, cover his head. And although he donned his robe for services, he rarely wore it otherwise. He was a big, strong man, who in ordinary clothes, appeared tan and handsome, a circumstance which made Cecilia meet him often in their copse. He spent many hours with his daughter, and nearly as many with William's son. He played the horse for hours on end and once watched patiently as the little boy crawled through his just planted seedlings, crushing them into lifeless mulch beneath his tiny knees. When the Abbot queried him about a loss of faith, Bartholomew's answer was surprising.

"Indeed, I have not lost my faith," he replied candidly. "In fact, my soul seems to have reawakened with my cock. I had grown to think myself abandoned in a godless world. Now I can see that I am blessed."

Dominic was first and always Cecilia's friend. She trusted him with her feelings and her body. When she was ill, she sought him out. When she was injured, she wanted him. When she found herself struggling with new ideas and unsettling thoughts, she went straight to him. Their nights together were long and satisfying for he alone fulfilled the burning desires of her intellect. And she, guessing his secret, knew that the one he burned for wanted her, and so assuaged her own guilt at his unhappiness by sharing with him forbidden pleasure and being his friend.

One evening, Bartholomew rounded a corner into view just as Dominic kissed her lightly and passed on through the cloister toward his own cell.

"He is very fond of you," he said.

Cecilia smiled. "He is," she replied mysteriously, "but it is not me that he truly loves." Bartholomew had no

The Monastery

idea what she meant.

Francis was the one whose life was most changed. Even outwardly he seemed a new man. With shoulders back and head up, he was somehow taller, now more stocky than fat. Eyes forward, ready to meet life's challenges, rarely did he trip or stumble; and although still unable to speak without stuttering, at least now he did not let the impediment deter him from expressing a view. He persisted, sometimes doggedly, until he had said what he wished to say. With Cecilia he could often speak without a stammer, especially after they had made love. Once able to control his body, he had learned to please her and now remembered often the first time he had heard her cry of pleasure. Amazed that he had been the cause of it, he had suddenly felt himself a man.

On a lazy August afternoon when the babies slept soundly under the watchful eye of Grandfather Paul, Cecilia wandered toward the barns into which she had seen Francis disappear shortly after the noon meal. It was his day.

She found him examining the fetlock of one of his horses. Lowering herself beside him she bent to look, too. Without conscious thought, Francis leaned into the softness of her. Squatting precariously, Cecilia toppled over onto the hay-strewn floor. Francis stretched himself over her, bringing his mouth to hers and realizing quite suddenly that he meant to have her here in the barn and now if she would consent. Cecilia laughed softly and pulled him to her.

"Do you want me then?" she asked in a sultry voice.

Afraid to trust his treacherous tongue, Francis merely nodded.

Unwilling to accept only that, Cecilia insisted, "Do you?"

"Yes," the man said clearly, "Yes, Cecilia, I do."

Cecilia smiled and wiggled out from under him, heading for the ladder to the hayloft. Thinking at first that she ran from him, Francis stood, dismayed. But when she reached the bottom rung, Cecilia turned. "Come on," she urged breathlessly. "Hurry!"

An hour later as they walked hand in hand back to the common rooms, Francis frowned. Cecilia had not used the prevention they had devised. Realizing, somewhat belatedly the possible consequence of their careless coupling, Francis started to apologize. Cecilia placed her finger to his lips. "Shhh." She whispered. "It's time to have another."

"And you would have it be mine?" he asked.

"I would," she replied with a slow smile.

Francis's heart soared.

By early October Cecilia was certain she was pregnant again. Only then did she stop using her loathsome precautions with the other men. As with Maggie, Cecilia allowed each of her husbands to discover the evidence of the expected child. When the Abbot raised an eyebrow in question, she lowered her eyelids and gave him a shy smile. "William, our methods are not exact. Surely you knew this would happen eventually."

"There is something about the look of you, my love, which suggests that this was not the capricious act of fortune but more an exercise of choice."

Cecilia smiled and reached on tiptoe to kiss his lips. "Life is an exercise of choice," she replied. Then she left him.

† *Chapter Ten* †

June 9, 1997

Gurinder Chopak had made no attempt to contact either Rebecca Kincaid or Cecilia for several days. Fearful of alienating the woman, Cecilia, he had decided to allow the passage of some time before trying to speak with her again. But it was frustrating to know that, as his time and hers were not related, he had no means of judging how much of hers was passing. Nevertheless, exhibiting tremendous strength of will, he had busied himself studying the history of the Middle Ages. If she would talk to him, he reasoned, then he should be prepared with questions which would glean the most information.

To that end he reviewed the popes from Innocent III, whose reign began in 1198, through Clement VII, elected in 1523, well into the Renaissance period. Surely, he thought, she was somewhere in there. Then he reviewed the European monarchs. This was far more difficult given the number of small kingdoms which had flourished during the period. He did, however, at least familiarize himself with the Spanish royalty, French monarchs and the Kings of England from Henry I to Henry the VII, a span of nearly 450 years. Since even the English spoke French during much of the period, the language of Cecilia's, or Rebecca's, dreams gave little clue to her geographic location. Still, he would be ready.

The staff of St. Vincent's reported no change in their patient; she remained unresponsive. After nearly nine weeks of this state, Rebecca was now fed through a feeding tube, secured surgically through the wall of her stomach. She was *turned, religiously, every two hours to prevent bedsores and, much to the chagrin of her family, she was diapered to minimize skin breakdown. This last circumstance had been the cause of her sons suspending their visits. Their father, also clearly disgusted, visited now only when Chopak requested his presence, his desire to meet the woman Cecilia apparently dampened by the need to do so in the presence of his insensible, deteriorating wife. Only Melissa still came daily, sitting morosely beside her absent mother, often weeping silently.*

Brian Kincaid entered the room just as Dr. Chopak was settling himself at the bedside. The dark doctor had learned over preceding weeks to make himself comfortable. Patience was the key.

He motioned Brian to pull up his own chair. The two men, pleasantries now forgone, spoke little, not from animosity or antagonism. That was past. There was simply precious little to say. Chopak began to chafe Rebecca's hand, calling softly, "Cecilia, can you hear me?"

Kincaid spoke, clearly irritated. "Her name is Rebecca."

Chopak met his angry gaze. "Rebecca," he said, his voice ice cold, "is gone. Cecilia lives. We talk to her or we talk to no one." Then he turned back to the sleeping woman and tried again.

Try as he might, Chopak could elicit no response. Finally, a disgusted Kincaid rose to find some coffee. A small, grudging courtesy, he asked, "Want some?"

Chopak shook his head. When Kincaid was gone, he tried again. "Cecilia, please. I ask only a few minutes. Help me."

The woman immediately opened her eyes, her gaze

The Monastery

sweeping around the room. "Is he gone?" she asked.

Surprised, Chopak nodded. "Yes," he said. "He went for coffee."

"He will return?" she queried further.

Chopak nodded again.

"Then we must hurry," she said. "He puts me in mind of the Bishop's soldiers and makes me fearful. What do you want, Saracen?"

Chopak drew a deep breath.

Cecilia interrupted even before he began. "Be quick," she advised. "No long tales tonight. Toland awaits me and," she smiled indulgently, "he does not wait well."

Chopak changed his mind. "I have many questions," he began.

Cecilia shook her head and frowned.

Chopak held up a restraining hand, "but," he continued, "I will not ask them tonight."

Cecilia smiled.

"I need help," he said.

Cecilia gave him her attention.

"Rebecca's family needs her."

Cecilia frowned again, only her expression communicating.

Chopak pressed on, "She has a place in this world. She has children. She has a husband."

"That man?" Cecilia asked, pointing a finger at the empty doorway.

"Yes," Chopak answered.

"And where are these children?" she inquired.

Chopak made no attempt to excuse the sons but instead concentrated on Melissa. "You have seen her daughter," he said. "She is the girl who weeps."

Cecilia's face softened, her eyes glistening with sympathy. Chopak could see that he had touched her.

"Rebecca," Chopak said suddenly. "Please come back."

Cecilia stiffened and gave him a hard look. "Saracen, she is not here."

"But what of her family?" Chopak argued.

"What of mine?" Cecilia countered.

Chopak remained silent. Then after a time, he responded, "Very well then, help me make them understand. Tell me about where you are. About your life. About your family."

Cecilia gave him a puzzled look. "Why?" she asked. "It has been some years since she left. It seems they have forgotten her."

"No," Chopak replied sharply. "It has only been a few weeks in our world.

Cecilia's eyes widened in disbelief. "I do not understand," she replied.

"Nor do I," Chopak conceded. "Help me. At least help me help the girl. She is heartbroken."

Cecilia thought for a moment of her own tiny daughter, her happy son and Francis's child, which grew within her. "Very well, Saracen," she said finally. "I will help you for the girl's sake. But," she admonished, "do not pester me for I am with child again and I am tired."

Chopak nodded gratefully. "How will I know?" he asked.

"I will come when I can," she said. Then she added a word of warning. "But each time it becomes more difficult. I think soon I shall not be able to come at all."

†††

Autumn 1322

They were at supper. Cecilia surveyed the men at table and listened attentively as they made quiet conversation with one another. Lucien sat beside her, his hand beneath the table, rubbing gently over the top of her thigh. Although the priest made no overt claim on her, she had realized, quite slowly, that he loved her very much. Still, the manner of his actions made obvious the fact that he had not yet forgiven himself for his behavior on their first night together and though Cecilia insisted repeatedly that it was of no consequence and all but forgotten, he continued to atone.

Toland sat across from her, angry as always. He alone seemed unable to come to grips with their arrangement. The others, even in moments of doubt, made no complaint about their lot. Each had come to love her in his own way, and Cecilia, getting from one man what another was unable to give, had all that she wanted and was well pleased with her bargain. Only Toland was discontent.

When it had become apparent to all that she was pregnant yet again his fury knew no bounds. He had come to her on his appointed night in a near rage. Acting the cuckolded husband, he demanded, "Whose is it?"

When Cecilia made no response, he grabbed her arms and shook her. "Whose?" he shouted. "Tell me!" His voice carried through the stone corridor and echoed into the locutorium, where the Abbot, Bartholomew and Lucien still sat. Bartholomew began to rise. "No," Lucien said. "Let me."

Both men looked to the Abbot for a decision. William

Seeth Miko Trimpert

Devon nodded to Lucien and then to Bartholomew he said, "Let Lucien manage him, please. There is a debt to be repaid." Bartholomew lowered his eyes in assent.

Lucien's knuckles rapped lightly on Cecilia's door, which flew open far too quickly to have been in response to his knock. Inside, Cecilia stood hands on hips glaring at Toland who glared right back.

"Out!" she ordered, pointing at the open door.

"This is my night and I will stay!" Toland shouted.

Lucien stepped into the room.

"Get out!" Toland bellowed.

Lucien stood his ground. "Leave now," he said quietly. "You make a fool of yourself."

Toland's face grew crimson. "This is my night! You cannot have her!"

Lucien gave Toland a look of pity. "I am not staying," he replied firmly, "and neither are you." Then he stepped aside making a path between himself and Cecilia.

Outnumbered, Toland had little choice. He stomped through the door and stopped abruptly just outside, waiting for Lucien. Lucien kissed Cecilia on the cheek and heard her whispered "thank you" before following Toland out. Toland winced as he heard her shoot the bolt he had made himself.

Late that night, when the silence was broken only by the sounds of wind in the trees, Cecilia fed Maggie and tucked her back into her basket. Unable to return to sleep she relived the angry scene with Toland and the sudden, unexpected feeling of security that had arrived in the person of Lucien. On impulse she checked her babies once again, grabbed her shawl and left them snug in their little beds, gliding silently through the monastery until she reached

The Monastery

Lucien's cell. Without knocking, she slipped soundlessly through the unlatched door and into the room beyond where he slept.

Seen without his cassock and the other accoutrements of his office, he was pleasant to look at. He was tall, nearly as tall as Bartholomew. His build was slight but pleasingly muscular with good proportion, his face too thin to be handsome and yet his features were agreeable. His nose was long, his cheek bones high, his mouth generous and tempting; but his eyes, now closed, were his strength. A startling green, with long straight lashes which presently lay against his cheeks, they dominated his waking face and drew attention from all else. Cecilia stood studying him. It was a rare moment when one caught Lucien off guard. His pride, receding with the growing acknowledgement of his humanity, still plagued him. Only Cecilia and the children were allowed to see him nearly at ease and even then he maintained a slight aura of reserve. In their most intimate moments she only glimpsed a vulnerable soul. Now, sleeping alone, he was defenseless.

†††

June 13, 1997

Dr. Chopak sat quietly evening after evening waiting for an opportunity to talk to his medieval woman, but Cecilia made no attempt to contact him nor did he "pester" the woman in the bed.

Earlier tonight, Brian Kincaid and his sons had visited. Their stay was brief. Chopak tried, without success, to convince Kincaid to return alone but the man claimed business commitments.

Disappointed, Chopak had already decided to go home to his own family when temptation overtook him. He picked up Rebecca's hand and called urgently, "Cecilia, please. Talk to me."

Amazingly, the woman responded immediately. She arrived breathless.

Although Rebecca was neat and clean, hair combed, nightclothes tidy, Cecilia exuded an impression of one harried and frightened. "Do not trouble me now, Saracen. We are in grave danger!"

Alarmed, Chopak pressed. "What danger, Cecilia? What has happened?"

"The Bishop," she responded, "he is in the courtyard with many soldiers. They are dangerous men. Do not trouble me again tonight. We must hide." With that she was gone.

† *Chapter Eleven* †

<u>November 1322</u>

The work courtyard was alive with men atop huge beasts. They wheeled and snorted in a state of high excitement, further incited by the shouts of their riders. Confused by their sudden confinement in a tight space, the lathered giants jostled for position and pawed at the ground, churning up funnel clouds of whirling dust. The Bishop, armed like his men, barked orders, which were swiftly obeyed.

They had arrived without warning, thundering into the compound while most of the residents of St. Fiacre's were still in the fields, making the most of the last days of a gentle Indian summer. Cecilia and the babies had been in the kitchen when the commotion began. Paul now whisked them quickly toward the guesthouse. Luis, who had been a bit under the weather for several days, scurried to remove all evidence of Cecilia and the children from her room. The Bishop, though not a recent visitor, had stayed within St. Fiacre's walls, and knew the location of his quarters.

Striding toward the Abbot's empty house, the Bishop pulled off his heavy gloves. When he saw Cecilia, one child under each arm and another clearly swelling beneath her breasts, he stopped abruptly. "Madam?" he scowled.

Cecilia curtseyed awkwardly. "Your Grace," she replied, dropping her eyes to his feet.

Brother Paul intervened without being asked. "Your Grace, may I present the Lady Cecilia, wife of Bartholomew de Carlisle?"

Seeth Miko Trimpert

The Bishop nodded curtly, offering Cecilia his ring to kiss. He watched with amused malice as she struggled, encumbered as she was, to kiss it. "Sin is its own burden, is it not, Madame?" he sneered.

Cecilia made no response but waited meekly for him to go on his way. Enjoying her discomfort, he waited until her arms ached from the weight of the children before tiring of his game and leaving her. Hurriedly she disappeared into the guest quarters where she placed her tiny burdens on the rough straw of the bed. She nursed each child in turn to keep them silent and waited for someone to come to her.

Brother Paul caught the Abbot as he entered the gate. He was running and out of breath. "He saw Cecilia," he rasped. "I told him that she was a visiting lady, wife of Bartholomew de Carlisle."

When the Abbot made a face, Paul hurriedly made his explanation. "I could think of no other name. Who else among us is truly someone and," he added, "someone from far away. Someone the Bishop does not know."

"You did well," the Abbot answered. "Bartholomew is in his shirtsleeves and has abandoned the tonsure. We will introduce him as my nephew, traveling with his family… headed home to England." He gave Paul a grim smile as the lie took shape. "Tell the others. Offer nothing. Follow my lead." With that he headed for his house to make his guest welcome. Nearly across the cloister garth, he stopped. "What of her things?" he asked in a hoarse whisper.

Paul made a dismissive gesture. Taken care of.

Bishop Antonio Giardina was a man of the age. The son of a rich and important family from Padua, he had come

The Monastery

to the Church a callous youth, lacking faith and goodness but with an abundance of what its hierarchy sought, money and ambition. Added to the prestige of his current office, the absence of the Papal court, now in residence in Avignon, had allowed him to amass far more power than was good for his immortal soul. Essentially a godless man, he enjoyed life to its fullest.

He traveled the countryside in the company of his own small army, hunting, drinking and generally marauding for sport. His sexual proclivities were known to be eclectic and while honorable men felt it necessary to hide their wives and daughters, he also traveled with a young cleric who was rumored to warm his bed in the absence of suitable female companionship. Although personally wealthy, he never hesitated to take what he wanted where he found it in the name of Mother Church, reasoning that there was no need to draw upon his own resources, if those of another might be expended.

This man now stood in the midst of William Devon's humble house, beating the dust from his clothing with his leather riding gloves and watching with disinterest as it settled onto the scant furnishings around him.

"'Tis a filthy ride up from the south," he complained. "There's been no rain for months and the road rises to meet you like the Devil himself."

"Your Grace," the Abbot bowed. "A bath might be arranged."

The Bishop, who smelled as though he would not know the word, guffawed. "I do not believe we need go so far," he replied. "Unless, de Carlisle might wish to share his wife. From the looks of her, one could hardly do her any harm." He laughed again at his own joke.

The Abbot feigned misunderstanding.

"The girl," the Bishop prompted, making a crude gesture to indicate her pregnant state.

The Abbot, a consummate actor, blushed modestly. "Your Grace," he said, his tone a mild rebuke, "she is my nephew's wife."

A faint look of annoyance crossed the Bishop's unpleasant face. "Never mind," he grumbled. "Anselm will do."

The Bishop was then shown to his room, warm and sweet smelling from Cecilia's recent habitation. Noting its condition, His Excellency looked askance.

"We had heard of your presence in the region," the Abbot explained, "and thought it wise to be prepared."

The Bishop made an odd sound of skepticism deep in his throat but before he could formulate an adequate response Brother Anselm entered, toting fine leather saddle bags, and began toadying about the room. The younger man's fawning and simpering nearly made William gag. At the earliest possible moment he excused himself and rushed to see what had become of his household.

The Bishop and his men had intended a stay of only two days, a brief respite in a journey to meet Giardina's summons to Avignon, but on the morning slated for departure their plans were thwarted by the abrupt end of the summer-long drought.

Shortly after sunrise, the blue skies of early dawn were overtaken as a menacing line of thunderheads marched, shoulder to shoulder, up from the south, a deluge of biblical proportions on their proverbial heels. The work quadrangle, already a dust bowl, became a bog and within the hour was

The Monastery

impassable. The manes and tails of the huge war horses stood on end, pulled skyward by the charge in each jagged bolt of lightening. Terrorized by that and crashing thunder, the beasts milled nervously, stirring the mud underfoot like cake batter and threatening at any moment to break through the gate and escape into the surrounding fields.

Francis stood, under cover of the open barn and watched. He could smell their fear. Just as he became certain that the leader would smash the gate and bolt, the storm suddenly abated. Towering thunderclouds, like huge grey ghosts, shape-shifted and bled into one another forming a dark, impenetrable mass. The rain settled into a solid sheet of water. As it did, the mounts, too, quieted and stood dumb and docile in the steadily pouring rain.

The Bishop's soldiers, heretofore camped haphazardly in the courtyard, sought shelter. They now appropriated the old dorter, evicting a number of small farm animals and the larger spiders and settled themselves for a few days of drinking and dicing, while the Bishop and his girlish young companion resumed residence in Cecilia's comfortable room.

The monks continued to keep to themselves, maintaining a hitherto nearly abandoned schedule of devotional services. Although not a silent order, their Bishop accepted their reticence to converse and attributed it to piety. Having already audited the affairs of St. Fiacre's and apportioned to himself a generous tithe, he spent the additional days, imposed upon him by the inclement weather, playing chess with the Abbot, eating, and amusing himself with Brother Anselm.

Eventually bored with the young cleric, and unwilling to challenge young de Carlisle for the favors of his pregnant wife, the Bishop's eye wandered to Peter but the older monks, wiser in the ways of corrupt Churchmen, had whisked him quickly from view.

When, finally, on the morning of the fifth day, the Bishop and his entourage decamped on their way to Avignon, the residents of St. Fiacre's nearly collapsed with relief. The charade had worked, but clearly contingency plans were needed. Their hospitality, though not lavish, had of necessity been sufficient to warrant another visit from their Bishop. And their stores, abundant from months of hard work, were riches the Bishop would not eschew. Next time they must be ready.

The monastery reverted quickly to the last days of its harvest but beneath the welcome comfort of returned routine was an unbidden whisper of fear. In departing the bishop had taken not only a substantial measure of their stores but left in its place uncertainty and a sense of vulnerability. Even a distant dust devil dancing across harvested fields, once a source of great amusement to the children, now became a menacing harbinger lest it be riders. No one felt at ease until the snows came, which they did with a vengeance, early and deep.

Winter's first blizzard, like a sea storm, howled around them for three days, refusing to retreat until the drifts topped the windward walls and blew in frozen spindrift into the northern quadrangle. When finally the sun wrested the sky from her opponent, snow, capped with a treacherously thin crust, lay six feet deep across the fields. They were marooned, their home an island on a sea of ice. But, they were safe.

The Monastery

Inside the monastery, huge fires kept them snug and warm. At first they roared in every common room but as the frigid, featureless days stretched endlessly on across barren fields the finite nature of even their mountain of winter wood asserted itself. At Chapter on a particularly bitter morning, it was decided that the library would be closed, the refectory table moved to the kitchen and only the locutorium and Cecilia's room kept heated. Days later the monks added the additional proviso that their sleeping pallets be moved from their icy cells to the locutorium. They were freezing. Even devotional services took on a brisk business-like air as their Creator received His praise with an economy of time and motion heretofore unknown. Still, it should not be thought that God was given short shrift for it was a rare evening indeed when each man did not offer his own silent prayer of thanks for his life and the way of it while sitting warm and happy before the evening's fire.

Once established, their new routine was pleasant. Meals in the kitchen took on the informality, and sometimes hilarity, of a street fair, jostling bodies in close proximity, eating and laughing, steeped in warmth and a myriad of tempting smells. When the weather was especially bitter and no chores called, Cecilia and the men often lingered over dinner until well past mid-afternoon, nibbling at the meal's remains and playing games. The children provided endless entertainment and thrived in their status as stars around which the planets of the monastery revolved. Young Will began to talk in earnest and ran from one thing to another, demanding with a point and a grunt to be told its name. Little Maggie staggered along behind him, her small, serious face taking note of each strange sound for use on the day when she would begin to speak in sentences, bypassing the cute baby talk of her brother altogether. When naptime came it was a contest to call whether the monks or the children protested more loudly.

As their sense of isolation grew, memories of autumn's terror faded. The Abbot had anticipated that living close would precipitate some difficulties but they were amazingly few. True, the men, unaccustomed to sleeping in the presence of others, did grouse and complain about one another's snores; and one morning, Dominic did announce with feigned gravity that he would not sleep again next to Toland if Paul insisted on serving lentil soup for supper. Toland blushed furiously while the remainder of the kitchen howled with laughter.

Too, there was the constraint placed upon those who were accustomed to stealing extra time with Cecilia, which none could now do under the noses of the others. There were no mornings in the barn or forge, no visits to the copse and no lazy afternoon with her door's bolt in place and William warm between her thighs. Cecilia solved this problem quickly and adroitly by revising her calendars so that each of her seven husbands spent one night each week in her bed. "I am cold," she said simply. "I want company." No one challenged her reasoning and even Luis, blue-lipped and thinning, gratefully took his nights in her bed. Only young Peter was a problem.

Prior to the Bishop's visit Cecilia and Peter had established an uneasy truce. Their relationship, not unlike that of a stepmother and her husband's son, though less than ideal was at least civil. Cecilia tried very hard. Peter gave no quarter. However, over the several months following the Bishop's sojourn with them Peter, now grown tall and handsome, became a serious problem. Fast approaching his

The Monastery

fifteenth year he grew ever more belligerent. Unbeknownst to the adults, he had engaged in considerable experimentation with the Bishop's bedmate, Anselm, and, although not cognizant of it himself, barely escaped rape when the Abbot confronted the Bishop coming upon the boy unawares in the latrine. Now sexually awakened, hormones raging, Peter took out his frustration on the pregnant Cecilia. When opportunity arose he bumped her, pressing himself against her body, letting a sly hand touch where he should not. Paul and Matthew each scolded him on more than one occasion. Finally, reluctantly, Cecilia appealed to the Abbot.

His behavior thus challenged, Peter retaliated, snapping angrily when required to speak with Cecilia and treating her small children cruelly. William counseled patiently at first, then, after seeing the boy trip toddling young Will with a birch branch, dragged the offending lad to the freezing barn for a thorough thrashing; all to no avail.

It was Bartholomew who finally brought the boy under control. Face to face in the deserted Chapter House, Bartholomew tried compassion first.

"Peter, I know this is difficult for you. A man's body is not always his friend, especially a young man's body. If you want a wife, you may leave here in time and find one, but you may not have Cecilia. The decision is hers and it is final."

The boy whined, "I am a man. I have needs."

"You are not a man," Bartholomew reasoned, "for if you were, you would know that even a man may not force himself on an unwilling woman."

"She will have me," Peter hissed.

Bartholomew sighed, the pain of regret clear on his handsome face, then spoke again his voice an angry growl.

"If you harm her… or the children, I will kill you," he warned. "Tell me that you understand. There must be no confusion."

"You will not harm me," Peter scoffed. "The Abbot will not allow it."

"I will, as God is my witness," Bartholomew swore. "Do not try me, son. You do so at your peril."

Now struggling under the twin burdens of fury and fear, Peter stalked away. But the problem was not resolved, merely deferred.

Of more immediate concern was Luis. Having absented himself from her bed in late fall, Cecilia was hard pressed to hide her surprise when he accepted the invitation to enter it again in winter. For some months afterward only he and Cecilia knew that he slept there, exhausted, pressed close against her warm young body, absorbing the warmth his own could no longer produce. He marveled at the growing child and often lay silently in the dead of night watching it somersault beneath the covers. He hoped to see it born, an affirmation that life would continue when he was gone.

Eventually, growing ever more concerned, Cecilia felt justified in breaking her unspoken rule of never discussing one man with another. Not wishing to arouse suspicion Cecilia waited for Dominic's night. Once they were comfortably ensconced beneath her covers, his hands warming themselves in the crevices of her body. Cecilia spoke.

"Dominic, I beg your indulgence for a moment or two. I wish to discuss Luis."

Even Dominic was taken aback by the mention of a rival while he was making overtures of love. He frowned.

"I am sorry," Cecilia persevered "Truly sorry, but

The Monastery

this is very important."

Dominic's face softened at her very apparent distress. "Of course," he replied gently, pulling his hands back to himself. "Tell me."

Cecilia quickly outlined the reasons for her concern: Luis arrived on his evenings exhausted. Walking from her chair to her bed, a distance of no more than five paces left him breathless and blue. He had breath for speech only after lying quietly for long periods of time and often required assistance to rise from the bed for nature's calls.

"He is cold, Dominic. I cannot warm him."

Dominic nodded gravely. He, too, had noted his old friend's decline. Even as far back as last summer Brother Luis had been unable to keep the pace of the other farmers. Bartholomew had reported seeing him more than once resting silently, uncomplaining, before moving on to the next task. Although not a young man, Dominic would have predicted that Luis's austere lifestyle augured well for longevity. Apparently, it was not to be.

"I think it is his heart," he said gently. "It lacks the strength to keep life flowing within him. Keep him close to you. Give him comfort."

Cecilia nodded then reached for Dominic, pulling him against her.

Dominic came willingly into the circle of her arms. "You are very special," he whispered.

"Thank you," she whispered back. Then, with a mischievous grin, she teased, "Shall I show you just how special?"

Dominic laughed, his own happiness, for the moment, crowding out the sadness of Luis's impending demise.

Seeth Miko Trimpert

†††

<u>July 1, 1997</u>

Gurinder Chopak had all but given up hope of further conversation with Cecilia. After fruitless weeks, he no longer sat patiently beside her bed but now came once, daily, to check her general condition and make appropriate notations in her chart. There had been no change except for a Stage I decubitus developing on her tailbone, inevitable. Today as he sat, chewing the end of a Waterford pen, and trying to decide what to write when there was nothing to say, a new aide scurried hurriedly in his direction. "Dr. Chopak?" she questioned.

"Yes," he replied.

"Your patient is asking for you."

"Mrs. Kincaid…" Chopak was shocked, "…is asking for me?"

"Well," the aide hesitated, "not exactly you. Sara somebody."

"Saracen?" Chopak offered.

The aide's crumpled brow cleared, "Yes," she said, "that's it. Who is Sara Sen?"

"Me," he replied, dashing down the hall.

The aide shrugged and returned to her duties.

Chopak entered Rebecca's room to find the woman sitting straight and serene, gazing around with interest. When she noted his presence, she smiled.

"Good Morning," Chopak offered.

"Is it morning?" the woman asked.

Chopak nodded.

The Monastery

Cecilia was napping through a winter afternoon. "It matters not," the woman said, brushing aside the inconsistency. "I have come to apologize. I promised to help you months ago and have not done so. I have my reasons, of course, but I have failed you and I am sorry."

"It is of no consequence," Chopak dismissed her concern. "I am most pleased to see you. Are you well?"

"I am," Cecilia replied, "as are my husbands and children. And you?"

"Well, too," Chopak responded.

Pleasantries dispensed, the woman looked askance. "What do you wish of me, Saracen? I have not dreamed of you since summer. You fade in my mind."

"I have a thousand questions, Madam," Chopak said.

"As always," the woman chuckled. "Perhaps, we might begin with fewer."

Chopak conceded. "What year do you live?"

Cecilia looked confused. Although aware of the century in which she lived, the exact year was of no real consequence and not firmly imbedded in her thinking.

Chopak thought quickly, "Who is King of England?"

Cecilia shrugged.

"Who is Pope?" *Chopak was becoming desperate.*

Cecilia, happy to finally be able to oblige, smiled. "John XXII," she said firmly. "And he resides in Avignon."

Chopak's mind reeled through the papal histories. John XXII had been pope from 1316-1334. A celebrated canon lawyer, he ruled the church during a turbulent time of transition, insisting on the supremacy of papal power in a contest between himself and Louis IV of Bavaria, later Holy

Roman emperor. "Can you find out for me who is King of England?" Chopak prodded.

Cecilia thought for a moment. "Bartholomew may know," she conceded, "He is from across the sea."

Abandoning more historical fact, of which she was obviously and perhaps understandably ignorant, Chopak turned to her personal life.

"Tell me of your family. Who are they and how do you live?"

Cecilia smiled. "I have a fine family," she bragged. "I live with them in the Monastery of St. Fiacre."

"Where is the monastery?" Chopak queried.

Again, Cecilia unlearned in geography, was unable to answer. Chopak prodded. "Is Avignon east or west?"

"West," she replied certainly.

"And Rome?"

"South."

"Venice?"

"Also south."

"Do you live near the sea?"

"No." Cecilia said.

"In the mountains?"

"No," again. "In the hills. We grow grapes."

"Is it cold?" Chopak asked.

"Bitter," the woman replied, shivering. "The winter is a hard one."

"Are you suffering?"

Cecilia laughed aloud. "Never!" she replied. "We have plenty and we are all warm and well... except Luis who grows old from illness."

"Luis?" Chopak's voice rose in question.

"Yes," Cecilia replied, sadness dimming the light in

The Monastery

her eyes. *"Luis is the oldest of my husbands. A fine kind man who asks little and gives much. He is a little in awe of me whether because I am young or female I cannot tell, but to him I am like a precious thing on loan and he treats me with near reverence."*

"And he is ill?" Chopak prompted.

"Very," Cecilia said again. "His heart cannot sustain him."

"How do you know this?" Chopak demanded.

"Dominic," she replied simply. "He is physician and friend. He knows much."

Chopak hesitated only a second. "Is Dominic your husband as well?"

Cecilia nodded.

"And Bartholomew, and Toland, and Francis, and Lucien and William?"

Cecilia's eyes widened in surprise. "How do you know them?"

It was Chopak's turn to laugh. "Rebecca talks in her sleep."

Cecilia blushed. "Not overmuch I hope," she worried.

Chopak brushed over the moment of embarrassment. "Tell me of your children."

Cecilia adjusted her position, frowning. "Her bottom hurts," she complained. Then, she continued. "Will is my son. He is just past two years, a strong healthy lad who greatly favors his father."

Chopak's eyebrows rose.

Seeing it Cecilia replied with a wry smile. "He looks so like William there can be no doubt."

"And the other?" Chopak queried.

"Maggie," Cecilia replied. "She is one year and she is Bartholomew's child."

Again the question on Chopak's visage.

Cecilia answered candidly. "I made it so." Then she smiled again to share her newest secret. "I carry another. Francis is father."

Chopak was too fascinated to observe polite convention. "Will you give each man a child?"

Cecilia nodded, "If I can… all, perhaps, save Toland. His need is too great and there is a cruel streak in him. About him I have not yet decided."

Amazed at his good fortune, Chopak sat back to catch his breath. Suddenly he noted a look he had seen before. Cecilia was alert to a summons from elsewhere. "Don't go," he begged.

"I must," she replied evenly. As Rebecca's eyelids drooped, Chopak called out quickly, "Cecilia, tell Dominic to make a fine powder of foxglove. Caution him to be sparing. A medicine is also always a poison, but in small amount it may help Luis for a time."

He could not tell if she had heard him.

† *Chapter Twelve* †

April 1323

Francis's son bounced his way through the winter, pummeling his mother mercilessly. Although nominally due in May, by early April it was evident that he was unlikely to keep to someone else's calendar. Cecilia took it all in stride. She ate like three men at every meal and napped in the afternoons, leaving Will and Maggie in the care of the monks. On April 16, in the midst of an unseasonably late snowstorm, Cecilia delivered a tiny boy one month early, ass-end first. Had he been full-term the breech presentation might have caused difficulty but, little as he was, his bottom slipped easily into the world. Like a foal, his legs came next, then his body and finally his head, topped with an amazing mop of bright red hair. Francis fainted dead away. Dominic and Paul roared with laughter. Frightened by the noise, baby Angus howled in protest.

After each husband had visited, Francis settled into Cecilia's chair. His paternity could not have been more certain had the child had his father's name stamped upon his back. Francis rocked him to and fro while Cecilia slept. The babe was the quintessential Irishman. He was beautiful, his skin like fine porcelain, his hands and feet perfect as though each small digit had been individually carved. His face was round with tiny elf-like features. His shock of red hair made him look as if his head were afire. Still, his worried father hovered for several hours until finally the child opened his eyes. "Are they crossed?" he asked anxiously.

Cecilia patted his hand. "They are blue like yours,"

she replied with a smile, "and they are looking straight at me." Francis was so relieved he nearly wept. "Good," he said finally. "He will be f-fine."

The season changed abruptly from winter to summer, spring forgone completely. With the break in the weather came rare letters. Lucien, returning from the year's first visit to the monastery's markets and a distant religious community, brought one for William from the Bishop, one for Bartholomew from England. The Abbot broke the ornate red seal on his anticipating a belated message of thanks for the monastery's hospitality. He found instead a demand for six oak casks of their finest wine, a gift for the Pope from Bishop Giardina.

For Bartholomew there was a long, sad missive. In a single stroke of her pen, his mother took from him his father and both brothers. Lord Carlisle and his first son, she reported, had succumbed to influenza on last All Hallow's Eve. Her second son, and favorite, had been lost along the northern borders in the service of the King. The monk stood, stunned. Edward II now demanded his return to secular life or forfeiture of Carlisle lands to the crown. The King, it was said, distrusted Bartholomew's brother-in-law, a good man whose only sin, a Scottish birth, brought his allegiance into question. The Bishop of Durham, under pressure from the King, had already granted Bartholomew a release from his vows. It was all arranged. He was to come at once.

The letter, written during the last of the harvest, was only six months old. It might reasonably have been much older.

Bartholomew sought the advice of the Abbot, then went directly to Cecilia. He was, at first, loathe to leave his

The Monastery

home and family. England was a world away, and his English family the same that had bought Heaven with his life nearly ten years past. However, the Abbot, a man of vision, advised further consideration.

"Think of the future," he counseled. "What will we do if His Grace, now that he has rediscovered us, visits often? He cannot see you again. Cecilia cannot be here. Much as we may wish it, the world may not leave us to ourselves. What is to become of Cecilia and the children? We may need a man of means to be her protector. You may be that man. Besides even a weak king can be a powerful ally," he added.

In spite of himself, Bartholomew briefly glimpsed a world where he was Lord of the manor, Cecilia by his side, her children around his feet. He would not have to share her. Desire twisted in his gut.

Then resigned, guilty, he pulled himself back to reality. "She will never consent," he argued. "Never."

The Abbot, too, was resigned. "She may have no choice."

The discussion with Cecilia involved considerably more emotion. At first she was furious. "You would leave me and Maggie? Are we nothing to you?" she raged.

When Bartholomew, explaining again and again what he and William had discussed, remained unmoved, she began to weep. First there were small tears rolling silently down her cheeks, then hitched sobs and finally a heartbroken wail. "You cannot leave me," she sobbed. "I cannot live without you."

Bartholomew was at a loss. As one among many he had not thought his importance so great. "The others will care for you," he offered. "I shall return before spring."

Cecilia's tears flowed unabated.

"How can you care so much for me," he challenged angrily "and want the others as well?"

"I do not know," she wept, "but I do. I swear it."

Thoroughly confused, Bartholomew pulled her against him, whispering fiercely, "I must be mad to love you so."

Two days later, on a swift mount, Bartholomew rode west, staying south of the still snow-capped mountains until summer could advance. Before leaving, he held her one last time and whispered softly in her ear, "Do not forget me. I will not forsake you. I will come back."

Cecilia wept pitifully for three days and then refused to speak or hear his name.

Luis died. Cecilia's dreamt remedy had helped him briefly allowing the monk a few additional weeks of happiness. Mindful of his limited time, he spent his final days with the children, playing quietly or telling to them the stories they liked best. The last day of his life was a good one. He played with Will, plaited little Maggie's hair and rocked young Angus to sleep at nightfall. Then he had a bit of his favorite custard and retired to Cecilia's bed. They watched the gloaming of the long summer day and talked softly of the days of his youth. Finally, the old man broached a forbidden topic. Cecilia stiffened and opened her mouth to object but a rough, dry hand brushed her lips.

"Listen to me, girl, and do not interrupt. Bartholomew did not wish to leave you. He has risked all that he loves to gain the means to protect you."

He waved away her attempt at further protest.

"The Bishop will return. He will know of our life.

The Monastery

We are not a secret."

Tears began to leak from Cecilia's eyes.

Returning to Bartholomew, Luis continued, "I know you love him, as well you should. He is a good man. Think kindly of him and pray for his safe return. Now give an old man a kiss and go to sleep."

When Cecilia woke at midnight to feed Angus, Luis slept easily beside her. When she woke again at dawn he was still, silent and cold. She wept alone and with a loving hand traced the lines of his weathered face, committing them to memory. "Good-bye," she whispered softly.

†††

July 7, 1997

Dr. Chopak arrived at his office early on Monday morning. He and his wife had been away on a much needed weekend. He felt rested and focused.

His first patient was not due until ten, allowing him the luxury of sifting through his stack of messages at his leisure. There was nothing of interest until the last. At the bottom of the pile, on pink paper, in Mrs. Pashar's lovely hand were the words:

"St. Vincent's called. They report Mrs. Kincaid keeps mumbling 'It's Edward II.' I hope that means something to you."

Chopak stared at the message. His heart raced and perspiration popped out on his forehead. She remembered, he thought with amazement. She actually remembered!

†††

Seeth Miko Trimpert

May 1323

The Bishop's men arrived to collect the requisitioned wine only weeks after its demand had been received. Four squalid men rode into the compound, frightening the hens so they didn't lay for a week and nearly trampling young Will. Paul dashed into the courtyard and snatched the boy from danger, then disappeared into the cloister.

Since it was not uncommon to find the children of visitors in a monastery yard, little note was made of the child until the soldiers were wending their way back to Avignon, six casks lashed with great care to a monastery wagon. Then the youngest among them, an exceptionally observant and ambitious fellow, remarked, "Do you not think that lad in the quad bears an uncommon resemblance to the Abbot?"

The others, all dim and unimaginative, pondered this possibility and its implication.

"If they've a whore about they might've offered her," groused a dirty fellow with no teeth.

Another agreed. "Them churchmen's a greedy lot by Christ."

Conversation, once turned to carnal pleasures, quickly degenerated to ribald stories of Hairy Mary and Moll the Mink and then to a ringing endorsement of bestiality put forth by one who claimed intimate knowledge of a wide variety of barnyard creatures. The soldiers thought little further of the matter of the Abbot and the boy until some weeks later when one fellow, well into his cups, made mention of it in the great hall, from whence the juicy tidbit, by a combination of bad luck and happenstance, found its way to the ear of the Bishop.

The Monastery

"I knew it," Giardina muttered. "I knew there was something there."

Irritation at having been both deceived and denied rankled, giving rise to a determination to extract retribution. However, in truth, the matter of profligate holy men, if such creatures could exist, was more common than not. Giardina would let the matter rest until the proper opportunity presented itself.

That opportunity was some time in coming. Due in part to the vagaries of history the Bishop's ecclesiastical star began to rise. An ambitious and unscrupulous man, with an army of his own, he was a valuable ally to a pope at odds with the Emperor of the Holy Roman Empire.

†††

July 8, 1997

Chopak did a quick physical assessment of his patient. Rebecca Kincaid was certainly failing. There was no question. Taking a seat beside her bed, he crossed one leg over another to make a surface on which he might write. He was charting his observations with only the scratch of his pen for company when he heard someone clear a throat. Glancing toward the open doorway he saw no one. When the sound was repeated he turned to the bed.

"Good evening, Saracen" Cecilia greeted him. "Are you well?"

The doctor nodded. "And you?"

Cecilia's brief smile and nod were followed quickly by a frown. "I am well," she stated firmly, "but she is not."

Chopak reached into his pocket, removed his small

tape recorder and clicked it on. "How does she feel?" he asked.

Cecilia moved gingerly, testing the foreign body. "She aches," she replied finally. "Her senses are dull; touch, sight and hearing muffled. And," she added, "her bottom still hurts."

Chopak waited for further comment.

Cecilia, anticipating the unasked question, answered it gently, "She will die, Saracen, and soon."

"You need not let her," Chopak challenged.

Cecilia smiled, an indulgent look. "Your estimation of me is too generous," she countered. "It is she who gave me life; I did not take it from her. That is not within my power."

"It is," Chopak argued. "The life that was hers is now yours."

Cecilia seemed to consider what was clearly an accusation. Her response was oblique. "It seems you believe that she and I are one"

Chopak nodded.

"You are wrong."

"You have the same soul," Chopak insisted. "You are the same soul."

*Suddenly Chopak's recorder snapped itself off, a low battery light flashing insistently. Without conscious thought he popped open the tiny access door and removed the dying Duracell, replacing it with another from his pocket. Cecilia watched with interest. Chopak switched the recorder to **PLAY** and observed carefully as the woman's eyes grew round at the sound of her own voice.*

"Magic?" she asked.

"No," Chopak replied. "Technology… a battery. This," he indicated the battery, "makes the wheels turn as a

The Monastery

mule does a water wheel."

Much to his surprise, Cecilia understood immediately. Intuiting the relationship between energy and action, she made a quick comparison. "Perhaps, that which you call the soul is like your bat tree."

Chopak looked dubious but Cecilia, caught up in her own analogy, went on, "Perhaps, the soul may power any life but," she reached forward, taking the recorder in one hand the discarded battery in the other, "the soul is not the life."

When Chopak still did not respond, Cecilia argued on unopposed. "Is it not possible that the soul is but a source of energy for the life but not the life itself? A candle gives light but it is not light."

Chopak could not hide his astonishment. "You could give Aquinas a run for his money," he grumbled.

Cecilia laughed, "So says Dominic," she replied.

† *Chapter Thirteen* †

Summer 1323

Bartholomew crossed Europe at a brisk pace, sending Cecilia a written message from west of Avignon, a city he circumvented to avoid the Bishop, and a horseman from Calais. The letter, delivered only a month after his departure by the hand of a Franciscan friend, was addressed to Cecilia. It was brief and to the point.

"Do not forget me," it read.

The rider took considerably longer and was a different matter altogether.

During the weeks it took to travel from St Fiacre's to the French port, Bartholomew had ample time and opportunity to become acquainted with his fellow churchmen, staying as he did in religious houses along the way. His impression was not a favorable one. Money slipped easily from the hands of the poor into the pockets of the clergy. Young oblates were buggered and virgins deflowered. He spent one night in a French convent, which in truth was little more than a brothel, and a prosperous one at that. He saw countless priests who appeared to have made gluttony and avarice, never mind lechery, a life's work. Bishop Giardina, he had learned, was not the exception, but the rule.

After nearly two months in the company of these prelatic scoundrels the new Lord Carlisle was more than pleased to find a family agent awaiting him in Calais. There was money to hand and his passage across the Channel was arranged. Bartholomew donned his legacy with the ease of a man shrugging into a well-worn cloak. The emissary,

The Monastery

a young knight, of late a member of the previous Lord Carlisle's personal retinue, was the second son of Edgar Tremont, a good man and a fiercely loyal one. The elder Tremont, a lesser nobleman in his own right, had been in thrall to Carlisle who was vassal only to the King. Blood will tell, Bartholomew thought as he took the son's measure.

"I need a man I can trust," he challenged. "Are you that man?"

The man drew himself to his full height. "I am, my liege. You may depend upon it."

"Very well," Batholomew agreed. "And so I shall."

The young gallant beamed.

"Mark me well, young Tremont. This is no small burden I place upon you. I put into your hands lives more precious to me than God."

Tremont started at the implied blasphemy.

Undaunted, Bartholomew continued. "I am my own man. Over the coming years, you will undoubtedly see that which you do not understand. You will hear what should not be said. I will want you at my back, never questioning, always loyal. My father trusted you and your father before you. So shall I."

"Thank you, Sire," Tremont replied.

"Serve me faithfully, man, and there is no boon I will not grant you. Your sons shall prosper, your wife ne'er go hungry, nor your daughters marry without generous dowry," Bartholomew promised. "But," he warned the smiling man, "fail me at the cost of your life."

The soldier sobered quickly.

By morning Tremont was mounted on the best horse to be found in the seaport and on reverse course from his master.

The changes wrought by Bartholomew's departure from St. Fiacre's were at first quite subtle: The loss of a strong back increased the workload of the other farmers, made greater still by Luis's death. His friends, Dominic, Matthew and the Abbot, especially, missed him. His quick wit and ready smile had enlivened many an evening's fireside.

Toland's mood lifted. Oddly, it was only Bartholomew whom he saw as rival. With the arrogance of one young and attractive, it was easy for him to discount the others: the Abbot was too old; Lucien too guilty; Dominic too casual; and Francis? Well, surely no woman would prefer a short, stammering man who fell over his own feet.

The children missed him. Young Will asked for Bartholomew daily for several weeks, trudging slowly through the kitchen gardens each morning, glancing this way and that as though checking one last time to make certain he was gone. And, although Cecilia did her best to explain, the little boy simply could not grasp the concept of an indefinite period of time and so finally thought his beloved playmate gone forever from his small world. Little Maggie, who at sixteen months had only just made the connection between the word and Bartholomew, called "Da" again and again. When her summons failed to bring her Da, even though others held and hugged her, she refused to say the word at all.

The worst was a gnawing ache in Cecilia's heart. For several months she was quieter than usual; kind, gentle and loving, as always, but somehow subdued. Although she still spent the occasional afternoon with William in her room, or Toland in his loft, or Francis in his barns, she was more often than not distracted and left more lonely than when she

The Monastery

had sought them out. But they were patient men, accustomed now to sharing her, and, but for one, they bore up well.

When Luis died, Cecilia began again the use of her crude birth control methods. The following evening, for only the second time since coming to the monastery, she broke her self-imposed vow never to speak of another man to the one occupying her bed.

"William," she said, cradling his head in her lap, "there can be no more children until Bartholomew returns."

"Why?" he asked.

She shrugged, tears slipping silently down her cheeks. "I..." she paused, her anguish clear, "...it seems wrong somehow. Like I am cheating him. To have another's child while he is gone, alone, trying to make a way to keep us safe." She shrugged again. "William, I cannot... please understand."

The Abbot nodded and wiped away the tear about to drip on him. "I understand," he said. "I truly do." And he did, for among them he alone knew the difference between loving and being in love. He alone knew what Cecilia did not. He alone understood that although Cecilia gave her love to each of them, it was Bartholomew who centered her, Bartholomew whose arms she longed for, whose body she ached to feel inside her own. It was Bartholomew who had captured her heart.

At Chapter the following morning Cecilia announced her decision and explained its rationale.

Toland exploded.

"Why?" he demanded. "Why? He has his child! You are well and healthy. I want my son!"

The others blushed and felt ashamed for him but he was too angry to notice.

In truth, the crux of the matter was simple jealousy. Toland had little patience with the children and only a vague desire for one of his own. He did, however, have a towering need to mark Cecilia somehow as his. The thought of her with her belly swelling, her womb stretched with his child, her screams as she pushed his son into the world drove him nearly wild.

Cecilia's position remained unchanged.

The others loved her as they always had and life became almost normal again until... Tremont arrived.

Autumn 1323

Charles Tremont, second son of Edgar and Gilda Tremont, husband of Sadie and father of Robbie and Alice, was as good a man as could be found. Raised by a father in thrall to the elder Lord Carlisle, he had come into service almost as soon as he could sit a horse. Ruggedly handsome with good solid proportions and craggy features, his face, already weathered from years out-of-doors, was punctuated by sharp blue eyes and a generous, often smiling mouth, centered below a crooked nose broken in his youth, topped with thick blond hair the consistency of hay. He was a fine horseman, a fair terror with dagger or broadsword and loyal to a fault. Bartholomew had not erred in trusting him.

As he rode south, Tremont pondered the many small hints his Lord had made regarding the unusual nature of things to come. Still, try as he might he could not have imagined life as he found it at St. Fiacre's. Arriving at the monastery in early fall, he proved as good as his word. It was evident that he had not been expected. The Lady was at first taken aback by his arrival and then so pleased she wept and

The Monastery

nearly hugged him. That she had been greatly worried for Bartholomew's safety seemed in no doubt. The monks, but one, were uncertain and reserved. The exception, Brother Toland, was clearly furious although on his life Tremont could not think how he had given offense.

Confused, cautious and considering it the wisest course, the knight simply faded into the fabric of monastery life, making himself useful and watching for the signs that would make explanation. At table as in life, he took up a place between Matthew and Peter. He worked willingly alongside any man and chafed at no task, however hard or humble. Always visible, but never forward, the sight of him on the periphery of her life was a comfort, a reminder to Cecilia, subtle but definite: Bartholomew had not abandoned her. Tremont was a living bookmark, holding Bartholomew's place in her life.

The signs Tremont wanted were not long in coming. First, he met the children. The paternal parentage of Cecilia's two sons was so evident in their faces and demeanors that Tremont trembled to contain his shock. Upon introduction, young Will stared at the monastery's newest inhabitant with the Abbot's big brown eyes. When Tremont looked from the child to the Abbot, a question on his honest face, William nodded gently. No such visual query was necessary where young Angus was concerned. His carrot top and sturdy, bowed legs were the image of Francis. At only seven months he was already pulling himself up to the hay bales in the barn, threatening to walk about unaided at any moment. The fact that Francis rarely went anywhere without the tot was further evidence if that were needed.

Only the little girl gave Tremont pause. Over those first weeks he studied her carefully but could see no resemblance to the monks, though she had Cecilia's fine features and curling hair. She'll be a beauty, he thought, perhaps, a match for Robbie. Eventually, he found reason to comment on the child's attractiveness to Cecilia, who took pity on him and answered. "She is a pretty thing," she agreed. "Bartholomew says she has the look of his sister but as I have not met her I cannot say. What say you?"

Tremont smiled... Bartholomew's daughter. Yes, he thought again, a very fine match for Robbie.

As the months passed and the monks came to know him, Tremont became a favorite. Like his master, he played hard, and worked harder. He could tell a story better than most men, and was always the butt of his own jokes. He spent many hours with the children, a means of assuaging his loneliness for his own boy and girl and became a good and much needed friend to Peter.

The youngster, with only the remaining monks and two priests to emulate, was starved for the example of a real man. Tremont filled that bill. Big and strong, he flexed glistening muscle with courage and gallantry. He could wield an ax, fell a deer and tease a baby all within an hour's time. He treated Cecilia with unfailing courtesy and expected no less of Peter, a fact which became apparent soon after his arrival. With growing concern Tremont watched Peter's inappropriate antics. His patience grew thin. The boy misbehaved in a variety of ways. He crowded Cecilia at every opportunity, staring boldly into her face while he did so. His hand would brush with pretended naiveté some part of her anatomy. Once certain that Peter's innocence was feigned and his advances unwelcome, Tremont determined to act. When next he saw the boy eye Cecilia suggestively, his untried penis stiff beneath his robes, the knight caught

The Monastery

him by the neck and dragged him from the refectory.

"You forget yourself," he chided. "A man does not lust after another man's wife."

Peter sneered. Though Tremont's face counseled otherwise, the boy hissed, "I could tell you things…"

Tremont's hand moved swiftly to the hilt of his dirk. "Say nothing," he warned. "Never speak ill of the lady."

Unaware of the danger in trying such a man, the adolescent snorted.

Tremont seemed to consider for a moment. Which, he wondered, was the wiser course? Would it be the carrot or the stick? He decided.

"Tomorrow," he said, "we will begin your training with a broadsword."

Peter's eyes grew round; a silly grin spread across his face. "Truly?" he croaked.

"Would you be a man or not?" Tremont challenged.

Peter swallowed hard, his Adam's apple bobbing in his scrawny neck.

Tremont took his silence for assent. "After breakfast then, in the quad. You must learn to be of some use to your Lord and the Lady."

At this reference to Bartholomew and Cecilia, Peter's sneer returned.

"Bartholomew," he spat, "is *not* my lord."

Tremont chuckled, his answer matter-of-fact. "He is," he asserted firmly, "and he will always be. Tomorrow, after breakfast. Do not be late."

Only Toland persisted in his animosity toward the knight. To be fair, it seemed more Tremont's relationship to Bartholomew than anything personal, which was its cause.

Still when the Bishop finally found time to visit St

Fiacre's once again, determined now to have his revenge for the monks past deception, it was Tremont, who saw the riders far off. It was Tremont who bolted from the fields, gathering children in his big arms, and Tremont who saw Cecilia safely ensconced in the old mill house before the scoundrel churchman rode into the gates. It was also Tremont who, upon the Bishop's departure, insisted that Cecilia and the children move from the Bishop's quarters to an empty cell on the far side of the cloister garth; he again, who assisted in devising a doorway which allowed escape from that cell to outside the monastery walls without detection from within. Bartholomew had indeed chosen wisely.

Bishop Giardina stayed but a few days. Certain of further deception, he grew angrier each day. But try as he might, he could not find the chink in their armor of deceit. There was no trace of either Bartholomew or the woman, no trace of children, only a small band of hardworking monks, enjoying the fruits of their labors; all unfailingly generous and pleasant company when their duties to God and their farm would allow. On the last night of his visit, angry at having to resort once again to the simpering Anselm when he had planned on the excitement of forcing himself on a young, attractive woman, Giardina sent his minion in search of Peter. Perhaps, the boy might be induced to tell the story.

Peter, full of his newfound manhood and awed by the Bishop's summons, rushed to Giardina's quarters feeling proud and important. He knocked boldly.

"Enter," the Bishop's voice was brusque.

Giardina plied the young man with brandy and flattery in equal parts, but gaining nothing decided to amuse himself with the lad, lest the entire evening be a loss. It was a brutal encounter. Temptation to tell their secret and save

The Monastery

himself at Cecilia's expense rose in Peter's throat, nearly choking him. However, blind loyalty to his idol, Tremont, made him loathe to lose the man's good opinion however dire the consequences. Thus he bore his rape in silence and limped miserably to breakfast on the morrow. The Bishop, his shameful appetite sated, but still none the wiser, had departed before dawn.

† *Chapter Fourteen* †

July 15, 1997

Gurinder Chopak watched as the dying body of Rebecca Kincaid gradually came to life. The animation brought on by the arrival of Cecilia was always startling and unexpected, like watching a great thespian don a role. The room, silent as a tomb, would suddenly take on a faint energy like rising wind. Then Rebecca's eyes would open and Cecilia would look about, orienting herself and checking carefully for a presence other than Chopak's. Only then would she speak.

In recent months, subconsciously aware of his desire for information about her life and anxious to please, Cecilia had become more inquisitive about the world around her. She harried William for news of the church, doggedly pursued Dominic about philosophy and politics, and undertook a veritable inquisition with Lucien about surrounding hamlets. Any man who would talk to her about his past and the world he had known outside the monastery was cross-examined to near exhaustion. At first each man was delighted with the attention but when her interest did not wane they wondered at its cause. Eventually each put it down to the natural curiosity of one who had no past and humored her until there was nothing more to tell. Chopak was the beneficiary of this intellectual mining.

Cecilia stretched and yawned hugely, wincing at the stiffness in Rebecca's unused body.

Chopak smiled. "Tired?" he asked.

Cecilia chuckled. "A mother of three tots is always

The Monastery

tired," she replied. "Add to that five husbands and occasional weariness is inevitable."

Chopak's brows knitted. "Five?" he queried.

"Five," Cecilia confirmed. "Luis died."

"I am sorry for your loss," Chopak offered. "Did the foxglove not help?"

Cecilia reached for his hand, squeezing in gratitude. "Oh, it did," she answered, tears glistening. "It did. For some weeks he was stronger. His mouth was not so blue and he could talk for long periods without becoming breathless. He even gained strength enough to play with the children. In the end, one night he simply went to sleep and did not wake. Thank you for your help. Those last weeks were a precious gift."

Chopak made no response but sat, heart pounding, holding hands with the 14th century. Finally, he nodded. Then certain that her tale was told he prodded, "but you said five. Who else has died?"

Cecilia blanched at the thought. "Do not say so!" she cautioned. "Evil may befall him."

"Befall whom?" Chopak asked.

"Bartholomew," she replied. "He has been summoned to England to the castle of his father. The King himself has called him," she added with a mixture of awe and pride.

"Truly? King Edward?" Chopak queried.

"Truly," Cecilia assured him. "His father and elder brother have died of some horror. His other brother was killed in battle. Bartholomew is to rule in their stead. The King insists."

"So he has left the monastery and returned to England?"

"He has."

Seeth Miko Trimpert

Chopak searched the face before him for some clue as to Cecilia's feelings on the matter of Bartholomew's departure and was once again frustrated by the limitations involved in communicating through a borrowed body. Although there was some expression on Rebecca's face, the ravages of her decline left it oddly devoid of the passion carried in Cecilia's voice. Finally, unable to divine her feelings, he was forced to ask, "And what of you and Maggie? Has he left you to the care of the others?"

The face took on a rueful look. "He has and yet he has not," she answered.

Chopak frowned.

"Forgive me, Saracen. I do not mean to toy with you. Bartholomew left in spring. The harvest is now passed. I sent him away in anger without so much as a wish for safe journey. My penance for that sin is to worry each night that he will not return safely and thus deny me an opportunity to atone."

"May I ask, Mistress, why you were angry?"

Cecilia paused, obviously considering whether she wished to share something so intimate, then conceded, "You may. I did not want him to go. I accused him, unjustly, of deserting me and his child, returning to a life of riches that did not include us."

Chopak nodded encouragement.

"But it was not so and I knew it. He went on a perilous journey to a cold and lonely place to…to…" She paused searching for a means of expressing his intent. Eventually, remembering Luis's last words to her, she finished, "to gain the means to protect me."

"And you believe he will return?" Chopak seemed somewhat skeptical.

The Monastery

"He will," Cecilia replied firmly. "He has promised... and he has sent his man Tremont to me in his stead."

Chopak nearly choked. "In his stead?"

Cecilia understood immediately Chopak's ill-concealed shock and the reason for it. Righteous indignation painted Rebecca's lifeless face. So angry was she, that the force of her fury began to superimpose her own countenance over that of the other woman's until Chopak found himself staring dumbly into the face of a beautiful young woman sputtering with rage.

"Saracen, I will tell you this but once. I am not a whore. I have six husbands to whom I am faithful. My children are their children and none else's. I do not sleep with the boy. I do not sleep with the Bishop, however much he may wish it. I do not sleep with any man who comes by the gate and I certainly do not sleep with my husband's good knight. Good day to you, Sir!"

"I am sorry," Chopak whispered. But there was no one to hear. He had blinked and she was gone.

For nearly an hour Chopak sat, alone, pondering what had happened. He had seen her, touched her. She was real. Finally, certain that she would not return this night, he returned to his own office where, checking his watch, he placed a call to Nigel Haversham's home in London. On the tenth ring a sleepy voice answered, "Haversham here."

"It's Gurinder," Chopak said.

"Excellent," the Englishman replied. "Been trying to reach you all day. Kept getting your service. I say, that girl seems a bit dim, eh."

"Never mind her," Chopak said brusquely. "You could never imagine what's happened."

"Right you are," answered Haversham. *"Nor could you."*

The conversation continued in this fashion, at cross purposes for another minute before the two men realized that each had something of considerable importance to report to the other and that they were not talking about the same thing.

Chopak was near babbling, something Haversham had never previously imagined let alone heard so he held his own news for the moment.

"Hold on there," he advised. *"Begin at the beginning."*

Chopak did, telling the tale of his most recent encounter with Cecilia as carefully and faithfully as he could.

"When she realized that I thought she was sleeping with Bartholomew's man, she was livid. That's when it happened. Her face was as clear to me as any I have ever seen. She is beautiful, Nigel, and very young. She's real. She's not a dream or a psychotic manifestation. She's real!"

Haversham chuckled. "Of course, she's real, old chap. But it'd have been a good deal better if you'd not pissed her off... especially given what I've found out."

"Which is?" Chopak queried, his composure regained.

Haversham began by way of explanation, "I've been a bit at loose ends the last several weeks, what with being between terms here and Lydia away at her mother's, so I've been contacting our fellow researchers to see what they know."

Chopak made no response but, as Haversham could still hear him breathing, he continued, "Joe Yamaguchi in

The Monastery

Hawaii has an old Chinese woman in an unresponsive state who mumbles from time to time in German. Family brought her in totally stymied. They all swear the old gal never even learned English. Hasn't spoken a word in any language other than Cantonese in 97 years."

"*Really?" Chopak replied, somewhat amazed.*

"*Really," Haversham confirmed. "But that's not the half of it, old chap. Manfried Kohl has a patient, too, a Swiss orphan child babbling about being an innkeeper. Manfried says the boy really knows his liquors," he added with a chuckle. "And Andy McMurtry, you know... that Aussie fellow who presented the paper on Time at our last symposium? Well, he's hospitalized a sheep shearer who keeps insisting he's a geisha. I've also heard from a colleague in Moscow that there are several unusual psychiatric cases in the Ukraine but you know the Russians... nobody will talk."*

"*What's happening?" Chopak mused.*

"*Damned if I know. Maybe we've got two realities snagged. Maybe our world and another have collided and they're stuck."*

Chopak could almost hear his colleague shrug but his thoughts had already returned to Cecilia. "Why do you suppose she was so angry with me? She does sleep with seven men... well, six now that Luis is dead. Why was she so offended?"

"*Vestigial morality," Haversham answered quickly. "She has something somewhere inside that questions her actions. Maybe it's the knowledge that however satisfied she may be with her arrangement it causes pain to the men she loves. To have one's actions cause pain to those one loves gives rise to doubt. You touched a nerve, my friend. You touched a very tender spot."*

†††

Late Summer 1323

With the dream-like remnants of her unpleasant exchange with Chopak in the recesses of her mind, Cecilia waited with impatience for an evening with Dominic. She was agitated and irritable. When he arrived she wasted no time confronting him with her quandary. "Is what we do wrong?" she demanded.

Caught off guard, Dominic cast his gaze downward, briefly hooding his thoughtful eyes. When he looked up again he waved a hand between the two of them, "Do you speak only of us or…" his gesture now became more expansive and took in the entire monastery, "…*us*?"

Cecilia was impatient. "Not you and I, Dominic. *Us*! Is it wrong to love you all? Is it wrong to live as we do?"

Dominic was in no hurry to answer and so parried her challenge with a question of his own. "Why do you ask?"

Cecilia blushed. "A dream…"

"Did you dream of damnation and the fires of hell," he teased. "Or have you been spending too much time with Lucien?"

Cecilia smiled. "Stop teasing," she insisted. "I am serious. Is it wrong?"

Dominic thought, then answered in a quiet voice, "I shall answer your question with another of my own."

Cecilia blew out a breath of exasperation. "You are no help at all!"

"No, wait," Dominic pleaded. "Think. Who is to say what is wrong? Are we hurting anyone? Is any man here or

The Monastery

you forced to this life?"

"Nnooo," Cecilia hesitated. "Well, perhaps, save Toland who would have it otherwise."

"Do we hold a dagger to his throat and drag him to your chambers?" Dominic laughed aloud. "I think not!"

"True," Cecilia admitted, "but mayhap we offer him two unacceptable choices and he has but taken that to which he objects less. He would not choose to share."

"Nor would most others," Dominic replied with candor, "but life is about making the most of choices offered. Not all options are open to all men."

"Granted," Cecilia agreed.

"Then who is to say that what we do is wrong or right?"

"But the Bible, the Koran…are there *no* rules, Dominic?"

"You speak of universals, Cecilia. I can only tell you that I do not believe in morality as divine decree but as evolving societal more'. In our small world we have chosen what suits us. Remember, we are men who lead an unnatural life. Look at our bodies. We were meant to recreate ourselves. Most other creatures do little else. They survive to reproduce and then die. You have offered us a limited physical life, one which enhances our spiritual and intellectual one. You ask is that wrong. I answer no."

Cecilia was not satisfied. "Then why is our way not permitted outside?"

"Outside a man may spend every waking hour toiling to put a roof over his wife and children and food in their mouths. Such a man is brave and selfless. He gives his all to the protection of one woman and her children. Paternity is of the utmost importance to that man."

Seeth Miko Trimpert

Cecilia thought of her conversations with the Abbot after the birth of Will. "And these things are not important to men such as yourselves?" she challenged, her eyes sparkling with amusement.

Dominic shrugged, his smile rueful. "I do not believe I said *that*," he replied.

† *Chapter Fifteen* †

October 1324

Bartholomew sat alone at the long table before a roaring fire, his brow etched with worry lest he had forgotten some small thing which, in his coming absence, could grow to rack and ruin. Finally, certain that he had done all he could, he refilled his cup from the flagon left full by a thoughtful serving girl and allowed himself the luxury of casting back over the past months, wondering how so long a time had passed so swiftly.

His arrival at Carlisle castle had been long awaited and much heralded but his position as prodigal son short-lived. He had arrived wet and filthy in a cold July rain, his joints aching, and longing for Cecilia and the warm Mediterranean sun. Anticipation of homecoming, however, buoyed his sagging spirits as he leapt from his horse and handed the reins to a waiting stable boy. Ignorant of the rider's importance, the boy pouted at the extra work until prodded sharply by an older man with a walking stick.

"Step lively, boy," the old man snarled. "Your master is at hand."

The boy's chin sank to his chest, head bowed. "Welcome home, my Lord. Milady will be well pleased by your arrival."

Bartholomew returned the nod. "Take great care of this horse, boy," he warned. "He's a fine beast and I shall test him again before many months have passed."

The boy bowed again and led the horse into the

stable.

Quicker than Batholomew could turn, the old man approached. Although ambulation was clearly painful, he walked ramrod straight, the only accommodation given to infirmity his walking stick, which helped hold him erect. Snapping blue eyes took in the new lord from head to foot. "You've grown to a fine looking man, my Lord, if I may say so. Your father would be proud." Then he waited.

Bartholomew took his own time studying the man. Although he did not recognize him at first, he made slow examination of his features and manner until a distant bell rang. The resemblance was unmistakable. "Tremont," he said with certainty.

The old man nodded. "Indeed, Sire."

By now a young woman with two children, a clinging babe and a son of eight or ten, had joined the old man. They waited patiently while Tremont and Batholomew observed the requisite pleasantries pertaining to Bartholomew's just-completed journey. Finally, the woman clutched desperately at the old man's sleeve. He brushed away her hand, then asked, "My son, Sire. Is he dead?"

Bartholomew suddenly, and quite belatedly, understood that this man and young Tremont's wife and children had expected him to return along with his liege. Bartholomew blushed in embarrassment. "Goodness, no," he burst out. "I've sent him on an errand, but he was well when he left me and there is little danger in its commission, save that in any journey. He is well."

The old man looked relieved. The woman burst into tears. The small boy popped forward. "My father's not dead then?" he piped.

"He is not," Bartholomew replied firmly. "Are you

The Monastery

Tremont's son?"

"Aye," the boy replied proudly. "That I am."

His grandsire cuffed him in the ear. "Yes, my Lord," he growled.

"Yes, milord," the boy repeated, barely cowed.

Bartholomew chuckled. "Your father is a good man," he told the boy.

"Aye, that he is," the boy agreed.

Bartholomew cast the old man a quick look before he could cuff the lad again, then crooked a finger to bring the boy closer. "Are you as trustworthy as your father and grandsire?" Bartholomew queried.

The boy turned serious. "I am, my Lord. Would you set me to a task?"

Bartholomew nodded. "I would. But first I must have your word that you can be trusted with a secret."

The boy's eyes grew round. "I'd die before I'd tell," he asserted. "They could cut my tongue out," he added stoutly.

Bartholomew smiled. "I wager that they could," he replied soberly, "but this secret is not so grave as that. I would ask a favor, though. I've two small boys, younger than you, who will want guidance and training. Will you help them learn the English ways?"

The boy grinned, showing a mouth full of large teeth, and bobbed his head. Immediately thereafter, a crease appeared between his two blond brows. "Does your mum know, Sire, and the Lady Gisselle?"

Now Bartholomew frowned, shaking his head. "Know what?" he asked. "And who is the Lady Gisselle?"

Skipping the first, the boy addressed the more important question. "Why she's to be your wife, Sire. A great feast is planned. It's been but waiting your arrival."

"So that's how it is," Bartholomew muttered.

"Aye, Sire," the boy confirmed. "And you with a wife already," he added glumly.

Bartholomew roared with laughter. "Aye, lad, and me with a wife already."

"Is she pretty, Sire, your wife?" the boy asked.

"She is," Bartholomew replied. "Why do you ask?" He pulled the boy close and tucked him beneath his own cloak to protect him from the pelting rain.

"Well, Sire," the boy confided, "my mum says the Lady Gisselle has a face like a horse and I thought it would be a good deal nicer for you if your wife was pretty."

Bartholomew laughed again until tears ran down his cheeks. "Off you go then," he said, patting the boy on the bum. "Be a good lad."

Bartholomew turned toward the stairway to the family quarters, but glanced back in time to see old Tremont raise his stick to his impudent grandson. "Do not strike him!" he shouted. "An honest man is worth his weight in gold, and that…" he pointed squarely at the lad's chest, "is an honest man."

Bartholomew mounted the exterior stairway, his thoughts tumbling. "Well, forewarned is forearmed," he thought with some resignation.

The Lady Ann de Carlisle, or the woman who thought herself still the Lady Carlisle, reclined on a mound of pillows before a huge fire in the family apartments. Her ample bosom answered gravity while her several chins rested on her breastbone. She was eating dried cherries, the juice leaking, quite unattractively, from the corners of

The Monastery

her mouth. To her right a rather sallow young woman sat erect on a three-legged stool, a needlework frame before her, fiddling idly with an unfinished and poorly executed tapestry. It was obvious from the staging of this domestic scene that Bartholomew's presence had been announced.

When Bartholomew entered the older woman exclaimed, "Oh, my son, I am so relieved to see you safely home!"

Bartholomew, still mindful of his mother's failure to protest his banishment to the austere and celibate life of the monasteries, replied with an equal lack of candor, "And I am so pleased to be safely home." Then he inclined his head toward his mother's companion, "Gisselle…"

The younger woman blushed and simpered, thrilled at the thought that this handsome man had remembered her name which, of course, he had not. But for the boy's warning, he'd have thought her the stranger that she was, and an ugly one at that. Young Tremont's mother was dead right; his horse had a handsomer face and smaller teeth.

"You remember Gisselle then?" his mother asked.

Suddenly, he did. Gisselle, eldest daughter of Lord Dansworth and his tongue-tied French wife; married, if he was not mistaken, the year before he left for the monastery, to a decidedly corpulent cousin of her mother's.

"And how is your husband, Madam?" He directed his question to Gisselle.

The woman feigned a look of great distress and toyed with her widow's weeds. "He died, my Lord, last winter of the grippe."

The Lady Ann added quickly, "Yes, poor thing. Gisselle finds herself quite alone in the world and greatly in need of a man's guidance regarding her lands."

Seeth Miko Trimpert

Remembering the towering man who had been Gisselle's father and the brood of rotund brothers who had been her husband's family, Bartholomew raised a skeptical eyebrow. This charade, he thought, has gone quite far enough.

"Mother, if I may," he said, indicating with a hand Gisselle's desired departure from the room.

Lady Ann balked. "Bartholomew, please, Gisselle has waited these many weeks for the sight of you. You cannot send her away. It is too cruel."

Bartholomew held his ground, gesturing again for Gisselle to leave. When she had, his mother held her temper in check and scolded as though he were an errant child, "Where are your manners? You have grown surly, my son."

Amused, the new Lord Carlisle chortled. "What I have grown, dear Mother, is married."

The Lady Ann de Carlisle paled and stared back at her smiling son, her well-laid plans crumbling to dust.

Within days the still widowed Gisselle, alone and disappointed, had decamped for the home of her mother-in-law, now destined to life as an extra.

As Bartholomew had expected, the Lady Anne did not take the news of a daughter-in-law well. Having ruled a husband, three sons and a household with an iron first for more years than she could count, she was not well pleased to be thwarted in her plan to install a complaisant fool of her own choosing in her son's bed. Still, she could see now that thinking him one of those milk toast monks, swooning at the prospect of crawling between any pair of thighs had been a serious miscalculation. The easy-going boy who had departed Carlisle Castle was clearly not the man who had returned.

To the contrary, the new Lord de Carlisle was a man to be reckoned with. Physically handsome and imposing, he caught the eye. In all matters he showed strength, character and an amazing resolve to set things right. He worked hard, took an active interest in everything which pertained to the estate and quickly gained a reputation as an honest man and fair arbiter of disputes. With his pleasant nature and friendly demeanor, he easily rekindled the fondness the peasants had felt for him as a boy, combined now with respect for the man he had become. Men, both highborn and low, already sought his advice and counsel. Rents were paid promptly; although a dispensation or delay, when asked and if justified, was swiftly granted. Moreover, Bartholomew involved himself in the lives of his people.

When Bridie, the smith's wife, lost her husband to a runaway draft horse, Bartholomew's own men harvested her meager fields, the Lord taking only half his portion as a show of sympathy for her loss. Generosity to the widow was not lost on Bartholomew's men for whom life was hard and death often only a step away; nor was his subsequent matchmaking lost on the women of the estate.

During the first six months of Bridie's mourning Bartholomew saw to it that a man in his service, always older, married and stable, darkened her doorway often enough to see to those matters which required the physical strength of a man. He made it his business to know that she and her children were clothed and fed without the young widow having to resort to unsavory means. When the smith had been six months and one day in his grave, Bartholomew selected a new man, young and eligible, to attend these chores. Within a few weeks the Widow Smith's new young man had sought and received the Lord's permission to marry her. Bartholomew rested easier knowing the young widow and her children to be safe and secure and was doubly pleased that a promising but rather wild and unruly young fellow had been brought to harness of his own accord. Bartholomew smiled secretly when some months later he came across the man at Saturday market, a tow-headed boy upon his shoulders, the former widow Smith obviously and happily pregnant at his side.

While busy regaining control of a substantial holding in near chaos Bartholomew left the running of the household to his mother, interfering only when he felt it necessary. Even so, he made it clear from the outset that he expected her to relinquish power when Cecilia arrived. Reluctant to do so, Lady Ann hinted rather slyly that a younger woman still bearing children might be unable to manage so large a household and so, perhaps, it should be left to her. Bartholomew recognized in his mother's actions a plan to reduce Cecilia's stature from Lady of the Manor to courtesan. He countered swiftly with an offer to build his mother a house of her own. Thus, in the least subtle of ways the battle lines were drawn; Ann de Carlisle would step aside gracefully or be removed.

Still, Lady Ann nagged and pestered, challenging first the wisdom of Bartholomew's marital choice and then the validity of the marriage itself. Eventually, making no headway against her son, she sputtered, "Has this dubious union the blessing of the Church?"

Bartholomew, alone in his knowledge of how many churchmen actually did bless this union, laughed until he nearly wept. Confused and angry, his mother continued to fume but in the end Batholomew prevailed with the simplest

The Monastery

of explanations. "I was not meant for religious life," he said, "a fact of which I repeatedly apprised my father, and thus when the happy opportunity presented itself I married. I have three children. There is nothing more to be said."

Lady Carlisle's opposing opinion and constant carping notwithstanding, nothing further was said.

Bartholomew made a visit to the King to pay his respects, then threw himself into the business of running a huge holding. His father, he found, had failed some in his last years and left much to his elder brother who had obviously had little interest in the business end of being in thrall to a King. A ladies' man, Lord Carlisle's elder son had sown his seed far and wide but never taken the steps necessary to produce a legitimate heir; he had thrilled to the power of riding through the countryside surveying *his* lands and people but never learned how they should be managed. He had taken more than one bride's maidenhead as his right, a fact which Bartholomew learned only when approached by the elder Tremont on behalf of an even more elderly wool merchant.

The merchant, father of a would-be-bride, had sent word to Bartholomew that his daughter wished to marry. Bartholomew nodded his permission absently and returned to the business at hand. When old Tremont cleared his throat and remained standing at his side, Bartholomew looked askance. Impatient at further interruption, he chided with uncharacteristic brusqueness, "What is it, man?"

The old man cleared his throat again, "Sire, do you wish to claim your right with the bride?"

At first Bartholomew looked blank. When he realized that to which the old man referred, his face grew crimson.

"God, no!" his voiced boomed throughout the hall. "What kind of man do you think I am, Tremont?"

"My apologies, Sire, but…"

Suddenly, Bartholomew understood. Giving his mother, who stood nearby, a murderous look, he stated in a voice that all could hear, "Never again. Not while I live." Then, feeling decidedly nauseous, he returned to his work.

As age had robbed Bartholomew's father, of first his stamina and then his mental acuity, rich land had lain fallow and rents gone uncollected. It was months before Bartholomew uncovered the extent of the neglect, and only then with the help of his brother-in-law, Roger McTaggart.

McTaggart, a forthright man born of an English mother and Scottish father, suffered the injustice of being trusted by neither camp with the philosophical grace of a man who recognizes those circumstances in which he cannot prevail and accepts them. Although he might easily have resented Bartholomew's return, he did not; and, in fact, dedicated himself wholeheartedly to the rehabilitation of the estate in the practical way of a man who knows where his bread is buttered.

Still, it was months more before the two men had things well in hand again and by the time all was rectified and running smoothly more than a year had passed. Bartholomew, grown sullen and short, was restless as an unbroken mount under saddle. "I miss my wife," he confided to Roger, "and my children."

King Edward, his northwestern border now secure, his taxes paid, and with twenty well-equipped knights and triple that number of archers at his disposal should he call, was reportedly well pleased with the state of Carlisle. Still, when

The Monastery

petitioned, His Highness initially denied Bartholomew's request to travel abroad so soon after his return home, citing as his reason distrust of the Scotsman with whom responsibility for Carlisle lands would rest in Bartholomew's absence.

Bartholomew sent a new pleading immediately. He must, he said, be allowed to retrieve his sons from foreign land. They must be brought up as proper Englishmen, men who could faithfully serve their King.

What man can ignore flattery?

Permission to travel was granted by return rider, the only proviso being that Bartholomew must return with all haste. And so, unwilling to delay another winter, Bartholomew left too late in the year, moving south through wind and cold rain as fast as his horse and small entourage could travel. Riding swiftly on its heels, they soon caught the gentle autumn moving down the European continent toward Africa and rode with it into the Mediterranean winter.

"We'll arrive home before the summer," he had promised McTaggart. "Hold fast until then."

†††

August 10, 1997

Gurinder Chopak made his daily round to the bedside of Rebecca Kincaid. It was a brief visit intended only to check her status before he left for the airport to meet Nigel Haversham. The two physicians would return together shortly.

After several months of transatlantic calls his English friend had finally invited himself to America. Nigel sat now, in first class, a neat scotch in hand, considering. While

Chopak watched and conversed with his medieval maiden and studied history, Nigel had done the grunt work, keeping in touch with dozens of doctors treating similar cases, following every lead, however dubious, from every corner of the world. There were now 37 documented cases in 21 countries; some already resolved. He would write a book when it was over.

The Swiss orphan had "recovered", returning to his own persona after only four days without apparent damage. Much to the Englishman's surprise, the Australian sheep shearer/geisha had died. Why one wondered would a man wish to become a woman who served men? Puzzling. Others had recovered or died, as well, leaving only 6, like Rebecca Kincaid, unresolved. When Chopak had reported the Kincaid woman "failing", Nigel had taken the next plane.

The two doctors sat at the bedside. Nigel did a quick physical assessment at Gurinder's invitation. The body – there was little evidence of an actual person – although that of a fairly young woman, showed all the signs of great age. The woman's facial features and muscle tone had grown slack. Her skin stretched and sagged, separating itself from the bone, fat gone, collagen melted. Her coccyx was home to a Stage IV decubitus, easily 2 centimeters in depth, 4 in diameter, with evidence of tunneling extending its width by perhaps nearly another. She had the sallow complexion of one who never sees the sun and her eyes, when the lids were lifted, had the opaque, lifeless look of the dead. Her heart beat a steady 56 times per minute; her blood pressure held at 100/60 and her respirations were 16. Her temperature was 97°.

"Has she spoken to you today?" the Englishman

The Monastery

asked.

"Not today," Chopak answered. "In fact, not since she became angry with me. I have tried but..." The man shrugged in resignation.

"Try again," the visiting physician urged. "Please."

Chopak sighed. He was more discouraged than Haversham knew and held no hope that the woman would speak with him again. Still, Nigel had come across an ocean for this; the least he could do was try.

"Cecilia," he called softly. "It is I, Gurinder. I know you are angry, but please, I have someone I wish you to meet."

Rebecca drew a deep breath and hiccuped.

Chopak frowned. "Are you there, Cecilia? Will you at least allow me to apologize? I was thoughtless, perhaps, but I meant no harm. Please..."

Eyes opened in the lifeless face. Someone groaned. "Saracen? I cannot see you. She is dying."

"Cecilia, can you come to us? As you did when you were angry? Can you do that?"

"Wait," Cecilia whispered. Rebecca's eyes closed.

The two physicians waited silently as the minutes ticked by. Finally, Nigel opened his mouth to speak but Chopak, still watching, raised a warning finger.

They waited another five minutes before Rebecca's eyes opened again. This time they were not the milky grey of those once blue but a deep brown, like pools of liquid chocolate. They moved around, taking in the room and its occupants. Slowly, the woman rose to a sitting position. Chopak quickly lowered the siderail to allow her to dangle her feet over the edge of the bed. Cecilia's face became clearer and clearer until Rebecca's was only a pale shadow *beneath the younger woman's beauty. Cecilia moved gingerly before she spoke.*

"Let her go, Saracen. She does not want this life."

Chopak reached forward. After a moment's hesitation, Cecilia let him take his hand.

"Forgive me," he said.

Cecilia nodded. "You are not to blame," she replied, candidly. "It is I, not you, who should be conscience-stricken."

"Tell me," Chopak implored. "Tell me everything, before it is too late."

Nigel Haversham sat, mouth gaping, as though thunderstruck.

Cecilia nodded and began her tale.

It was winter again. Bartholomew had not returned. Life was quiet and lonely. Toland, once certain that Tremont would not share her bed, seemed resigned to his presence and soon ignored him completely. The other monks were well; the children healthy and growing.

"How many children?" Chopak asked.

"Three," Cecilia replied firmly. When the East Indian's eyebrows peaked in question, Cecilia said but one word. "Tremont."

"Tremont?" Chopak queried.

Cecilia nodded. "Tremont is Bartholomew's man, a good man. He accepts all; questions nothing. Still, how would it seem if I were to have a child in Bartholomew's absence. Bartholomew would seem a cuckold, a fool. I cannot…"

Chopak squeezed the woman's hand, an acknowledgement of sympathy. "Ah," he said softly, "the world intrudes."

The Monastery

Tears welled in Cecilia's eyes.

"Do you wish to have another child?" he asked gently.

The young woman nodded.

"Whose?" Chopak asked.

"Bartholomew's," she whispered.

Understanding the significance of her statement and wishing to avoid any painful topic, which might induce her to flee, Chopak steered the conversation elsewhere.

"What of the Bishop? Has he come again?"

"Yes," Cecilia replied, shuddering, "again and again. He has searched high and low for us and would have found us twice over but for Tremont. At his insistence, the children and I have moved to a cell on the far side of the cloister garth. We are no longer the heart of our home, but now on the periphery. My husband's knight has fashioned us a bolt hole by which we escape to the old millhouse when horses enter the gates. Tremont takes us there while the others press on with daily life. The Bishop knows something is amiss but cannot put his finger upon it. Still, he is cruel and persistent. Given time, he will find us."

"What will he do if he finds you?" Nigel spoke for the first time.

Cecilia shuddered again, acknowledging his question. "He raped poor Peter when last he came. I will not fare better than the boy."

Before either man could speak again, Cecilia picked up her chin, listening. "Someone calls," she said. "I must go."

Rebecca's body, without the support of Cecilia's will, slumped suddenly and slid to the floor.

† *Chapter Sixteen* †

<u>January 1325</u>

Hard as he pushed Bartholomew could not reach St. Fiacre's before Christmas. Two days past the New Year, a fierce blizzard breathing down their necks, he rode into the gates with six men on horseback, causing unintended mayhem. Tremont, having seen the riders from afar, had already whisked Cecilia and the two younger children to their cell. Unable to find Will, he had dragged a sobbing Cecilia out the secret gate, assuring her again and again, "I will find him, my Lady. I will."

Four year-old Will had been playing in the barn with a new litter of kittens. Terrified of all riders and now trapped with six of them between him and his Mama, he made a frantic scramble, burrowing deep into a mound of hay and hoping against hope that the bad men would not find him. Although not fully cognizant of the damage done Peter on the Bishop's last visit, Will was still bright enough to know that the older boy had been badly hurt and greatly feared a like fate for himself.

Bartholomew, filthy and bearded, dismounted, leading his lathered beast toward the barns and fresh hay. With a wave of his gloves he indicated that the men should make themselves comfortable in the old dorter. Striding forward, he shouted, "Francis! Where are you?" Passing under the lintel and into the shadow of the cold barn, he yelled again, "Francis!"

The only reply was a small sob, definitely not Francis.

The Monastery

Stopping, he ran a hand over his steaming mount to silence its snorts and listened again.

Another sob, stifled, but certain.

Bartholomew followed the sound to the back of the barn, then further into a mound of hay.

A hiccup.

The man reached a huge hand into the haystack, grasped a handful of cloth and warm, wriggling flesh and withdrew a small, sobbing lad.

"Please, sir," the child cried. "Do not kill me."

Bartholomew frowned and held the child at arm's length. He was tall for his age, wiry and looked so like the Abbot that Bartholomew smiled. "Will? By God, boy, but you've grown some."

At the use of his name, Will stiffened. "Do not kill me," he sobbed again.

A cold fear snaked up Bartholomew's spine. This boy was in mortal terror of being murdered, but why?

Pulling the boy close, Bartholomew hugged him hard. "I'll not kill you, Will. I love you. It is I, Bartholomew."

The boy's eye grew wide in disbelief. Could this huge, fierce-looking man be his friend, his playmate of near half a lifetime ago?

Bartholomew, seeing the lad's confusion, rubbed at his beard. "Truly, I am under here. Say you have not forgotten me. Please…Will?"

Suddenly the little boy threw his arms around Bartholomew's neck. "I thought you were the Bishop's man come to kill Mama and Maggie and Angus and me!" he wailed. "You'll not let them hurt us, will you? Mama said when you came we would be safe."

Bartholomew swallowed a lump in his throat. "Did

she say that?" he asked.

Will snuffled, his tiny chin bobbing in assent.

"And where is she?"

"Tremont took her to the mill," the boy replied. "We hide there when *he* comes."

"And do you hide often?" Bartholomew asked, anger mounting.

"Often enough," the child said. "We must. The Bishop did a bad thing to Peter. Grandfather says he must never see us."

Their conversation might have continued for some time had not Bartholomew noted Will's eyes growing round again as he gazed over the former monk's shoulder. Will's mouth opened, then, as if in answer to a warning, closed again. Bartholomew spun on his heel, using a swirl of voluminous riding cloak to wrap the dagger-dressed hand of the man behind him and, in doing so, buying enough time for each of the would-be combatants to ascertain the identity of the other.

"Tremont!" Bartholomew bellowed

"Milord," Tremont replied, blushing furiously, his hampered hand dropping to his side, the dusty cloak with it.

"It seems I have come none too soon."

"None too soon," Tremont agreed. "The danger grows daily. But for the Lady's intransigence I would have brought her and the children to you last summer." Then realizing his apparent criticism of Bartholomew's wife, he bowed his head. "I did not mean to offend, Sire, but the Lady's will is stronger than that of most men."

Bartholomew gave his man a rueful smile and clapped him on the back. "No offense is taken. Intransigent, eh? You've a most generous way with words. I thank you for

The Monastery

your loyalty."

Bartholomew turned back to Will and lifted him effortlessly onto his shoulders, carrying him as he had done when he was smaller. "Where are the others, Tremont? Cecilia and the children? The monks?"

"The Lady and the children are in the copse beyond the vineyard. You will know it…just over the rise?"

Bartholomew knew it, better than his man imagined.

"She would not go farther until I had recovered Will. The monks are about the business of the monastery. Only the Lady, the children and I flee. The others proceed in a normal way, hopefully giving little cause for suspicion."

Bartholomew nodded, seeing the wisdom of Tremont's plan. "Tell the others I am back. Ask Paul to feed my men. Oh, and see my page. He has letters from your family. I shall go and collect mine."

Tremont smiled gratefully and set out upon the tasks assigned.

Bartholomew, with Will aloft, strode toward the copse where Cecilia huddled with the Maggie and Angus, peeking every few minutes through the evergreens toward the monastery below. The hue and cry that normally accompanied the arrival of the Bishop and his men was lacking. There was no shouting. No dust from stamping horses rose from the courtyard; no dogs yapped and bayed. Afraid to think what new menace stalked them now, Cecilia held her children and trembled in the cold.

After what seemed an eternity she spied a tall figure passing out through their secret door. It was not Tremont. The man, for someone so large could only be a man, walked with great purpose. At first Cecilia thought him a giant for he was taller than anyone she had ever seen. But as he drew closer the shape was wrong. Long legs rose to a broad body. Arms, with hands placed upon shoulders, bulged with muscle, but where a head should have been rose a slender shape, much too long for a neck, topped with what might have been the head of a much smaller person. The oddly made man moved steadily upward on the steep hillside with no hint of fatigue. Puzzled, Cecilia watched. Her heart sank when she realized that this giant, was no giant at all but a large man with a child atop his shoulders, a child who was her son. With Will as hostage, there would be no escape for her.

Cecilia instructed Maggie and Angus to remain hidden until Tremont came for them, then rose, squared her shoulders and stepped free of the evergreen foliage, which hid them. She walked with a sure step toward Will and the man who held him until she heard her son giggle, then laugh aloud. His captor appeared to be tickling him. Confused, she faltered and nearly fell. Seeing her stumble, the man quickly set Will on the ground and bounded for her, catching her up in a bone-crushing embrace. Will scampered along behind him.

"Mama! Mama!" he shouted. "Bartholomew is home!"

Cecilia did not hear the tiny voice but knew the feel of the man as soon as his arms surrounded her. Her cheek found its place against his broad chest, her ear against him, listening to a thundering heart. Tears ran in a silent torrent down her pale cheeks.

"Cecilia," he whispered.

She could not reply. Her arms tightened around him and held fast as the sobs, long swallowed, wracked her too-thin body. When finally they subsided, Bartholomew lifted her chin and smiled at her tear stained face, "So, you've

The Monastery

missed me then?" he asked quietly.

Surrounded now by excited, dancing children, Cecilia drew a sleeve under her dripping nose and tried for a weak smile. "Not a bit," she hiccuped.

Bartholomew sat comfortably ensconced in front of the locutorium's blazing fire, trying to absorb the changes in monastery life. Tremont, who would have withdrawn to the dorter with Bartholomew's other men, now sat, at his liege's insistence, in his accustomed place. He, Peter, Matthew and Paul played at an old game of chance recently grown popular among young nobles. They gambled polished stones, Peter having the largest share at the moment. Will watched, delighted when anyone would deign to let him throw the dice for them. Bartholomew smiled and wondered what others might think, seeing monks, soldiers and churchmen's children rolling dice across a monastery table. Still, no one's soul seemed in jeopardy.

Turning back toward the gathering at the fire, he studied each of his fellow husbands. Having been so long away, he had come to regard Cecilia as *his* wife and the notion of once again being one among many discomforted him. He did not want to share. With a deep sigh he resumed his perusal.

The Abbot was the man most changed. Though Bartholomew had been away but nineteen months, William Devon had aged many years. His hands, once merely gnarled, were now so misshapen they hardly seemed human appendages. And, although covered by his robes, Bartholomew knew from the stiffness of his movement that the Abbot's other joints must be the same. His back was bowed as well as though under some great weight.

Bartholomew thought it was pain as much as disease that brought him low.

When William caught the younger man watching, he nodded and whispered, hoarsely, "Yes, my friend, I have grown old."

Bartholomew could think of no reply.

Brother Francis sat, legs splayed, on the floor before the fire, rolling a ball back and forth with Angus. He hummed a little tune and spoke softly to the child who grinned and jabbered his nonsense responses, all the while pushing his ball of woolen yarn back and forth, back and forth. When the boy finally became sleepy, he crawled into his father's lap and, yawning hugely, closed his eyes and went to sleep. Eventually, Cecilia rose and picked up the child, carrying him to a makeshift crib in the corner where she tucked him up in warm blankets. Francis rose, too, and placed a soft kiss on Cecilia's ear as they put their son to bed.

Dominic and Lucien sat in quiet conversation. Bartholomew knew from the tenor of their voices, though words could not be discerned, that the topic was serious, which with Lucien meant either business or religion. Dominic caught Cecilia's eye from time to time and seemed to smile encouragement. Tonight was to have been his but he had willingly relinquished it to Bartholomew, reasoning, perhaps rightly, that his friend should have 18 or 19 credits for the months of his absence. Lucien looked merely sad.

Toland, who had gone to see to the smithing needs of a distant village in exchange for precious seeds, was, blessedly, away.

Little Maggie fluttered like a moth. At first terrified of the bearded giant who was her father, she cautiously circled the room in concentric, but ever decreasing circles until she

The Monastery

had ventured close enough to touch him. Even bathed, with his beard trimmed, as he was now, he was no less imposing. Will saw her reticence and chided. "Touch him, you silly goose. He'll not bite!"

Made bold by her brother's taunts, the child stretched a finger to within an inch of Bartholomew's hand. Still, too timid to follow through, she withdrew. Cecilia watched from a distance until she was certain that Maggie would not close the gap on her own. Then she left her chair, walking behind Bartholomew and placing a hand on his shoulder. She stood caressing the muscle in his neck until goose flesh rose on his arm.

Missing nothing, Maggie chirped, "Have you taken a chill, Sir?"

Shivering, Bartholomew nodded. "Perhaps, I have. It was a long, cold ride from England."

"I could warm you," the girl offered. "Grandfather Paul says it always warms his old heart for me to sit in his lap." With that she crawled into Bartholomew's waiting lap and snuggled close. Then stroking his beard, she asked shyly. "Is that not better?"

Bartholomew kissed the top of his daughter's head. "Hmmm...much better. Thank you, Maggie."

As the fire burned low and evening subsided to a murmur, Cecilia began gathering blankets to move the children across the now frozen cloister garth to their beds.

"I hate this the most," she grumbled. "The Bishop has driven us from our home, from our warm place in the heart of the house, to the edges of our life."

Before Bartholomew could think of an answer, William had placed a twisted hand on Cecilia's arm. "Leave them here tonight, Cecilia. Francis and I will stay with them…" When Cecilia looked afraid, he added, "…and Tremont. Tremont will stay, as well. They will be safe and warm. Take tonight for yourself… and Bartholomew."

Suddenly, Cecilia realized what William offered. A night alone with Bartholomew; no fretful children; no others nearby. Alone. With a shudder of anticipation she nodded. "Thank you," she whispered.

The old man smiled.

Bartholomew, Cecilia's heavy cloak already in his hands, wrapped her tightly in the warm wool and pulled its hood over her curling hair, the simple gesture so intimate that the others ached to see it.

Snow had begun to fall again. Their heads bowed against a howling wind, the two walked together out into the night. All who watched knew that life was now changed and would never again be as it had been.

The first hours of Bartholomew and Cecilia's night were spent in breathless, mindless passion. With no more than a glance at the fire dying in the hearth, they tumbled into Cecilia's icy bed completely unaware of anything outside themselves. Clothes were loosed and tossed with no thought for where they might land. For the first time in her life, Cecilia wept with wanting and Bartholomew, for all his good intentions, took her fast and rough. They moved from the first fierce, bruising climax of long separation to another still urgent, grasping coupling without pause, then to a languorous, searching lovemaking where their hands ran over one another, tracing faces, nipples, scars. Their eyes looked for changes, signs of what had passed while they were apart; their lips whispered what their hearts knew. They slept briefly and woke to love again before at last settling to

The Monastery

talk.

"Tell me everything," Bartholomew begged.

Cecilia stopped. The words echoed, so familiar. Who had said them? When?

"Cecilia?"

Cecilia shook off a shiver. "Yes. Yes, I shall but will you not tell me of your adventures first? You have seen how it is with us."

Bartholomew shook his head. "No. I will tell you everything but after I know what has happened here."

"What would you know?" she asked, her voice reluctant and low. "What? That the Bishop comes whenever weather permits? That he brings horsemen and archers, filthy men who drink and sport within the monastery walls? That his men bring whores to the dorter? That once they killed one and left her for us to bury? That he sometimes stays for weeks, steals our stores, makes us live in hiding?" She began to weep. "That he buggered poor Peter so that he did not sit for a month? That he kept promising the boy that he would stop if only Peter would tell him where I was?" She drew a breath and continued in a near whisper. "Shall I tell you that life without you is unbearable? That I am so afraid?"

Bartholomew silenced her with a finger to her lips "Yes, my love, all that and more. I am sorry to have left you so long. I would have come sooner if I could. But now there is a place where you and the children will be safe. There is a home... a castle... in a distant land and it is yours if you want it."

Cecilia wiped her eyes and tried to smile. "What else would you know?" she asked softly.

Bartholomew did not hesitate. "The calendar is gone from the kitchen wall. Where is it?"

"In the Chapter House," she replied.

"Why?"

"So Tremont did not see," she answered.

Bartholomew understood. "And the children? Does he know?"

Cecilia nodded her head.

"Has he said as much?"

"No," she replied. "But his face gives him away. He is an honest man."

"As is his son," Bartholomew chuckled.

Cecilia looked puzzled.

"Never mind, I shall tell you later."

Bartholomew opened and closed his mouth several times, a question formed but afraid of its answer. Finally, he took a deep breath. "There are no other children? Have you lost a babe in my absence?"

"No," Cecilia whispered.

"Did you…are you…why, Cecilia?"

Blushing, Cecilia tried to explain. "I have used the methods we devised before Angus and have only let them come to me once each month. William is unwell and Dominic… Dominic asks little." Embarrassed beyond belief, Cecilia protested, "Bartholomew, I cannot speak of this with you."

"You must," he insisted. "If you are to be my wife in the world outside, there can be no secrets between us. None, Cecilia. Do you understand? Now tell me, why? Why have you done this?"

Cornered, Cecilia answered. "I had no choice. What would Tremont think if he watched me swell with someone else's child. He would think you cuckolded, married to a whore! What would he say of you to other men?!"

The Monastery

Bartholomew let out a long sigh and pulled Cecilia to him. He kissed her once, long and hard. "You did this for me," he said finally.

"Yes," Cecilia admitted. "for you."

When Cecilia woke later, a fire blazed in the hearth and Bartholomew, chilled to the bone, snuggled against her trying to get warm again. "Now I shall tell you my tale," he began and proceeded to talk almost uninterrupted until dawn.

He told her about his trip north and the things he had seen in religious guesthouses.

"They are all like the Bishop!?" Cecilia was horrified.

"Not all, but many," Bartholomew replied.

He told her about meeting Tremont in Calais and his relief in knowing that he could send someone to protect her. He told her selected bits about his mother, his sister and his sister's husband, his friend Roger McTaggart. She was wide eyed at his recounting of his audience with a King. But mostly he told her of the differences between their small world and the one outside. "I had forgotten," he said, "how the world smells, how infrequently most people bathe. Men stink like something rotten. Women with their courses nearly gag you when they pass. City streets are ripe with human and animal waste. Everyone is covered with lice! And I had forgotten also how they look. Children are ragged. Women just past childhood are already old with screaming babes and sagging breasts. A man can go a week without seeing a woman with all her teeth. You've spoiled me, Cecilia. Clean and beautiful as you are. I cannot want another woman, nor a world without you in it."

Cecilia's eyebrows peaked in surprise. "Are you saying that you have not been with a woman since you left me?"

Bartholomew took his turn to blush. "I had opportunity," he declared firmly. "I had offers."

Cecilia laughed. "Yes, but did you…?"

"No," Bartholomew admitted. "I did not. I could not. But I shall make up for it now."

When the two arrived at breakfast they were still talking. While Cecilia saw to the needs of her children and coaxed them to finish their porridge Bartholomew spoke with William. He was direct.

"She cannot stay here," he reasoned. "She is not safe."

William posed the question foremost in his mind, "Will she leave?"

Bartholomew replied, "She will."

"Have you asked?" the Abbot wondered.

"I have not," Bartholomew answered. "But, she has no choice. Given an opportunity, Giardina will make her watch while he tortures and kills her children, your son, Francis's son and my Maggie, and then he will make her beg to die. We are too few and he is too many. I repeat she has no choice."

"And the children?" William queried. "What of them?"

Bartholomew's face softened. "In the world they must be mine," he replied. "I love them. I can give them a home, a future. You cannot. Francis cannot."

Sadly, William agreed. "Cecilia thinks we will all go together from this place. You and I know that cannot happen.

The Monastery

No one who sees my Will or Angus will think them yours if Francis or I are nearby. They are too like us."

Bartholomew made no argument. Much as he wanted Cecilia and her children for himself, he could find no joy in the other man's pain.

It was a strange winter. For the first time in memory there was no talk of spring planting, crop yields or breaking weather. Although never put into words, this lack of plans was tacit acknowledgement that when spring came everything would change. The monks met in the Chapter House, gathered at a time when Cecilia would be occupied elsewhere with her children, another open admission that this decision they would make for her. All were grateful that Toland was still absent.

Bartholomew spoke first. His offer was generous in the extreme.

"My holdings are substantial," he said simply. "There is Carlisle Castle, large, well-fortified and overlooking the Irish Sea. There are several other houses, as well, along Scotland's southwestern border. There are monasteries and convents to the east in West March and a prosperous hamlet in Carlisle itself. The castle staff is huge. I am expected to have my own household priest, monks for the education of my children, a cellarer, a personal physician, and trusted advisors as did my father before me." Thinking of Toland, Bartholomew added, "The village smith died last year. A replacement has not been found. A place will be made for any man who wishes to accompany us either in his religious capacity or in any other."

He paused while the monks digested his invitation, leaving the larger issue yet to be addressed. In his soul, each man squirmed, discomforted by the certain knowledge that had he been in Bartholomew's place he would have been hard-pressed to make so generous an offer.

When no one spoke, Bartholomew squared his broad shoulders and continued "But, in the world outside, Cecilia will be *my* wife. Although it might be possible for her to slip away with one of you from time to time, it is inevitable that her secret would be discovered. A castle, however large, is always small. Living is close and privacy outside my family apartments scant." He paused again.

"Cecilia will be my Lady and, as such, must be above reproach. There can be no scandal if she is to have respect. And," he added gravely, "as your children and mine grow older there can be no vicious gossip about their mother."

Throats were cleared and nervous feet shuffled as Bartholomew's words sunk in.

William was the first to speak, his loss of Cecilia a foregone conclusion. Therefore, putting aside his own pain, he went directly to what was for him the heart of the matter – his son. "What about the boys?" he challenged.

"What about them?" Bartholomew replied.

"You will have your own sons," the Abbot said with certainty.

Bartholomew nodded. "God willing."

"Then what of *ours*?" the Abbot queried, including Francis in his question with a gesture of his hand.

The determined look on Bartholomew's face suddenly eased. "Your sons," he said, facing the two men, "are my sons, too. We agreed when first we took Cecilia that her children would be *our* children and so they are." Now he looked straight into the Abbot's dark eyes. "Will is your son, true, but he is my son as well. He is the first son of this house

The Monastery

and he shall inherit in accordance with English law." Then he turned to Francis. "Angus is our second son. As such he will likely serve the King, but not if he chooses otherwise. I am a wealthy man."

Embarrassed by what might seem braggadocio, Bartholomew paused while his face reddened slightly. "I can and will provide for him a happy life, one he desires and one which suits him."

Tears stung the Abbot's eyes as he bowed his head in agreement.

Francis, fearful of sobbing aloud, turned and fled.

"Think on it," Bartholomew advised the rest. "We must have a plan. Cecilia must agree."

The others had nearly three weeks to think while Bartholomew cashed in his credit of nineteen nights. He had asked to have them in succession and, since Cecilia clearly wanted it so, the monks had little choice but to accept his wishes. It was not, however, only simple lust which prompted his request, though God knew that was a factor. Bartholomew understood that as the others took leave of Cecilia's bed, the necessary farewells would be painful, perhaps, even passionate encounters. Although he could not bear to dwell on them in detail, he did recognize that the only means of insuring that Cecilia did not arrive at Carlisle Castle heavy with another man's child was to make certain that she carried his. On their third night together, he told her this.

"Your sons seem always to favor their fathers," he said smiling. "The one you bear this year must be mine… and all those after him," he added in a whisper.

To his surprise Cecilia did not argue but pressed her lips to his neck and pulled him to her bed.

Toland returned home when Bartholomew had four nights left. He arrived in the middle of the afternoon on a snowy Saturday while the children played happily under the watchful eyes of the monks in front of a huge fire in the locutorium. He had thought the horses and men evident in the barns and dorter to be those of the Bishop and was, therefore, surprised to find the children in residence.

"Whose men?" he asked without greeting.

All eyes turned to the Abbot.

"Bartholomew's," William said quietly.

Toland scowled. "Where is he?" he snorted.

"With Cecilia," William answered.

Toland made a strangling sound, spun on his heel and headed for Cecilia's cell.

"Toland, don't...." the Abbot tried, but the younger man was gone, striding angrily across the frozen cloister garth.

His fist met the oak of Cecilia's door, the repeated pounding reverberating throughout her small house. Otherwise engaged, it was a moment before either she or Bartholomew recognized its demand. Fearing injury to one of the children, Cecilia slid quickly from beneath Bartholomew and, hastily donning a discarded woolen shift, pulled open the heavy door.

Toland was thus confronted with a tousled Cecilia, barely covered, her face chafed with whisker burn, a mark of passion peaking out from the top of her left breast. Bartholomew lay naked in Cecilia's bed before a blazing fire, only a thin blanket covering his lower body. The room was warm and pungent with the musky smell of sex.

Heedless of the outrage on Toland's face, Cecilia

The Monastery

demanded, "What's happened?"

Toland growled and locked eyes with Bartholomew, who rose and wrapped the bedclothes around his waist. "Close the door, man," he ordered. "Cecilia will freeze." When Toland began to take a menacing step forward, Bartholomew amended, "I meant with you on the outside."

Intent on the safety of her children, Cecilia ignored their conversation. "What has happened?" she pleaded. Her voice rose in panic. "Toland! Tell me!"

Finally, realizing that Cecilia thought his presence due to illness or injury to one of her brood, Toland answered, his tone dismissive. "They are with the others. They are fine."

Cecilia shivered, her nipples hardening in the chill wind. "Then why are you here?" she asked.

Toland pointed a finger at Bartholomew's chest.

Cecilia gave the uninvited man a cold look. "Not now," she warned.

When Toland opened his mouth to object, she repeated, "Not now, Toland." Then she carefully closed the door in his face and set the bar.

Cecilia turned to face her lover, a new look of understanding dawning across her face. "This is going to be very difficult," she said.

Bartholomew, at first, only nodded. Then he reached out for her and with a gentle tug pulled her back into bed. "We will manage," he promised. "You will see."

Bartholomew and Cecilia returned together to the common rooms just before the winter sun set. Supper was tense, but Bartholomew, accustomed now to power, remained serene and certain. Cecilia grew more dependent on him each day; the children more comfortable in his presence. Little

Angus, mimicking Maggie, had today for the first time said "Da", but much to Francis's consternation, the tyke spoke the word to Bartholomew, who in response picked up the small boy, laughing happily and tossing him into the air. Angus squealed with delight and shrieked again and again, "Da! Da! Da! Da!" Maggie danced around her father's feet giggling. Then young Will, loathe to be left out of the hilarity, tugged shyly at Bartholomew's stocking.

"What about me?" the child whined.

Bartholomew stooped to place Angus beside Maggie. "What about you?" he chuckled, lifting the Abbot's son high and tossing him, too, into the air.

Will crowed with delight as Bartholomew tickled and teased.

Later, when the children had been herded to the kitchen for their bath, Francis approached, his jaw set in anger. "Angus is mmmm-y son," he stuttered. "Mmm-ine."

Bartholomew shrugged helplessly. "He is," he agreed. "But if that were known at Carlisle what would they call him? Hm? And his mother, Francis, what would they call her?"

There was no answer. Francis was beaten.

Over the following weeks Bartholomew strengthened his position by speaking in a forthright manner with each man and remaining stone-faced when Cecilia showed affection for the others. His stoicism paid off as one at a time the dominoes fell.

The Abbot was the first.

"There is a Franciscan monastery a day's ride east of Carlisle in West March. It is not so comfortable as this," Bartholomew's gesture took in the warmth of their

The Monastery

surroundings, "but provision could be made for you. Will could be sent with Tremont to visit once or twice year. It is not ideal, I know, but what choice is there?"

The old Abbot sighed. "I thank you for the offer, my friend" he said. "But I will not come with you. You have made your point too well. Will grows more like me with each passing day. There can be no hint of scandal if he is to inherit. I will not jeopardize his future... or Cecilia's," he added. "I will go south to Sicily where I can spend my last days in warmth. Though it breaks my heart to lose them, I would risk Heaven before their safety."

Bartholomew nodded.

"But," the Abbot entreated, "you will keep your word, Bartholomew? My son will inherit?"

Bartholomew nodded again. "On my life," he swore.

For her own part, Cecilia, realizing the coming necessity to choose, made her own inquiries of her husbands. When the Abbot's night came in February, William knocked softly and entered Cecilia's house only at her invitation. The children, long asleep, were snuggled together on the warmer upper floor. Cecilia and William spent the early part of their evening at chess, as usual. When finally they curled together in her bed, Cecilia asked an unexpected question.

"William, did you love your wife?"

The old Abbot started in surprise, then settled to serious consideration of her question and the implications of his answer. "I did," he finally replied. "More than my life."

"More than me?" Cecilia asked.

A denial all but escaped his lips before he clamped tight his jaw. After some minutes he answered, "I loved her differently, Cecilia. We were young. I thought I could not survive without her. She was the passion of my youth, the promise of a happy life." Then he added with a pained smile, "She was my Bartholomew."

Cecilia smiled, too. "You know then?"

"Yes," William replied. "I know."

She persisted. "So, you do not love me as you did her?"

The Abbot drew a long breath before giving Cecilia her freedom. "No," he lied, "I do not."

Satisfied, Cecilia curled into the circle of his arms, a great weight lifted from her heart. In the early hours before dawn, while she slept, the old Abbot slipped away, across the silent cloister garth, weeping quietly.

Bartholomew, who no longer had a cell of his own, slept in the Abbot's upper workroom. When he heard the old man enter the house he crept down the creaking stairs and clamped a hand on the Abbot's trembling shoulder. "I am sorry," he whispered.

"Go away," the Abbot begged. "Please, man, have mercy on me. Go away!"

Bartholomew closed the door quietly as he left and plodded through deep snow toward Cecilia's house. He slipped in and silently crawled beneath the covers of her bed where she snuggled close against the man of whom she dreamed. When dawn came, she awoke to find her dream come true.

Toland was an altogether different matter and, in Bartholomew's estimation, by far the more dangerous. When early one evening the two men found themselves, quite by accident, alone together in the barns Bartholomew seized the

The Monastery

moment.

"Toland," he began carefully, "we must talk."

The other man stiffened, his mouth hardening into a grim line. "You cannot have her," he growled. "I will not step aside."

Bartholomew, menacingly calm, only inclined his head to indicate that he had heard. "And what of the children?" he asked reasonably. "How will you provide for them?"

A rustle like the scurry of mice sounded in the doorway, but intent upon the impending contest neither man noticed. The murmur of their voices, however, had warned the visitor of their presence. In the intervening silence, barely reigned tempers arced like lightening before a storm. Cecilia, now on hushed feet, stepped quickly back into the shadows.

Toland continued to stand, still, silent, and belligerent.

Bartholomew prodded again, "Tell me, Brother, how will you feed them, clothe them, keep a roof over their heads? How?"

Toland shrugged, his indifference clear. "I am a talented blacksmith," he bragged. "I can provide handsomely for Cecilia and myself in a town of any size."

"Perhaps," Bartholomew conceded. "But what of Will, Maggie and Angus? What can you offer them?"

Toland shrugged again, an ugly sneer twisting his mouth. "Keep them!" he spat. "They are your bastards, not mine. I only want Cecilia."

When Bartholomew did not reply, Toland laughed, a mean sound. Then ignoring the fact of his steadily deteriorating relationship with Cecilia, he told a bold lie.

"You cannot even imagine what we do together," he

taunted. "She wants me in her bed, rich man, not you. She will chose me."

The barb struck deep. Gut-wrenching agony twisted through every muscle in Bartholomew's tall frame. The picture in his mind, Cecilia with Toland, seared his eyelids as he lowered them, shuddering, and drew a long breath.

Toland knew he had hit the mark.

Even so, Bartholomew considered for only a moment before replying. "If you are right and she chooses you," he offered, "I shall provide you with work and a house in Carlisle. Neither you nor she shall be hungry but you must promise that the children will remain with their mother. They are only babes. They need her."

Like one struck, Cecilia sucked in a silent breath. She knew the passion Bartholomew felt for her; it was returned in equal measure. But more, he offered a deep, steadfast love, a rock on which she could build her life. And yet… he would do such a thing for her, should she choose another in his stead. Had there been any doubt, here was final confirmation of the rightness of her choice.

She cleared her throat as though just arriving. Smiling pleasantly at both men, she spoke, "I heard my name. I hope you spoke kindly."

"Always," Bartholomew said quietly.

Cecilia stepped forward, reached on tiptoe and pulled his earlobe down to her mouth. She let her lips feather over his ear, her words quiet as breath, "You would do that for me?"

His face grave, his heart upon his sleeve, Bartholomew nodded.

Cecilia kissed him on the lips. "Midnight," she whispered.

The Monastery

Then she turned to Toland. "Come with me," she said, extending a hand.

Thinking himself the winner, Toland cast Bartholomew a look of triumph. He wrapped a possessive arm around the departing woman and together they headed for her house.

Bartholomew saw to his horse, unnecessary since his men would have done so, and returned to the locutorium where he played with the children, then brooded over what was happening elsewhere.

Cecilia's door was no sooner closed than Toland began to divest himself of his clothing. Still angry at the slights he had suffered since his rival's return, he meant to take his due. Cecilia watched for several seconds, a look of mild distaste on her face, before he stopped. Seeing that she had not even begun to remove her own things, Toland pulled at the ribbon of her cloak to hurry her along.

Cecilia brushed away his hand. "I wish to speak with you."

"Later," he groaned. "This night is mine."

"No. Now," Cecilia replied, in her tone an odd note of warning.

Toland slowed the shedding of his clothes.

"*And*," she corrected, "this night, like all others, is *mine* to share with whom I please."

When she saw that she at last had Toland's attention, Cecilia continued, "Bartholomew proposes that we…"

"Do not speak of him in my presence," Toland snarled.

It was as though she had not heard. "Bartholomew," she repeated softly, "proposes that we flee the Bishop. We will leave this place and go to England. He says there is work for all…"

Toland tried again to interrupt but was silenced with a wave of Cecilia's hand. She was not to be deterred. "… there is work even for you. There is no blacksmith in Carlisle."

Toland snorted in disgust. "Woman, surely you jest. What *Lord* Bartholomew de Carlisle proposes is that I… we… become his vassals… chattel! That we shoe his horses and plow his fields while he plows you."

Ignoring the crudity of his comment, Cecilia defended Bartholomew. "I think his offer generous."

"And *I* think his offer self-serving," Toland retorted. "I can take care of you. You need not go with him."

Cecilia drew a long, thoughtful breath; it was time for truth. "I wish to go with him," she answered. "He loves me and he loves my children."

"I love you," Toland argued.

"In your way," Cecilia conceded, "mayhap, you do. But you do not love my children. You would not love even your own child."

The mention of a child drew Toland's eyes toward Cecilia's almost imperceptibly thickening waist. For a moment his heart leapt. "You're pregnant!" he crowed.

Cecilia hand stroked the already tightening skin over Bartholomew's son. "I am," she confirmed.

Then the reality of past weeks ran headlong into Toland's fantasy. He had spent only one night in Cecilia's bed since Bartholomew's return. One night, spent in a jealous temper, not love.

Cecilia shook her head in answer to the unasked question. "No, Toland, it is not your child. It will never be."

Anger flared like dancing flame in the jealous monk's eyes. Without hesitation, he raised his hand, palm open, and

The Monastery

slapped Cecilia so hard she saw stars.

"You will regret this," he swore. "You will rue this day."

When the sun rose Toland was gone, his meager clothing, fine tools and one of Bartholomew's best horses with him. He had said no good-byes; still it did not seem likely that he intended a return.

Plans were made. Some would accompany Bartholomew; some would not.

Paul stated firmly that he would not see his little people taken to a barbarian land without him. He would go, he said. He would cook. Bartholomew laughed. "English food could use your help," he chortled.

Dominic, too, would go to England. At first he had hesitated. Cecilia wept. Dragging him to her room, she had pleaded. "I am breeding again, Dominic. I cannot do this without you. I will die. You must come, please."

Happy for the excuse to go with them, Dominic quickly agreed. He would be household physician. Neither he nor Cecilia had any real qualms about the necessary change in their relationship since both knew that theirs was essentially a deep friendship. Both had always known that Dominic's heart lay elsewhere.

Brother Matthew declined repeated invitations to join Bartholomew's household, finally declaring firmly that he would travel south to Sicily with the Abbot and remain with the old man until he was no longer needed.

Peter, to the surprise of a few, agreed to join their company as Tremont's page. Although old for such a station, the position did provide a means of integrating the lad

~~into Bartholomew's household. In addition, Bartholomew~~ suggested that Peter assume the role of Cecilia's nephew giving him the added status of family. Peter at first demurred, still reluctant to be indebted to Cecilia. Eventually, however, at Tremont's urging, he accepted.

Greatly pleased by the news, Bartholomew clapped a hand on the boy's shoulder.

"You make me proud," he told an embarrassed Peter. Then he added, "Shall we begin negotiations for an suitable wife?"

Peter blushed beet-red and stammered.

"You do want a wife?" Bartholomew teased.

"Yyy-yes, milord," the boy replied.

Upon hearing Peter's response, Tremont smiled to himself. "*Milord*, indeed," he thought.

Francis chuckled, "He sounds l-like mm-me." Only the little monk, sole inhabitant of a special place in Cecilia's heart, steadfastly refused to discuss his future plans. And Cecilia, despite numerous attempts on Bartholomew's part, declined to discuss Francis with him. Bartholomew, afraid for Angus's future, had begged, "Cecilia, please."

"No," she replied softly. "Bartholomew, let it be."

That left only Lucien's fate still hanging in the balance. Bartholomew, of course, offered the priest the position of household cleric at Carlisle Castle. He would have been only too happy to see his friend replace the drunken sot who now shepherded the Carlisle flock. It was a generous offer of a comfortable post in a wealthy household but, still, not so great as the not-forgotten prospect of rising within the hierarchy of the Church herself. If Lucien accompanied them to England, he would never be *Your Grace*, nor ever wear the rich, red garments of a Cardinal. Bartholomew

The Monastery

watched and wondered as the other man brooded. Cecilia remained serene, giving the troubled priest the necessary room to make the right decision.

When his night finally came in March Lucien came to Cecilia early, something he rarely did. He played quietly with the children until they retired to their loft for sleep. Then he sat with Cecilia, his hands across her writing table, firmly grasping hers.

"I cannot go," he finally said.

A mixture of pain and relief flickered across Cecilia's face.

"Why?" she asked.

"Because," he said gently, "you are all that stands between me and what I want in this world."

Cecilia looked as if he had struck her.

Lucien flinched at the pain he had inflicted.

"Please, Cecilia, listen to me."

Cecilia struggled to withdraw her hands, but Lucien's grip only grew tighter.

"Please listen," he begged. "Please… if I could have you for myself, or even stay as we are now, I would never leave. But I cannot, we cannot, and we both know it. You will be Bartholomew's wife, much as I might wish it otherwise. I have gladly risked all to be with you, and would just as gladly continue to do so, but I will not jeopardize your life and happiness, nor that of those little imps." He nodded toward the loft where the children slept.

"I cannot have you, Cecilia, and since that is so there is something else I would have. I will stay here until you are safely away and all is done and then I will make my way to Avignon. I have a future there. I need only find it."

Then the priest pulled her to her feet. He traced the

contours of her face with a finger.

"Come," he whispered, leading her toward her bed. "I love you, Cecilia, but if our lives go as they must, when you are gone I will never make love to you or any other woman again. Come."

Although tentative plans were made for an April departure, winter held fast during the early part of the month. Deep snows and bitter cold persisted until a sudden and disastrous warm spell swept over them, causing flooding and calamity. Lakes rippled where last year wheat had grown; old, gnarled trees which had stood for hundreds of years gradually pulled their rooted feet from the sucking mud and toppled, stately limbs crashing and breaking as they fell.

Finally, the waters began to recede. At first only the uplands were dotted with island hilltops. Then slowly, some pasture began to reappear. On a warm day, while the rivers still shimmered like mirrors in boggy lowland fields, Bartholomew took all but one of his men on a hunting party. Expecting to be away no more than a few days, he gave strict instructions to the man who remained behind.

"Keep a sharp eye to the west. Send Peter at the first sign of riders. He knows where we hunt. Take my Lady and my children to the mill. Do not fail me."

In truth, however strict his instructions, Bartholomew had no thought that the Bishop would travel through lands still mired in mud and covered with the detritus left by rivers of melting snow. If he had he would never have gone.

† *Chapter Seventeen* †

Spring 1325

Toland, who as Cecilia had once observed did not wait well, sat on the edge of a chair he had warmed for five successive days. But for his overwhelming need to extract some retribution he would have left long since. Saddle sore and weary he grew ever more impatient. Members of Bishop Giardina's staff glided past him, robes flowing, a dozen times a day, sometimes with a condescending smile, sometimes with no notice or acknowledgement at all. Still he sat.

During Monday and all of Tuesday, he sat, the Bishop unaware of his presence in the palace. On Wednesday, Anselm passed by and recognized him. After a brief conversation with Giardina's minion Toland felt certain that he would be granted an audience. But Wednesday came and went, as did Thursday, before Anselm reappeared to say that perhaps the Bishop might find time for him on Friday. In truth, it was Monday again before Giardina agreed to see him.

The Bishop played a satisfying game of cat and mouse. He knew, of course, who Toland was and, further, even suspected what he might want. Nevertheless, he let the feckless monk sit for day after endless day as a lesson to him on the relationship of power to humility. When finally he tired of his game, he had the monk brought before him.

Toland wasted no time. "Do you want her?" he demanded.

The Bishop, unprepared for such candor, studied the seething man.

"Can you give her to me?" he finally answered.

Toland nodded.

"Why?" Giardina asked.

"I have my reasons," Toland growled. "Yes or no?"

"Yes," Giardina replied. Beneath his opulent robes, he could feel himself stiffen in anticipation. "What is your price?"

Toland did not hesitate. "When you are finished with her," her answered carefully, "I want her."

The Bishop licked his thick lips. "I may use her for a time," he warned.

"I will wait," Toland agreed.

"And if I should wish to share her with some special friends?" Giardina asked.

Toland shrugged. "So long as she is mine in the end."

The Bishop had one last question. "And the children?"

Toland shrugged again. "As you wish."

Too busy with the business of a besieged pope, the Bishop was forced to send a trusted lieutenant and a dozen men to collect his prize. His orders were clear. Travel to the Monastery of St. Fiacre. Take the woman who resided there into custody and return her to the palace. On pain of death, let no man lay hands on her before the Bishop. Deal with the children and monks as necessary.

Thirteen riders left at dawn.

†††

The Monastery
August 24, 1997

Nigel Haversham stayed a full two weeks in America before he despaired of having another chance to see Chopak's medieval woman and left for home. Every case he had been tracking was now resolved save Rebecca Kincaid and her condition made the prospects for her survival virtually nil. Gathering his voluminous notes and promising to keep in touch, he boarded an afternoon flight to London.

Chopak concurred with his colleague's assessment and had begun the slow, disappointing process of weaning himself away from the long-held hope that Rebecca Kincaid might actually return and somehow be induced to remember her other life.

It was, therefore, with some surprise that he took a call from the weekend charge nurse at St. Vincent's, informing him that Mrs. Kincaid was stirring.

Upon arrival Chopak found his patient restless and flailing against the rails of her bed. The staff had already padded them but was still awaiting the necessary order before applying protective restraints to the patient herself. Chopak, however, declined to write that order and sat himself at the bedside to monitor his patient. As though somehow sensing his presence the woman opened her eyes.

"Cecilia?" Chopak queried.

The woman, her countenance nothing but a blank stare, did not respond.

Chopak chafed her hand and repeated, "Cecilia? Are you there?"

Blue eyes, once milky, continued to clear and gaze back at him. Then an unfamiliar voice rasped, "Who is

Cecilia?"

Chopak nearly fainted. "Mrs. Kincaid?"

"Yes," the woman replied. "Who are you?"

Heart thudding, Chopak introduced himself, "I am Gurinder Chopak," then added, "your doctor."

The woman's voice grew firmer and more certain with each word. "Miles Winston is my doctor," she countered. "I don't know you."

Chopak's answer was evasive. "I am a specialist called to consult."

The woman seemed to accept this. Then, glancing out a west-facing window toward a late after sun, she asked, "What time is it?"

Chopak consulted his watch. "4 p.m." he replied.

Frowning, the woman asked another question. "What day is it?"

"Sunday," Chopak answered.

The woman's face showed her surprise and some consternation. "I've been asleep for four days?!" she gasped.

"Four months," Chopak corrected.

"Four months!" Rebecca repeated. "Impossible! What's the date?"

"August 24," Chopak said with certainty.

"Oh, my God!" Rebecca whispered. "Oh, my God!"

Brian Kincaid arrived within the hour, followed only moments later by Melissa and Evan. Brian Jr. was out of town. The family babbled in incoherent bursts of emotion until Rebecca, more confused than ever, nearly collapsed with exhaustion.

The Monastery

"*Go home,*" *she begged them.* "*Please, I have to think.*"

When they all had gone she agreed to some weak tea and crackers offered by an aide and then lay in her room listening to the world outside her door.

She eavesdropped as one aide spoke to another. "*What happened to the other woman?*" *a voice asked.*

"*Who knows?*" *another replied.* "*She's just crazy...*"

Uneasy, Rebecca shifted, dislodging her feeding tube. She rang for a nurse. When a young aide rose to answer the summons, Chopak, still seated at the nursing station, placed a gentle hand on her shoulder. "*I'll go,*" *he offered.* "*Finish your dinner.*"

In Rebecca's room, Chopak removed the offending feeding tube and placed a small dressing over the opening in her skin.

"*Why are you still here?*" *Rebecca asked.* "*I thought you'd have gone home.*"

Finished, Chopak sat beside the bed. "*I thought I might stay awhile,*" *he replied.* "*You needn't talk if you don't feel like it.*"

The woman gazed around her. "*I don't mind,*" *she replied.* "*It's just that my family is exhausting. They always were.*" *An almost familiar look of annoyance crossed her face.*

The hairs on the back of Chopak's neck stood on end.

Then in a sudden non sequitur Rebecca demanded, "*Does it seem especially noisy in here to you?*"

Chopak listened. There was soft music overlaying the usual sounds of evening shift. He shook his head. "*No. What do you hear?"*

"Noise! It's deafening! Can't you hear it? There is that sound," she pointed to the intercom speaker over which the music came, *"and clanging like cymbals and a shrill ringing. There is a thumping somewhere and water running."*

When Chopak did not respond Rebecca continued, covering her ears with her hands. "And listen to the noise outside. Horns, sirens! How can you bear it?"

Chopak sat, listening. She was right. There was the Muzak, of course, plus the crash of empty dinner trays being shoved into the now cold food cart. Telephones were ringing; someone in the next room was hammering on a wall; a toilet was flushed and a shower ran. Outside the building there were the sounds of auto traffic, including a police siren wailing in the distance.

"I am not accustomed to all this din," she *complained, the inconsistency of her statement lost in her own confusion.*

"And that constant hum…what is it? A thousand bees?"

Chopak listened again. Air conditioning. He got up and closed the door. Although the noise persisted, it was at least somewhat diminished.

"Thank you," Rebecca said. *"Now, tell me Doctor, what is wrong with me?"*

Chopak hesitated, his slight frown evidence of his reluctance to explain. He removed his glasses, cleaned them methodically, then placed them carefully in a breast pocket.

"Come on. I can take it," the woman encouraged.

"There is nothing wrong with you," Chopak assured her. *"You have simply, and I might add quite inexplicably,*

The Monastery

been sleeping."

"*For four months?*" Her skepticism was clear. "Hog wash!"

"*You are like her,*" Chopak said.

"Like whom?" Rebecca demanded.

"*Tomorrow,*" Chopak answered. "*We shall talk tomorrow.*"

August 25, 1997

Gurinder Chopak arrived in Rebecca Kincaid's room shortly after 10 a.m. Her daughter and younger son had come and gone, while her husband remained at her bedside. Husband and wife were engrossed in a deep and conspicuously acrimonious discussion of her recent whereabouts. Kincaid, angry and aggressive, hurled insult and accusation . The physician wondered how the man had so quickly forgotten that he had nearly lost his wife. Rebecca, baffled by his allegations, made few replies.

When she noted Chopak's arrival Rebecca dismissed her husband with a weary gesture. "Go away, Brian," *she said.* "I need to see my doctor."

A parting shot, Kincaid scoffed, "Then have them call Miles, Rebecca. This guy's some kind of pseudo-shrink."

As the proverbial dust settled, Rebecca Kincaid straightened her clothing and relaxed against her mound of pillows. She leveled an uncompromising look at the small brown man before her. "You have some talking to do," *she warned.*

Chopak flushed beneath his smooth dark skin.

"Don't play the shy guy with me," *she counseled.* "I have little patience. Now tell me, where have I been? What *happened to me? Was I raped?"*

Chopak hid his surprise. "Why do you ask?"

Rebecca gave him a look of pure exasperation. "My daughter came at six and wept until nine... not unusual for her, granted, but distressing nonetheless. My younger son acts as though he has seen me naked. And Brian? Well, Brian seems to think I've fucked a football team. What the hell is going on?"

Chopak choked in astonishment. "You're so like her!"

"I've had enough of these vague exclamations. Begin at the beginning. The last thing I remember is looking in my mirror and thinking I could not face another day. That day was in early April. Now talk. And by the way, what is a pseudo-shrink?"

Chopak hardly knew where to begin. "Before I begin, please, will you tell me what you remember."

"I just did."

"No, about your dreams. What can you recall about your dreams?"

Rebecca wrinkled her brow. "There are only wisps, but I have a hazy sense of men, monks perhaps, and children. Very small, lovely, children. There was snow and huge fireplaces and a wonderful feeling of being happy." She smiled. "And," she added with great emphasis, "it was blessedly quiet... not like here."

"Hold on to those memories," Chopak urged. "Write them down. Time will try to steal them from you but they are very important."

Over the next several hours Doctor and patient talked. Rebecca was fascinated by Chopak's theories but unconvinced. Yes, she admitted there were odd dreams but

The Monastery

another life? That seemed unlikely. Chopak tried, through a variety of methods to jog her memory but nothing seemed quite right. He left discouraged but determined.

August 26, 1997

It was late afternoon. A crisis precipitated by another patient's attempted suicide had kept him from visiting Mrs. Kincaid until nearly 5 p.m. Now Chopak met Melissa, departing, as he arrived.

"How is she?" he asked.

Melissa seemed noncommittal. "Distant," she replied. "I've left some of her favorite music. Maybe that will help."

Chopak entered the room to the sounds of Celtic ballads filling the room with ancient Ireland.

Rebecca smiled at him. "For some reason Enya always puts me in mind of the Middle Ages," she said. Then, chuckling to herself, she added, "It makes no sense, I know. They didn't have the instruments to make any of these sounds in that time. Still it's just a feeling."

Wary of the lure of the other life, Chopak snapped off the CD player. "Let's walk," he said briskly. "Come, I'll help you into the wheelchair."

They roamed the halls, Rebecca riding, Chopak pushing, until they had seen all there was to see. When they tired of their explorations, they sought, then eschewed, the dayroom, already full of a large family celebrating Grandpa's birthday. Finally, Chopak suggested they enjoy the summer evening in the garden.

Rebecca gave a long sigh of relief as Chopak pushed her chair through the double doors and out into the peaceful gloaming. She sniffed tentatively, then took a deep, slow breath, inhaling the fragrance of lilacs surrounding the seating area. With eyes still closed Rebecca sniffed again.

"It needs rosemary," she said, as if the air were a soup, its prime ingredient missing.

Some miles to the east, a summer storm flashed like a beacon, then rumbled. "God must be hungry," she murmured.

When Chopak looked puzzled she explained. "I always say that to the children. It makes them less afraid."

Her use of the present tense was not lost on the good doctor although he refrained from comment.

In a comfortable silence they sat, watching the fireflies' Lilliputian imitation of the distant lightening. Across the way, a small boy escaped his aging grandma and darted toward them. He was a bow-legged little thing, red-headed and very fast. When Rebecca saw him, a hand flew to her throat.

"Angus!" she gasped, "What are you doing here?"

The tyke stopped, stared and then with a slight squeak stated firmly, "My name is Tommy!"

The boy's grandmother was a scant five steps behind him, embarrassed and slightly out of breath. "I'm sorry," she wheezed, "but he is so fast." Then to the child she cooed, "Come, love, let's go back and see Grandpa."

Chopak said nothing, only stared.

Suddenly embarrassed, Rebecca said quietly, "I thought I knew him."

† *Chapter Eighteen* †

April 29, 1325

Bartholomew brooded. It was as though time had stopped. After nearly two years of patient work and sacrifice, when finally Cecilia was within his grasp, everything had been snatched away. He sat now, head in hands, staring at her sleeping form. If sleep it could be called. In truth, the difference between that restful state and Cecilia's, however subtle it might seem, was like day to night. Though nominally alive, Cecilia responded to nothing. Not whispers, not shouts, not touch. She was warm and she breathed but she was gone.

Heartbroken, the young Lord Carlisle relived, again and again, the horror of that fateful day, that awful day which had stolen her from him, from them all. It had taken time to piece the tale together. But what else was there? Bartholomew sighed. Time stretched before him, a long empty road, devoid of meaning without Cecilia. He could not bear to look forward, only back.

The scene played in his mind's eye. The weather had been warm. While he hunted only a few miles away, a happy Cecilia, at home in the monastery, tended to her children amidst the scent of spring flowers, wafting here and there on the light breeze. As evening fell, fireflies made their shy debut and danced as the sun dipped low and disappeared in a last blaze of color. The future had seemed assured. How wrong he had been.

Content, Cecilia and Maggie watched as a patient Will taught Angus a game of tossing stones. Francis, who played with them for a time, had already retreated to the barn for evening milking. The other men were engaged in the various activities deemed suitable for a late Sabbath afternoon. William read; Dominic tended his medicinal herbs; Lucien went over the accounts; Paul kneaded the morrow's bread; and Matthew prayed. Soon all would heed the summons of the bells for Vespers. It was like any one of a hundred Sunday evenings since she had come to the Monastery. Life was in balance, suspended in a perfect moment in time.

Only Bartholomew's man was disgruntled. Resentful at being left behind with a woman not his own, along with children and churchmen, he had drunk himself into a stupor, then fallen into a deep and lethal sleep.

Bartholomew, just camped, had watched as his men built a crackling fire and began the messy task of dressing out the large buck, the yield of a day's hunting. Without warning, a prickle of fear raised the hairs on his neck. Keen eyes searched the horizon as he sniffed the air. There was blood on the wind… but only the deer's? To the west, a faint cloud, like cottage smoke, rose in a lazy column and was lost in a darkening sky.

A shudder of premonition ran through Bartholomew. He spun on his heel and sprinted for his horse. "Mount up!" he barked.

Tremont looked askance. "…but, milord? The deer?"

"To your horses, I say!" roared Bartholomew, already in the saddle. "Now! 'Tis worth your life!"

St. Fiacre's had no such warning, for the monks, accustomed now to the noisy comings and goings of riders

The Monastery

on large mounts, had paid no mind to the clamor of arriving horsemen until it was too late.

Mindful of Tremont's careful training, young Will fled at once. With little Maggie in tow, he darted across the courtyard toward the chapel. Like two lithe wood sprites they went, swift and silent. Past the forge they flew and out the back gate into the woods, where they disappeared amongst the tall ferns, invisible to the Bishop's rampaging knights and their deadly archers.

Little Angus, only two and still unsteady on his feet, was left far behind, stumbling blindly in a fog of dirt raised by the huge war horses. Terrified, he spun in a panic, trying to find where his brother and sister had gone. Cecilia saw him, small and weeping, about to be trampled by a heedless mount.

The new life within made her less quick than she might otherwise have been. With a pounding heart, she sprinted across the courtyard, snatching up her small son without breaking pace and making for the escape her other children had made before her. An archer, heeding the admonition to take the woman alive and thinking to slow her progress by killing the child, nocked an arrow and drew back his bow.

Francis, having heard the commotion, rushed from the cool quiet of the barn into a scene of sheer bedlam. His crossed eyes swept across the compound, taking in the scene in an instant. Too far from the archer to hinder his aim, Francis bolted instead toward Cecilia and his son. As he neared his wife and child, he threw himself at their retreating backs, making of his body the largest shield possible. His agonized scream echoed through the courtyard, "Nooooo!"

The archer's aim was deadly. A grim smile crossed an ugly face as the disappointment of having missed the child turned to mild satisfaction at the twang of a feathered shaft stopped in full flight. The monk would do as well, he thought.

His arrow, straight and true, pierced Francis's back near its center and passed though, protruding far enough beneath the monk's breastbone to scratch Cecilia's arm as he knocked her from her feet.

Bartholomew, his men in close pursuit, thundered into the compound. Too late, he charged the archer at full gallop, and trod him into the dirt. The hapless man, his victory short-lived, lay without moving as Bartholomew held his prancing horse in place until the man was no longer recognizable as human. Only then did Bartholomew dismount and stride toward Cecilia who now sat upon the ground with Francis's head in her lap.

Cecilia raised a hand to stay his approach.

Bartholomew stopped, bowed his head and stood aside, understanding that there was nothing to be done.

Francis lay, his life seeping into a red halo around him. The little monk beckoned Cecilia closer to ease the pain of speech. Looking from her to his son and back again, he gasped, "One favor…"

"Anything," Cecilia sobbed.

The dying man reached out for his small son. His words came in short, breathy bursts.

"Promise me… when he is grown… do not give him to the Church… find him a good wife…" He reached up to caress her cheek, "…one he does not have to share."

Then he beckoned again to the child and drew a last painful breath trying to strengthen his voice. The boy moved closer, staring and frightened by the red stain, which grew ever larger.

The Monastery

"Come," Francis coaxed, giving his hand a gentle tug. "Angus," he wheezed, "my son, mind your mother."

Cecilia's wail could be heard forever.

While the tragedy of Francis's death played in center courtyard, Bartholomew's men quickly dispatched twelve of the Bishop's thirteen marauders. On the whole a motley lot with few real soldiers, they were no match for the men of Carlisle. The unlucky thirteenth evaded them for the greater part of a day before he, too, was seized and sent to meet his Maker; his additional punishment, a death something less merciful than those of his comrades.

Meanwhile, Bartholomew strode across the embattled courtyard, side-stepping the bodies of the dead. A cold fury etching every line in his face, he roared into the old dorter like a whirlwind, breaching the bolted door with a ruthless kick and casting aside a huge trestle table in his path as though it were kindling.

The man left to watch over his family still lay in a drunken stupor, snoring softly and oblivious to all that had happened. Huge hands clamped, vise-like, on the man's upper arms as Bartholomew shook the sorry bastard until his neck snapped in protest.

The man yelped as pain shot both north and south through his spine. Arms flailing, too groggy for real thought, if ever he were capable of it, the fellow slurred, "Wha-? What ith it? Unhand me, you cur!"

Beyond reason, Bartholomew continued to shake until the man's bones literally rattled beneath his skin. When finally alert enough to see Bartholomew's face, the man knew his fate and promptly pissed himself.

A look of disgust crossed Bartholomew's face as the

odor of urine seeped into the air. He dragged the man, reeling and stumbling, into the courtyard. The scene before the dazed man was almost more horrifying than the look in his Lord's eyes, a fixed glare so fierce and pitiless that he stood, slack-jawed and drooling. Bodies were strewn about, each in its own ghastly repose. Blood soaked the dust, leaving dozens of blackening circles, like spots before the eyes. Worse yet, four solemn monks moved the lifeless body of Brother Francis onto a carrying canvas and walked in slow procession toward the Chapel. As the dim-witted man began to realize the enormity of his blunder, his eyes widened in mute terror.

Judging him to have had ample time to see the results of his crime, a merciless Bartholomew drew his dirk. With his free hand, he grabbed the man by his hair and pulled backward, stretching his neck to its fullest extent thus exposing, beneath a fleshy jowl, a throat white as fish belly, Adam's apple bobbing in swallowed sobs.

As the last shadow of Francis's body disappeared into the Chapel, Bartholomew growled, "He was a good man…" His gaze turned to a weeping Cecilia and Francis's trembling little son, "…and much-loved."

Then in a voice grown cold and monotonous as a chant, he pronounced the biblical judgement, "An eye for an eye, a tooth for a tooth, and a life for a life."

With one vicious slash Bartholomew went from judge to executioner. He drew his blade across the condemned man's throat with the swiftness of light, cutting deep and twisting so that blood spurted from the arteries on both sides of his neck.

Reeking of his own fear, the man barely whimpered before a sickening gurgle heralded choking, then drowning.

The Monastery

Released from the iron grip at last, the guilty man crumpled into a heap in the dust, adding his own blood to that of his enemies.

Tremont and Bartholomew's other men looked on without comment, their faces wanting all expression.

Fury spent, Bartholomew sighed and squared his broad shoulders.

"Bury him," he said icily. "Leave his grave unmarked. Any who wish to remember him may visit Brother Francis, for his part in that good man's death is the only act of consequence in his worthless life."

"Yes, milord," Tremont replied. Then under his breath he urged, "Make haste, men. The children must not see this."

Cecilia, alone with Angus behind the sturdy bar on her door, lay on her bed and wept. Will and Maggie were found and fed by Paul. When dark fell their mother's keening, an eerie inhuman sound, could still be heard throughout the monastery. Instinctively each child sought his own father. Will found the Abbot in the library, alone and staring into the fire, and curled up at his feet to sleep. Maggie crept up to her huge bearded "Da" and tugged shyly at his tunic. Batholomew, deep in conversation with the other men, barely noticed her until she pulled his sleeve a second time. Then he reached down and scooped her into his lap, making a cradle of his arm, kissing her forehead and allowing her to cuddle against him until she was comfortable.

When morning came Cecilia's rooms were silent but for the whining of a hungry Angus. No amount of begging or cajoling would elicit a response. Finally, a desperate Bartholomew kicked in the door.

Cecilia lay tear-stained, but silent, curled around the weeping boy. Although her breath came in slow even strokes, he could not wake her.

And four days later, she remained so.

†††

September 13, 1997

Rebecca Kincaid waited patiently for Dr. Chopak to arrive. A concession to her uneasiness in his office, they now met thrice weekly in the comfort of her home. Although there was no thought on either side that she was somehow in need of psychiatric help, both were intent on understanding what had happened to her and why. Over the last several weeks they had been making some progress. With carefully directed encouragement, Rebecca now remembered more than just snatches of her other life. And, though not yet completely convinced that it was other than a dream, she did feel interested enough to pursue it.

At first, she had been so overwhelmed by family and the drama of her recovery that she was barely able to recall anything. But now that life had settled back into its unhappy sameness, entire days of fourteenth century life would drift like clouds in and out of her consciousness. She would remember a place, a taste, a smell and, despite olfactory stimulation's reputation as memory's most evocative sensory stimulant, usually it was sound which drew her into that other world. She remembered half-familiar faces, healing silence and most often, unbeknownst to her new Indian friend, she remembered making love with a handsome man who still touched her face and called her.

The Monastery

Tonight Chopak came, unscheduled, in response to a vague telephone summons, "I don't know who I am," she had said. "Do you?"

That call, preceded as it was by a visit from a bitterly complaining Kincaid – "She isn't herself," he had raged. "Her speech is odd. Half the time, she is somewhere else. What the hell is going on?" – made him uneasy.

From the first moments of tonight's session, Rebecca had been dogged in her pursuit of the past. "It's time," she insisted, "to tell me about her. I've told you all I know, but there is more. I'm certain of it. There are feelings, things I can't describe. Now it is your turn. Tell me. Tell me everything you know."

When Chopak hesitated, Rebecca played her trump. "Tell me, Doctor, or these sessions are over. I will not speak with you again... ever."

Half expecting this threat, Chopak sighed. Rebecca Kincaid was a strong-willed, intelligent woman. It was a wonder she had been patient this long, he thought.

"I am sorry," Rebecca apologized, "but I must know, Gurinder, and you are the only one who can tell me."

Chopak nodded. "Very well."

Rebecca smiled, pleased at his capitulation. "I was happy, wasn't I?" she asked.

Noting her use of the first person, Chopak agreed, "Yes, she was. Quite happy."

"Alright then." Rebecca drew up her feet and tucked them neatly beneath her. "Make yourself comfortable and start at the beginning. I won't mind repetition and I have all night."

Chopak settled into a large chair with care, like a

man preparing to row a long distance. He began, as always, in his own way. With lilting voice and graceful hands, he drew the picture of Cecilia's life as he knew it. There were gaps, of course, which the man through no fault of his own could not fill, making the story seem a bizarre series of non sequiturs. Rebecca, however, listened patiently to the zigzagging tale.

Chopak did his best to describe the monks. "Toland," he said, "was the first and, I thought for a time, the favorite. But I soon learned that Cecilia saw something special in every man. I began to see that each had qualities, often missing in the others, for which he was dearly loved. Francis, for example, allowed Cecilia to wield a kind of power usually reserved for men. She literally made him a man."

Rebecca interrupted. "How? How did she make him a man?"

Chopak blushed. "I had thought to describe the men to you first, before trying to explain their arrangement," he evaded.

Rebecca shook her head. "No," she insisted, her voice low and firm. "I have waited quite long enough. Now we do it my way. How did she make him a man?"

Chopak drew a long breath, made the now familiar steeple of his fingers and sighed. "Rebecca... may I call you Rebecca?"

Rebecca gave him a weary look, "Yes, Saracen, you may," she answered.

Chopak caught his breath. "What did you call me?"

"Saracen," she replied evenly.

"Why?" Chopak asked.

Rebecca shrugged, "I don't know, but I suspect I soon will. Continue. How did she make him a man?"

The Monastery

Evasion at an end, Chopak's answer was direct. "She took him to bed."

A look of mild surprise dawned on Rebecca's face, then a slight smile. "Did she?" she queried. "Good for her!"

Chopak went on. "But not only him, Rebecca. She also took the Abbot, the other priest – Lucien, and four other monks."

Rebecca calculated quickly… "Seven men?"

Chopak nodded.

"Well, I'll be damned," she chortled. ""So she sleeps with everyone?"

Chopak shook his head. "No," he replied. "Not everyone. There was an older man, Brother Paul, who declined her favors citing paternal feelings as his reason and another young monk who preferred to remain celibate."

"How odd…" Rebecca mused.

"And," Chopak added, "there was a youngster, an oblate he is called, who caused considerable trouble when denied Cecilia's favors."

Rebecca chuckled. "Remembering my own sons in their early teens, I have no difficulty imagining that!"

When Chopak did not continue his tale, Rebecca prodded, "Don't just sit like an ass at the bottom of a steep hill."

Chopak gasped again. "She said that to me once. Just as you did, in just that tone. She was exasperated."

"As am I," Rebecca replied. "Talk! I want to know about each of her men and the life she led."

Defeated, Chopak agreed. "There were seven husbands…" he began again.

Rebecca nodded encouragement.

"William, the Abbot, seemed a strong steady presence who loved deeply. By all accounts, he was dependable and true.

"Lucien, the second priest, was different. It was he who allowed Cecilia to play Eve; he who eventually risked every shred of his being to be with her.

"Dominic was her tutor and friend.

"Luis, the one who died, was, I believe, simply the beneficiary of her desire for the others."

When Rebecca's brows rose in silent query, Chopak gave an all too practical explanation: "It was all or none, as it had to be."

He spoke in great detail of his strange talks with Cecilia; tried to explain her views of the world, both theirs and her own.

"They were always too brief," he said of her visits. "She would arrive unannounced, behave quite normally and then, with almost no warning, disappear. It was unsettling, to say the least."

He spoke of the children, painting with words a colorful picture of each so that Rebecca could see them in her mind's eye. As Angus came to life, Rebecca laughed aloud, "...the little boy at the home!" she exclaimed. "I thought he was Angus."

"Yes," Chopak replied. "He seemed very like him."

The night wore on as the hall clock tolled each hour in its turn – one, two, three. Still they talked. By daybreak, Rebecca could almost see the Abbott, dark brows, furrowed over deep-set eyes, a kindly, appealing old man content with a young wife and his growing son. She had a sense of Lucien, his haughty pride humbled by the need to be loved. She knew Toland, who seemed to her much as Brian had been in the *early years of their marriage and Francis who had bloomed into manhood, fatherhood, needing only the nourishment of love and acceptance.*

Discussion of Dominic lasted longest since Rebecca found him fascinating. She peppered Chopak with questions: "Are they lovers? What does he look like? They sound like friends, but you say she sleeps with him?"

Chopak was patient for he knew Dominic well. "He was her friend," he insisted. "There was something physical, yes, but it was different. He was different."

"He loves another," Rebecca said with certainty.

Chopak noted again her consistent use of the present tense, then challenged, "How do you know?"

Again the shrug. "I just do," she asserted. "Go on."

Chopak accepted her statement and continued, "Then there was Luis. He, too, was older and never figured greatly in her conversation except when he was ill. I believe he died of heart failure."

An inexplicable sorrow settled over Rebecca. She waved a hand in sad dismissal. "I cannot speak of him tonight."

Chopak sat back as though his story were complete. Trying to signal the session's end, he turned off his tape recorder, wondering as he did so how many times Rebecca had switched from third to first person, from past to present. He was anxious to replay his tapes. The apparent mixing of two lives was troubling.

Rebecca caught his gaze, held it.

A patient man, he remained stoic.

Minutes passed before Rebecca prodded, "Saracen, at the beginning of your tale you mentioned seven husbands and three children. Throughout this long night, you have spoken freely of six husbands and two other men. You have described a troublesome teen-aged novice and introduced two young sons, whose paternity is in no doubt. You have, however, assiduously refrained from any description or comment on the seventh man who, I can only assume, must be the father of Maggie."

Wary, Chopak shifted in his chair.

"Explain," Rebecca demanded.

"Tomorrow," Chopak pleaded. "You are tired. I am tired."

Rebecca gave his plea a moment's consideration. "It is already tomorrow," she advised. "But I will grant you a brief respite."

Chopak released a breath held.

"Tonight at seven?"

Chopak nodded his head in mute agreement, then rose and left.

Rebecca showered before climbing wearily into her bed. It was 8 a.m. Brian's key could be heard in the snap of the front door latch.

While quiet footsteps climbed the stair, passed her door and moved away again toward the guest bedroom and bath, she pretended to sleep. Within minutes a distant shower thrummed on Italian tiles. A bare squeak of the faucet announced its end. Then, more minutes later, a well-dressed Brian returned and plunked himself on the side of her bed, bending to plant a perfunctory kiss on her cheek.

His greeting was time-worn, "Morning, Beck."

When she fluttered her eyelids in feigned awakening, he gave her a practiced smile; his lie followed, smooth as silk, "My meeting ran later than I expected last night. I didn't want to wake you so I slept in the guest room."

Rebecca didn't even blink. Her reply was cool. "I appreciate your consideration," she said.

Brian smiled again. "Remember please that we are having guests tomorrow night."

"Are we?" Rebecca's dismay was clear. "I've told you, Brian, that I'm not up to entertaining yet."

Kincaid's lips compressed into a thin line. "I'm afraid you'll have to be up to it, Rebecca. This is important. Twelve for dinner, tomorrow at seven. Miss Quinn sent them invitations two weeks ago."

"Then perhaps Miss Quinn should entertain them," Rebecca snapped.

Kincaid rose and left the room.

Rebecca rolled over and went to sleep. Later she would call Claridge's Catering.

† *Chapter Nineteen* †

April 30, 1325

Young Will scampered across the cloister garth shouting as loudly as his tiny voice would allow. "Bartholomew! Bartholomew! Come quick! Mama's awake!" Like a small madman he dashed from cell to cell, then through the refectory and into the kitchen beyond, searching everywhere for someone, anyone to tell. Finally, he ran headlong into Tremont who, upon hearing the news, scooped the lad into strong arms and bolted toward the Chapel and his liege. Good tidings shared, the three ran back across the garth to the door still held open by a little sentry.

Round-eyed and silent, Maggie pointed to the woman who sat bewildered in her mother's bed and body. As Bartholomew crossed the threshold, the girl took his hand and led him to Cecilia. His voice choked with emotion the huge man dropped to one knee beside the bed, grasping Cecilia's hands and pleading, "My love, are you well?"

The woman only stared in blank wonder. Bartholomew recognized the signs of amnesia he had seen years past. He turned to Will.

"Go quickly, son. Find Brother Dominic. Bring him here."

Once again, Will dashed away across the garth, while Bartholomew stayed close.

Little Maggie began to pat her mother's hand. "I missed you, Mama," she whispered. "Did you miss me, too?"

A faint smile turned up the corners of Cecilia's mouth.

The Monastery

"I did," she answered softly. "Very much."

Needing no invitation, the child clambered up onto the bed and snuggled against her mother's side. Cecilia kissed the top of her head, wrapping an arm about her. With the other hand she reached up to stroked Bartholomew's damp cheek. "She's yours?" she asked.

"Of course, she is mine," answered the confused man. "Cecilia?"

The woman hesitated only a second before she answered his query with one of her own, "Bartholomew?"

But Rebecca Kincaid knew the answer before it came. Here was the man in her dreams, the seventh husband, father of Maggie. Little wonder Chopak had been reluctant to confirm his existence. He was young and handsome, taller than she had thought and broader. He exuded a subtle strength that drew like a magnet and, at once, a passion for the woman that burned in his eyes and overflowed in rivers of relief down his sun-browned face. Rebecca reached again to offer solace. Speechless, Bartholomew pulled her, child and all, against a thundering chest.

Surprised at the depth of his emotion, Rebecca couldn't help but ask, "Were you so afraid?"

Unashamed Bartholomew dashed a tear from his cheek. "I thought you were gone," he whispered. Then, he squeezed her hard and, without any sign of embarrassment, prayed aloud, "Thank You, Lord. Thank You."

Rebecca covered her surprise in the arrival of a number of men who now crowded through the low doorway to Cecilia's tiny home. She studied each face as it passed beneath the lintel. The Abbot, limping painfully, was first. Then another old man, tall and erect, holding Will's hand. Hawk-featured Lucien hung back, while Dominic, Angus on one hip, strode forward.

"Do you know me?" he demanded.

Her uncertainty betrayed only by a slight rise in inflection, Rebecca guessed, "Dominic?"

A look of plain relief dawned across the man's face.

Delighted with her accomplishment, Rebecca shivered. "I'm right!" her heart crowed, but she offered her visitors only a tentative smile.

Still, Dominic remained unconvinced. He pointed to each man, demanding to be told his name. Thanks to Chopak's faithful reporting, Rebecca knew them all. She named each in turn, "William. Paul. Lucien. Matthew." Then, made bold by unwarranted success, she pushed her luck, "Where are Francis and Toland?"

The man who held her stiffened. "You do not remember?"

Rebecca shook her head.

Bartholomew rose and motioned the others to take the children and withdraw. When all were gone, he sat again beside her on the bed.

"Toland has betrayed us," he said. "Francis is dead. We must leave here at once for England. You are not safe. The children are not safe."

Rebecca absorbed his words trying mightily to complete a puzzle with too few pieces. Then in a flash of insight she took a bold chance.

"Tell me about us," she pleaded. "My head is fuzzy."

"Fuzzy?" Bartholomew repeated. The word was strange and had no meaning.

Rebecca nodded. "I am confused. My thoughts are… jumbled." She waved her hands in the air.

The Monastery

Bartholomew understood. "It is like the first day in the garden," he said, wrapping his arms around her. "You are Cecilia. You have said so to Brother Dominic."

It was Rebecca's turn to weep. "Tell me more," she begged.

Bartholomew began, "We live in the Monastery of St. Fiacre. William is our Abbot; Lucien also a priest…." His voice sure and soothing, he described their lives in poignant detail from the first days of her time with them; he took his time, weaving the fabric of their lives into its bright, happy pattern. When he spoke of the early days of their arrangement, Rebecca wondered if even Cecilia understood what a blessing these men thought her to be.

As the hour passed, Bartholomew talked more of the good, prosperous years, then the advent of the Bishop, his own sojourn in England and its purpose, the loss of Luis, Toland's perfidy and Francis's death. Finally, the trail of his words led to the present. Bartholomew took the woman's hand and held it, looking into her eyes as though they held the future.

"Now, you shall be my wife only, if you can be content to be so. We must go to England, you and I and the children."

After all that had been said, Rebecca asked one simple question, "Do you love me?"

Bartholomew released a slow breath. "More than my life…I swear it."

September 14, 1997

In the distance a bell chimed with maddening insistence. Rebecca Kincaid pulled a pillow over her head. Still unable to ignore the noisy demand she rose like a bubble from the depth of sleep. By the time she had achieved the periphery of consciousness, a worried Chopak stood at her bedside shaking her shoulders with considerable vigor.

"Go away," she whined. "Go away!"

"I will not," the doctor replied firmly. "Get up."

"What time is it?" she snarled.

"Seven," Chopak responded.

Rebecca came alert. "Seven!? Seven in the evening? I've slept the day away!"

"Indeed, you have," he replied.

Rebecca let her heavy eyelids close for a moment more. Bartholomew flashed before her. Naked, he towered over her. She could feel the heat of his skin, smell the sweetness of his breath as his mouth closed over hers.

"Go away, Gurinder," she begged. "I'm not up to this tonight."

Suspicious, Chopak lingered. "Why?"

"I'm just not," Rebecca insisted. "I'll meet you in your office tomorrow at ten. I promise."

Chopak was not easily dissuaded. "Let's talk for just a while. You were so anxious to know about Cecilia. Have you changed your mind?"

Eyes closed again, Rebecca shook her head. She could hear Bartholomew calling...calling...

"No, but I will not talk tonight, Gurinder. Please, go."

When Chopak gave her a hard look, she repeated, "Not tonight." Then a brusque dismissal, "Let yourself out."

With that she rose and walked to her bathroom. The door closed behind her with a soft click, on its heels the snap of a lock.

Without alternative, Chopak did, indeed, let himself out.

Desperate, Rebecca opened her medicine cabinet, rummaging frantically until she found what she sought. In the back, behind a row of over-the-counter preparations, was a full bottle of sleeping tablets, prescribed for Brian years ago. With shaking hands she breached the childproof cap and shook three tablets into her open palm. Hurriedly, she tossed them to the back of her throat and swallowed. Within minutes she was sleeping soundly...

...safe again in Bartholomew's arms.

She woke once to the feel Bartholomew's rough hands navigating the terrain of her skin. Unbidden her body moved toward him and opened. This, she thought, is mating. To be driven to make love with a man by a need so great, so primitive, that it cannot be denied. This is how it was meant to be.

While Bartholomew slept, Rebecca climbed the stairs to look at Cecilia's children. She kissed each small cheek and lay a hand over the next babe who fluttered below young, swelling breasts. Cecilia's last secret, she had discovered only hours ago. Unaccustomed to Cecilia's body, the child had gone unnoticed until, as discarded clothes fell around her feet, she had noted the mound of belly. A look of mild surprise had changed to sublime satisfaction when Bartholomew's lips placed a light kiss in its center. Without being asked, he had murmured, "Mine."

Returning now to the warmth of Cecilia's bed, Cecilia's man, Rebecca took Bartholomew's face in her hands and woke him with soft kisses.

"Listen to me," she whispered. "Listen carefully. She may sleep again for a time, but as you came back to her, she will come back to you. Wait for her."

Bartholomew sat up. "Cecilia, you frighten me. I do not understand."

"I know," Rebecca answered. "But trust me. She won't be long. Promise you'll wait."

"...a lifetime, if I must," Bartholomew replied.

†††

September 15, 1997

Gurinder Chopak was in his office at eight a.m. He had begun his day, as he had so often over the past few months, by reviewing the case of Mrs. Rebecca Kincaid. His notes were precise and complete. From the time of Miles Winston's first call to this very moment, he had been convinced that this was the case. This was the patient who would prove, or disprove, all his theories, all his suppositions. But even now, near as they were to the end, he still didn't know which it would be.

At nine he had placed a call to Nigel Haversham.

"He's on the continent," his secretary had said. "Not due back until late tonight. Shall I have him call?"

The Monastery

"Please," Chopak replied. "Tell him... whatever the time. It's urgent."

Rebecca Kincaid was always punctual. She looked rested and, Chopak thought, a bit smug. There was a satisfied curl in the corners of her mouth that was clearly happiness, but happiness tinged with regret, like a painter's canvas awash in brilliant red, marred by a single, inexplicable, almost imperceptible, streak of blue. Her step was light, her movements quick. Her eyes, once the color of an ocean, had changed to hazel.

"You are well," Chopak said. It wasn't a question.

Rebecca gave him a cat-like smile. "I am," she confirmed.

"And you want to know about Bartholomew?"

Rebecca's smile broadened.

"And his child?"

Rebecca laughed aloud. "I'll wager that I can tell you more than you can tell me," she challenged.

Chopak reached for the intercom. "Mrs. Pashar, there are to be no interruptions. Absolutely none."

"Yes, Doctor," the pleasant voice replied.

Chopak turned back and settled into his chair. "Tell me, Rebecca. Tell me everything."

Rebecca talked for two hours without interruption. In that time Chopak learned of Toland's betrayal and Francis's subsequent fate. He learned many details of Bartholomew's trip to Carlisle, of William's resolve to go south, of Dominic's and Paul's decision to accompany Bartholomew's family northward. In short, he learned all that Bartholomew knew of Cecilia and more, for Rebecca had gleaned a good bit on her own.

Chopak listened, alternating between intense interest and outright astonishment. Sometimes his brown brow furrowed in concentration; at others his mouth gaped. At the end he asked, "But how do you know all this?"

Rebecca chuckled. "I spent all of yesterday and last night with Bartholomew. In fact, I was with him when you interrupted. At a most inopportune time, I might add."

Chopak blushed.

"There isn't much time, Gurinder. They have to leave soon, before the Bishop knows his men are dead. They won't leave without her."

"But she's gone. She's here. She's you!" Chopak sputtered.

Rebecca reached out in a soothing gesture and patted his hand. "Yes, yes, in a way, she is me. And I am her...or is it she? But, Gurinder, the events which have allowed this... whatever this is... to happen are almost over. I can feel it."

"This is not her time, Rebecca. It's yours." Chopak argued.

"Perhaps," the woman conceded, "but, somehow our wires got crossed. There must be a reason. Gurinder, I've made a muddle of my life. Hers is lovely. Her babies are beautiful. Her husbands are good."

When Chopak would have interrupted, she waved a warning hand.

"Please, let me finish. Bartholomew is a man in a thousand and his baby, her baby, will die if she does."

"But, you could die having that baby! It's the fourteenth century for Heaven's sake! Then what would your noble gesture be worth?" Chopak was shouting. Rebecca's calm was maddening.

"You forget your own theory, Gurinder," Rebecca chided. *"She could die, not I."*

"But you're linked, somehow... aren't you?"

"We are. I'm stronger than she is at the moment but I can feel her struggling to save her child."

Chopak's voice was a choked whisper. "Can you?"

Rebecca nodded. "It's as though the distinction between us is blurring. Have you noticed the color of my eyes?"

Chopak nodded.

"Bartholomew is real to me. Sometimes, I can still feel his baby. Cecilia is here, somehow, begging for her chance."

Alarms went off in Chopak's head. "She told me once that she didn't take your soul. That you weren't the same person. That she didn't have the power to give you back your life."

Rebecca considered this for a moment. "She may have been half right or maybe she lied. I can give her my soul, as she could give me hers. I don't think she can take it, nor could I have done so except when she was distraught over the loss of Francis. In that brief period, her will to live was weakened by sorrow. But, she would never have remained in that state. She is too strong, too happy. It was a momentary lapse, a fleeting grief."

Chopak had no words.

Rebecca did. "I, on the other hand, have very little to live for and am, therefore, a less formidable opponent. She might wrest this soul from me if she is determined enough. I can feel her, but I'll wager that she has not felt me."

"You're wrong," Chopak argued. *"She told me once that your bottom hurt."*

Rebecca chortled. "She was right."

"She begged me to let you go."

"As would I, in her place. Had you done so, this would not be happening. She would be on her way to merry old England and I would be pushing up daisies."

Chopak frowned at her grim attempt at humor. "Stop that," he commanded. "This is serious."

Rebecca's answer was a mild rebuke. "No one knows that better than I, Gurinder."

Suddenly, Rebecca rose from her chair. "I need to be alone. I need to think."

Chopak tried to protest, "I don't think that's wise."

Rebecca ignored his comment and changed the subject. "We're entertaining tonight," she said. "Please come."

Chopak's body language clearly communicated his relief that she had definite plans for the evening. "Of course," he replied. "What time?"

"A little before seven."

"Alright," he said. "I'll be there."

That decided Rebecca picked up her purse and headed for the office door. She passed through and closed it behind her. Then, as an afterthought, she reopened it and stuck her head in. "Gurinder?"

Chopak's head came up in surprise. "Yes," he replied.

"It's black tie."

While the dazed man organized his notes and thoughts, his intercom buzzed. Mrs. Pashar was apologetic. "I know you said no calls, but since Mrs. Kincaid has left I thought..."

The Monastery

"Of course," Chopak murmured. "Who is it?"

"Dr. Haversham from London," the secretary replied.

"Put him through," said a relieved Chopak.

A cool clipped voice came crackling over the ocean, "Chopak? Nigel here. My girl says you called. Frantic is what she said, actually? What's happened?"

Chopak wasted no time. "Rebecca Kincaid has discovered Cecilia."

"Discovered? What do you mean discovered?" Haversham demanded.

"I mean," Chopak replied, "that she knows about Cecilia, her life, her husbands, her children."

"My God man, how the bloody hell did she learn about them? I thought we'd decided long ago not to discuss alternate lives with these patients except under hypnosis."

"Yes, I know," Chopak hedged, "but, Nigel, Rebecca is different. She's much more aware. She knows things, feels them. She's lived with this woman too long. Their personalities are beginning to blur and..."

Haversham prodded sharply, "And what, old man? Spit it out. Don't dither."

"And she crossed the Dreamline. She lived Cecilia's life for a day, met her husbands, held her children. She knows Cecilia is pregnant."

"Bloody hell..." Haversham swore again. "Bloody, bloody hell!"

Chopak sighed. "That's not all, Nigel."

The Englishman groaned aloud.

"Do you remember the HCG levels."

"Ummm," Haversham responded.

"Well, there's more. Rebecca says now she can feel

Cecilia's baby and her eyes… her eyes, Nigel, have changed to hazel. They aren't blue anymore."

Haversham, like a broken record, muttered again, "Bloody hell."

"She, Rebecca, is beginning to compare the two lives in value. She hinted that she may relinquish her soul to Cecilia."

"Relinquish?" Haversham was incredulous. "You're talking suicide, aren't you?"

"Perhaps," Chopak replied.

"Stop her!" Haversham nearly shouted.

"But you said not to interfere," Chopak reminded.

"Well I've changed my bloody mind! If she dies the door is closed. We may never get another chance like this one. Put her on a suicide watch, Chopak. Put her in restraints if you must, but stop her. I'm on the next flight."

Late, Gurinder Chopak turned onto the Kincaids' street at half past seven. A lump rose in his throat as he noted red and blue flashing lights. To his dismay, in the midst of their manicured front lawn, surrounded by dozens of welcoming luminaries, he saw two fire rescue trucks and an ambulance. A newsman's camera flashed. A score of curious neighbors milled about chatting among themselves.

"Such a nice woman…" one clucked.

"A lovely couple…" said another. "Never a hint of scandal."

A policeman, just arrived, tried to bring order to the scene. "Step back, folks," he pleaded. "Step back. Go on home, now. Please. Let these fellas do their work."

As if on cue, two paramedics wheeled a stretcher onto the dew-dampened grass. That they seemed in no hurry

The Monastery

told Chopak all he needed to know.

Inside the front doorway, a dozen beautiful guests stood as though frozen in time. Soon wraps were donned in a whirl of rustling skirts and shuffling shoes. Half-full glasses found their way onto tabletops, their clinking ice awash in expensive liquor quickly abandoned. Murmured good nights and vague expressions of condolence were tossed into the air in the faint hope that they would drift on the evening breeze to their host's ear. The doorbell, which one man bumped in his hasty retreat, chimed two bars of Clare de Lune.

Chopak entered unimpeded.

Dozens of flickering candles, which an hour ago had provided ambience, now gave the rooms a decidedly funereal air.

In the dining room two little serving maids could be seen clearing a table still set for twelve, while an older woman in black bombazine, obviously in charge, hovered in the doorway, her hawk-eyed glare taking in each detail. Apparently satisfied that all proceeded as best it might under the circumstances, she disappeared without a word like a diver into a smooth pond, leaving barely a ripple behind her. Death or no death, she knew her business.

Kincaid stood in the living room, leaning on the mantle, a tumbler of amber liquid in hand.

"Good evening," said Dr. Chopak.

Kincaid turned, frowned. "I'm afraid I wasn't aware you'd been invited," he said.

A caterer, noting his host's lapse in manners and gracious to the last, offered, "A drink, sir?"

Chopak declined. "Thank you, no" he replied.

Kincaid cleared his throat before he spoke, his voice flat and unemotional. "She's dead," he said.

Chopak nodded, turned and left the room.

On impulse, he took the more circuitous route to his car, detouring up the stairs and into Rebecca's room. One man challenged him.

"I'm her doctor," he murmured and was henceforth left to his own devices while the professionals gathered the requisite evidence for a finding of suicide.

As he wandered he noted the empty bottle of Nembutal, neatly bagged and tagged.

"She was dressed for the party," one policeman said.

"Must have changed her mind," replied another.

While a hive of activity buzzed around her, Rebecca Kincaid lay stretched full length on top of her bed's counterpane. She wore a silk wrapper of oriental design which gapped slightly at breast and knee allowing only a peak of expensive lace undergarments. Her hair was curled softly to frame a face to which simple make-up had been artfully applied. Her cheeks were dusted every so lightly with rouge; the rosy hue on her lips cruel mimicry of life's blush.

Chopak stepped to the bedside, a hand extended to grope needlessly for a pulse.

"Don't touch her!" a homicide sergeant admonished. "She's evidence."

Chopak withdrew his hand and continued to wander. An envelope lay in plain view on the night table, the name of its intended addressee written with a flourish. When he reached for it, the same voice that had once chastised him growled again, "Ain't you listenin', buddy. Don't touch."

"But it's addressed to me," Chopak replied.

All eyes turned to study him. "You're Chopak?"

The doctor nodded. "I am."

Rebecca's stationery, like her home, was understated and tasteful. A scroll of initials centered the single sheet of beige linen paper on which she had written her farewell. The growling policeman read over Chopak's shoulder.

<u>**September 15, 1997**</u>
<u>**5:50 p.m.**</u>

My Dearest Doctor,

I have just taken 13 little tablets from the bottle at my bedside. If you should discover me before they have done their work I must ask that you respect my decision. It is final and your intervention would only force me to find a less pleasant end to this segment of my journey.

You were right, Gurinder, I have not died but simply moved on. With luck, Cecilia and her family are already en route to England and safety.

Perhaps, I may see you in that next life, or failing that, in another. It would be too cruel for two such as we, two who have shared something so momentous, never to meet again.

Rebecca

From somewhere deep in the officer's throat came a single noise, an ambiguous vocal economy, which said at once everything and nothing.

A second officer, less circumspect, muttered, "Had a

little thing with her, did ya, Doc?"

Chopak smiled sadly and shook his head. "Not the kind of thing you have in mind," he replied.

† *Epilogue* †

Gurinder Chopak climbed steadily up the steep hill, its rocky terrain making a mess of his bared, now bloody, feet. Although the sun shone brightly, he shivered in the chill wind that blew against his lightly clad back. His gauzy white shirt and baggy trousers whipped in the salt-stiffened air while the unaccustomed smell of kelp invaded his nostrils. Behind him, the Irish Sea, dressed for a summer dance, wore a gown of cobalt festooned with whorls of lacy foam from which ribbons of spindrift beckoned gaily.

The man shivered again. Why, he wondered idly, was he dressed for the steamy clime of India when he was clearly elsewhere? The inconsistency, however, seemed essentially irrelevant and did not trouble him greatly.

Breathing heavily, he crested the low hill, before him a scene which comes to the mind of everyman who contemplates pastoral English life. He took a moment to survey and catch his wind.

His hilltop, one amongst several, fell away sharply into an undulating pasture of green, its high grasses rolling like ocean waves. In the distance were creatures of indeterminate species, some moving with varying speed from place to place, others stationary. Beyond these to his right was a semi-circle of trees, dark, dense and tall enough to merit the appellation forest. To the left, and a bit farther, rose a grey, many-turreted castle, flags and pennants waving from every visible peak. And beyond that a deep fjord. Ah, he thought, a peninsula.

Recovered, Chopak began a careful descent. Once at

the bottom of the granite-strewn slope, he increased his pace to that of a brisk walk. As he neared the hollow, it became clear that some of the, heretofore, generic creatures were sheep, a great number of them in fact, which grazed with singular intent upon the grass. Closer still, several dogs could also be divined, yapping and running in circles around… ah, yes, those were children.

As in a dream, Chopak approached without fear. Of a sudden, a woman and two toddlers came into view; she reclined on a blanket, audience for the antics of other children and two men who cavorted with them, the babies, tumbling over one another in play like two puppies. Chopak stopped and studied the scene.

Without warning the woman turned and spied him. She smiled a slow, warming smile, as though, perhaps, he had been expected.

"Saracen," she said softly. "How lovely to see you."

Chopak gasped. "Cecilia? Is it really you?"

Cecilia chuckled and gave him a wry grin, "And who else might I be?"

Wanting further assurance, Chopak sank onto the blanket beside her and grabbed her hands. "You *are* real," he whispered.

"As real as ever I was," she replied.

The would-be puppies, lured from their game by the arrival of this exotic stranger, toddled up to Chopak, one tripping over his outstretched foot, the other plopping a crushed bouquet of herbs and wild flowers into his mother's vacant lap.

"Yours?" he asked.

Cecilia nodded.

"And Bartholomew's?"

The Monastery

Cecilia grinned again. "Oh, yes, Bartholomew's," she laughed. "Meet Hamish and Nathaniel. Not to be outdone by the others, nothing would do but that Bartholomew must father twins!"

Mention of Bartholomew and the other men drew Chopak's gaze to those who still romped in the field. Seeing his interest, Cecilia pointed to each. Indicating a tall, handsome man who strode across the fields, laughing, a shrieking boy under each arm, Cecilia said "Bartholomew."

Then her hand shifted in the direction of a slim, blond man who trod through a blaze of wildflowers, a little girl in tow. "Dominic," she said, adding, "…and Maggie, of course."

Finally, she pointed toward the sleeping form of an old man, who dozed, like Rip Van Winkle, beneath a distant tree. "Paul."

The sound of a bugle crossed the meadow, riding high on the afternoon sea breeze. "You must go soon," Cecilia said. "It grows late."

"No, please! Not yet…" Chopak pleaded.

Cecilia placed a finger to her lips. "Close your eyes," she said quietly. "Open your hand."

When Chopak complied, the woman withdrew a spiked stalk of green from her crumpled bouquet and placed it in his open palm, closing his fingers around it.

"Smell," she said.

Eyes still closed, Chopak drew a long breath, inhaling the clean scent.

"Rosemary is for remembrance," she whispered. "Remember me."

Chopak's eyes flew open at the finality of Cecilia's words. He nearly sobbed as he surveyed the orderly appointments of the bedroom he shared with his wife, Mari. He could hear her now, humming in the shower. Hopefully, he closed his eyes and opened them once again; the scene did not change.

Only a dream, he thought sadly. Only a dream.

With a heavy heart he pulled himself erect, then swung his legs over the side of the bed, groping blindly for his slippers. Once found, he slid his feet inside, pushed himself upright and trudged slowly into the bathroom.

Mari, her shower finished, dressed quickly and began to tidy their room. She picked up her husband's discarded robe and yesterday's newspaper, then turned her attention to the rumpled bed. Whipping back the sheet, she snatched up the nearest pillow to plump it. Beneath the bolster was something odd. Reaching gingerly, she grasped a sticky bit of greenery – a sprig of rosemary, aromatic and fresh, sap still leaking from its bruised stalk.

She shook her head in amusement. One simply never knew, she thought, what Gurinder might do next. With a wry smile, she turned toward the open bathroom door.

"Gurinder, my dear," she called, "however did this weed find its way into our bed?"

Acknowledgements

The author would like to thank Kim Trimpert for so generously allowing the manipulation of her photography in the production of the cover art for this work and Eugene Trimpert for creating just the right rendition. Also owed a debt of gratitude are my generous and patient readers: Rachael Trimpert, Linda Cohan, Lauren Miko and Sheila Mandell and my parents, readers and all around supporters, Mike and Sally Miko.

About the Author

Seeth Miko Trimpert, a Registered Nurse and technical writer, has twice been recognized by the National League of American Pen Women (NLAPW) for her fiction work – once in 1999 for her short story The Widow and again in 2001 for her novel Hard Over. Ms. Trimpert is now a member of the NLAPW.

Married to a military officer, she is the mother of three grown children. She has lived and traveled throughout North America, Europe and the Western Pacific. Currently, she and her husband divide their time between their home on central Florida's Withlacoochee River and their sailboat in Key West.

The Monastery is her second novel. She is also the author of *Bear Crossing.*